Summer Shore

NOVELLA COLLECTION
REBECCA REED
JESSICA WAKEFIELD
TABITHA BOULDIN

FRAMED

WITH

Love

Rebecca Reed

Chapter One
Six days before the Wedding

Olivia Perez closed her eyes against the brilliant dawn firing the water and breathed in. Her long, slow exhale reached all the way to her bare toes, worries eased by the extravagance of having the beach to herself. The velvety bundle in her arms wriggled, threatening to conjure the long list of items on today's to-do list. She lifted the rabbit until they were nose-to-nose. "Which way, Sable?"

After a moment, she lowered the protesting bunny and raised her face to the horizon. A sea breeze caressed her cheeks in welcome. Salt clung to her frizzing hair. Shoving her cares away, she traversed the shifting sand until it firmed, glancing toward the cluster of high-rise buildings half a mile up the beach. Nothing moved at this early hour except the retreating tide and a few sandpipers and scuttling crabs. Overhead, the discordant cries of gulls broke the soothing rhythm of the waves.

After a moment's hesitation, she turned her back on the hotel district and the pier stretching far into the Gulf and faced the stretch of cottages and homes that lined the beach road winding westward from Summer Shore. Her step faltered at the dark silhouette crouched at the water's edge, face to the sea. Her eye tracked to the large dog bounding through the surf. Perhaps today wasn't the day to change direction.

An echo of Mama's voice gripped her. "*There's never a good time to step into the unknown.*" God knew she'd been in stasis the last few years, but decisions had never been her friends. Her shoulders rounded, courage leaching away. Maybe tomorrow.

She rotated east as Sable squirmed again. Olivia placed the rabbit on the sand and looped his leash over her wrist. They made their meandering, hopping way toward the pier, an echo of a hundred similar walks she'd taken since moving back six months ago.

The skin on her neck prickled. Something felt off. She glanced around, seeing nothing.

Wishing for her camera, she pulled out her phone and bent to photograph her pet's tiny trail then added more shots of the rabbit. Standing, she scrutinized the results. Not as good as the Canon could do, but not awful. She admired how the sun's rays crossed the sand to dust Sable's brown shades with gold.

A rhythmic pounding registered seconds before the leash pulled taut, the jerk sending her phone tumbling––exactly why her camera was safe in her third-floor room at The Summer House.

A bark and passing blur triggered her lunge toward Sable. She caught the slobber-furred rabbit as a sharp command delivered it from the black dog's jaws.

"Stella, sit," rumbled a second command.

She spun to face the voice, legs tangling, rear plopping onto the sand. Her phone skidded out of reach, but she clutched the bunny tight to her chest. Squeezing her eyes closed, she quivered in anticipation of the dog's onslaught. When seconds passed with no attack, she cracked one eyelid to find bare tanned feet beside the dog who sat on her haunches, pink tongue lolling.

Some magnetic force dragged Olivia's gaze up muscled calves to fuchsia flower-patterned board shorts riding low on narrow hips. A white tank accented rather than covered the man's toned abs, chest, and shoulders. White-blonde hair flowed past his ears in silky filaments, making her want to gather them between her fingers. But his stunning, cut-glass eyes stole her breath––the blue so intense, she forgot everything else.

He cleared his throat, severing their connection by squatting in a ripple of muscles to retrieve her phone. A swipe of his long fingers cleared it of sand. His gaze landed on the photo she'd taken, and his lips pursed as he studied it. The quirk of his brow sent an odd ripple through her middle. "I love the angle. How you caught the sun across the fur." He stepped forward and stretched toward her.

She accepted his help before she remembered he was the enemy––or at least the owner of the enemy––snatching her hand away as soon as she hit her feet and rotating so Sable was as far from the dog as possible. The bum's mouth quivered as if he fought a smile, and she jerked her gaze away.

"I apologize for Stella. She gets a bit too enthusiastic over the prospect of meeting new friends."

Frowning, Olivia glanced over her shoulder. She expected sarcasm, but instead, sincerity softened his features. "Your dog tried to eat my rabbit." Her tone warbled with what she hoped he took for righteous anger, though in reality, she fought the tears confrontation always conjured.

He ruffled the fur on the labrador's head as the dog stared at him with what could only be described as adoration. "Aw, Stella wouldn't have eaten your puffball once she realized it wasn't some sort of fluffy new toy. She'd have dropped it after a circuit or two none-the-worse-for-wear. Labs have soft mouths."

She narrowed her eyes in an attempt to glare--an expression she'd never mastered. "That makes it all right?"

His brows shot up and he leaned toward her. "I'm sorry she scared you, but taking your pet rabbit for a good hop on the beach isn't exactly normal."

"Aren't you the charmer." She'd mumbled, but the way his hands found the pockets of his shorts told her he'd heard.

His gaze didn't leave her face, conveying a softness that both challenged and unnerved her.

Her chin raised against the squeeze in her stomach. "We come here every morning--early--to avoid dogs and their owners."

"Look, uh--"

He paused in an obvious invitation for her to share her name. She may have supplied it under the spell of his unusual eyes had Sable not taken the opportunity to wiggle free and scamper toward the lapping water. Stumbling after her suddenly speedy friend, Olivia was certain Stella would show her true colors. Instead, the dog stayed put while her quick and agile owner scooped Sable up before the next wave's froth could tickle the rabbit's toes.

The sight of her bunny cuddled against the man's broad chest, his hair spun silver in the rising sun, broke the back of her resolve and sent another shiver through her midsection. She could only stare as he approached, placed Sable in her waiting arms, and retrieved her phone from his pocket.

"Here you go, Shutterbug."

Her nose scrunched at the nickname, but he continued without pausing.

"Stella and I'd best move on before we get in any more trouble." He dipped his head to the phone still in his hand. "I'd say if you aren't already pursuing photography, you should. Though, of course, you've no cause to take the advice of your lowly, resident beach bum." He held out her device.

Olivia cradled Sable in a football hold and accepted it. Stella had yet to move from the spot where he'd ordered her to sit. None of Olivia's prior experiences had prepared her for this pair, and it appeared she'd misjudged them both. By the time she'd cleared the knot from her throat, man and dog were jogging away.

She screwed up her courage. "Hey, Silver!"

He hesitated as if leery, then turned and backpedaled.

"Thank you." She added a smile.

Maybe one side of his mouth tipped in a lopsided grin, but he was too far away for Olivia to be sure. He sent her a jaunty salute before resuming his jog toward Summer Shore. Gorgeous hair streaming behind. Dog loping alongside.

Her stomach pitched with uncertainty. The morning's calm prematurely shattered. She stared into the retreating tide where thousands of undulating peaks and troughs broke the sun's fiery reflection. A fitting image for her life at present––everything out of kilter and her dreams retreating.

A glance toward the barrier island town with its seasonally swollen population revealed the dog and her owner as specks in the distance. Resort workers moved like ants among the tables and loungers, wiping away the accumulated grit and preparing for the day. She brought Sable to her neck, relishing the warmth and his velvety fur. Inhaling, she trudged through the deeper sand toward The Summer House and LOVElegant where her friends and different problems awaited.

Pausing for a final look, she studied the heaving water as if it might spit a videographer onto the beach. Every delay buried her friends' dreams a little deeper. She had two days to find a qualified replacement or they'd lose the celebrity event that promised to put their wedding planning business on secure financial footing.

Time to conquer her fears and reach out. Someone had to be available on short notice.

She closed her eyes, one hand flattening the poofy mass of curls. Failure wasn't an option because the thought of even one more rejection sent her mind spiraling into places she never wanted to be caught in again. If only she could pray like her counselor had suggested, perhaps her confidence wouldn't be as shaky as her steps across the shifting sand.

Stirling's imagination refused to let go of the woman he'd just jogged away from with her thick cloud of dark curly hair and rich tan skin. Deep mournful eyes that shot sparks at him and matched her pet rabbit's fur––sepia with a creamy undertone. Her indignation made him chuckle until he recalled the sadness ringing her eyes. Familiar. Reflected in his mirror every morning.

Stop it! He couldn't afford to take on another cause. And that girl looked as lonely as he felt. Even if his isolation was his own fault.

The pier grew closer, a few patrons milling about on the cool sand. He'd have enough time to check the equipment before his first private lesson was set to arrive, barely. Stirling, or Mac as he went by nowadays, slowed to a walk, breaths puffing from his exertion. His hand found the loyal lab's head. Soft fur quieted the wrestling within. Her pink tongue lolled, and she smiled at him, the golden brown of her eyes another reminder of the girl he was trying, and failing, to purge from his mind.

The photo had been stunning. Especially considering her phone wasn't the newest model. She definitely had an eye, capturing the sunrise as it flowed across the sand and onto the rabbit's fur.

Once he'd used similar gifts as he filmed his family's underwater treasure hunts. If only they hadn't lied to him, perhaps he'd still be in the Keys.

"Naught but trouble comes from lies." His grandfather's words.

Gramps had been full of quotes and quips both wise and comical. How he missed the man he counted as much of a father--if not more--as his real dad.

He shook off the melancholy thoughts and unlocked his hut. The place was more of a shack--shed even--though hut evoked *Robinson Crusoe* or *Treasure Island*, the stories that had fueled his love of trea-sure hunting as a boy. He opened the screened windows in the back room, checked the snorkeling gear, and set out everything the small private party would need. Then he doublechecked today's reservations on his iPad. Booked solid--the first time in a week. Maybe the con-stant flow of clients would keep his thoughts focused in the present.

Two hours later he bade his third group farewell as Tian rushed up carrying the sign he'd commissioned last week. Her brother Hai saun-tered behind, hands in pockets and elbows at jaunty angles--ever the too-cool teen. Stirling was proud of how far the pair had come in the three years since he'd caught them sleeping in his kayak more than half starved and a bit feral.

"The sign looks good." He smiled as Stella nudged the girl's hand.

"Did Tian catch your vision?" Hai repeated the phrase Stirling had used while explaining his ideas.

"Flawlessly." He gestured to the polished and preserved driftwood post. "Excellent workmanship, Hai."

"About time you advertise. You're the best teacher and guide in the Panhandle." Hai tugged at the sideways bill of his cap.

"When are you going to take advantage of the free lessons I offered, so you can say those words from experience?"

The siblings shared a glance, then shrugged.

He paid the pair the balance of their fee then pondered the circular sign declaring his presence to all those strolling the beach—Scuba and Snorkeling by Mac. His stomach unsettled for the second time that day. He pressed his lips together. He'd been hiding long enough. Though he'd stopped short of using his given name. So, maybe still avoiding his parents.

"You need another." Tian indicated the back of his building. "For those coming from the cottages and the boardwalk."

Hai nodded. "I snagged another piece of driftwood this morning perfect for a stand."

Stirling squinted in mock accusation. "I think you two are plotting how to siphon all my profits."

"Oh no, Mr. Mac." Tian's mouth and eyes rounded. "We would never cheat you."

He mussed her pixie-cut hair. "Of course not. I was only kidding." Her brother grinned. "Right, Hai?"

The boy crossed his arms and stretched taller, though he wasn't more than five feet on tiptoes. With an air of superiority, he cocked his head at Tian. "She doesn't get man jokes."

"Ah." Stirling winked at Tian who rolled her eyes like any dramatic teen. "I'm sure you're right."

They worked out details for another sign, then Stirling guzzled water and wolfed down an empanada from the stand to his east. Stella devoured the crusty edge while he welcomed his next group of clients.

He worked through the afternoon guiding a youth group's snorkeling excursion at a nearby cove and a wedding party's scuba session at one of the beginner-level artificial reefs scattered off the coast. He'd nearly nixed the last dive because one of the groomsmen had argued with him over safety protocols, but in the end, the bride had convinced the man to cooperate. One good thing he'd gained from working on *The Treasure Hunting MacAllisters* was the ability to remain firm through calm authority and tact.

Gramps had drilled it into his head that those who lack self-control quickly lose the respect of those around them. Stirling sought to model himself after his grandfather. His one epic fail occurring during the argument with his father hours before he'd left without goodbyes or explanations.

Color streaked the west when he checked and stowed the last piece of equipment, grateful for the panorama that allowed him to view both ends of the day, but groaning knowing he'd have to wake extra early to switch out scuba tanks before his first lesson tomorrow. He secured the windows and doors, then patted his new sign with affection as it reflected the crimson and fuchsia shades of the drowning sun.

He and Stella crossed the packed sand to the small marina where his boat was moored, his thoughts drifting to this morning's encounter with the dark-haired woman and her rabbit. His lips quirked. If only she knew how close she'd come to his given name when she called him Silver.

Satisfied the craft was secure, Stirling patted his leg. "Come on Stella. Let's find something to eat and then head home."

The dog rose, shook her black coat, and trotted to his side, licking her chops.

At the fish market Stirling purchased some fresh fillets.

The owner, a compact woman with smile lines around her eyes, wrapped them in several layers of paper before handing him the package. "One of these days Barry and I'll get around to those snorkeling lessons you promised a year ago."

"If you two ever take a day off, come on down." Stirling paid her husband then retraced his steps toward the cottage.

As they passed his hut, the new sign glinted. It seemed to hint maybe he was ready to put down some roots.

Insecurity had kept him holed up in the shadows for the last four years. He wasn't sure he was ready for his family to find him, but he was beginning to think reconciliation might be possible. Maybe he could even pursue a relationship.

The image of a feisty woman with sparks in her eyes and a fondness for animals lit his imagination.

Chapter Two
Five days before the Wedding

Olivia harnessed Sable and padded through The Summer House's open gate half an hour earlier than usual. Chill pre-dawn winds eddied the loose sand, and she was glad for the windbreaker she'd tossed over her T-shirt and leggings.

She headed toward the pier at a brisk walk rather than her normal leisurely pace. Sable squirmed, wanting down, and Olivia slowed for the rabbit. Her gaze darted about half expecting the silver-haired man to surprise her or maybe the big black dog to come bounding from the surf. But wasn't that why she'd left earlier, so she wouldn't have to see them again?

Olivia's attempts to purge the image of his unique hair flowing behind him as he jogged away hadn't been successful. Nor had the golden eyes of the dog left her in peace. After considering the incident, she realized she'd overreacted. The dog had not been about to eat her rabbit. And the way it had sat without even a twitch at Silver's command, revealed its training and discipline.

The sky lightened by degrees, but the day was overcast, so Olivia couldn't see the sun. Appropriate since she hadn't found a videographer to replace the one who quit. She'd called all afternoon and tried online services, but everyone with experience was already booked. The secret pre-Christmas wedding had her rattled enough without the holiday's nearness making finding a replacement nearly impossible.

Worse, the social-media-star bride and groom were due to arrive later in the day, and she had yet to tell Viana, the mastermind behind LOVElegant, or Lauren, former model and wedding cake designer extraordinaire, of her dilemma. She didn't deserve best friends like them, and she couldn't let them down.

Olivia shuddered, a fragmented memory stirring her aversion to the myriads of people on social media. If she could stick to the nature and animal videos––the subject matter that had captured her teenaged imagination––she might be able to handle it, but faces exposed her weaknesses, left her vulnerable, and reminded her how much of an oddball she was. Irony of ironies, she was employed as a wedding photographer. That is, if they could pull this one off.

A glint of metal in front of the mysterious shack she passed every morning caught her gaze. Tucking Sable beneath her arm, she veered closer to investigate. *Scuba and Snorkeling by Mac. Lessons and guided adventures.*

"Oh, Sable, I've always wanted to learn to scuba dive. So much life beneath the water." When her family had gone to the beach with relatives, she'd tracked the boats ferrying divers out of the marina while her siblings and cousins swam and held dance parties. She'd never asked for lessons because there hadn't been money for such extravagances.

The death of Olivia's father before her first birthday had made her mother into a strong woman. A woman who'd yanked five children across the state the summer before Olivia's freshman year and started her own restaurant featuring the Cuban food from their Miami neighborhood. The business had thrived, but Olivia had hidden in corners that first day of high school. If Viana and Lauren hadn't grafted her into their friend group and given her a place to connect--a place worlds removed from the sister who'd warned Olivia to stay quiet and leave her alone--Olivia might have been crushed beneath the shame of her sister's rejection.

Olivia stepped onto the pier, loving the weathered wood beneath her feet. As she ambled farther out amid the waves and roosting pelicans, considering how she would capture their pewter feathers against the lighter grays of the sky, the memory of her sister's disdain faded, and she felt more at ease. Nature was relaxing. People stressed her out.

So why had she forsaken her dream?

She sighed. If her hunt for a videographer didn't turn up someone soon, she might have to trade her Canon for a spatula or waitress's apron so she could eat. Worse, she'd be disappointing her only friends--friends who'd taken a chance by inviting her to be part of their business. Friends she couldn't bear to lose.

Sable squeaked, and she relaxed her hold. "Sorry."

The sentiment was true, but she was tired of apologizing. Of the energy spent reading others and blending into their perceptions.

In the quiet water the dark shape of a sea turtle glided past, kick-starting Olivia's heart. She raced to the other side, catching a better glimpse before it disappeared from view. "Too large for a Kemp's ridley," she told Sable, stroking the velvety fur. "They're so rare anyway. But, no streaking on the shell. Probably a loggerhead swimming for the seagrass in Bartlett Cove."

A moment later, a pod of dolphins arced above the waves, their gray skin shiny in the wan light. Olivia watched their departure, wishing she'd had her camera but able to breathe deeply once more.

"Gracias a Dios," she intoned, the Spanish of her youth returning in the reverence of the moment. How long had it been since she thanked God? Or asked Him for help? Too long, for certain.

She stared into the moody sky. *Please let a videographer cross my path.*

Sounds floated over the water, shaking her from the moment. Voices, people stirring. She'd lingered longer than usual. "Time to go home, Sable. The people are awake."

Striding along the pier, she passed a few gruff fishermen who nodded, but declined to speak. She liked these men who understood how to communicate without words. Perhaps she should have become a sign language interpreter. That career may have suited her better.

She groaned inwardly. Unless a miracle happened soon, exploring options may be her next move.

"You're not doing your share, Stella."

The dog's ear twitched from her shady spot as Stirling hauled the final tank to the tiny front room and paired it with flippers and a dive belt. Maybe he should hire a helper. This group of six divers was the largest he could accommodate with his limited equipment and the size of his boat. Of course, growing his business had been the last thing on his mind when he rented the dilapidated shack just over three years ago.

He'd thought only to keep his mind and hands occupied after nearly a year of living the beach bum life. The phrase pulled the image of Shutterbug and her rabbit to mind. He'd used the name at the time to irk her into providing her real one, but he'd thought of her that way so often in the last twenty-four hours, he wasn't sure another name would stick should she decide to gift it. *If* he ever spoke with her again. A big *if*, since he knew barely anything about her.

He grabbed two waters and poured one into Stella's bowl, then downed half the other while exiting onto the sand. Swirls of white and gray clouds greeted him. The horizon blended with the surf, squeezing the world in a tight embrace. Movement caught his eye, and he focused on a figure power-walking near the foam.

Could it be?

His senses attuned to the shoulder-length hair tossed like a black cloud by the gusting wind. His hands itched for a camera to capture the wildness caged beneath her monotone outfit. Several strides later, the rich brown of her rabbit's fur peeked from beneath her arm.

Shutterbug.

He canted his head toward the sky that seemed close enough to touch. *That Your doing, Lord?*

He heard no answer. Not that he expected one. He'd only recently stopped trying to hide from God. Though maybe he already knew, since coincidence wasn't a word according to Gramps. The familiar pinch reminded him of the empty place left by his grandfather's passing even as his legs carried him toward the approaching woman.

She could move. He had to hand her that as she'd nearly passed him by the time he reached her, despite being almost a head shorter than he was.

"Shutterbug! Hold up a minute."

When she neither slowed nor turned, Stirling hurried forward and matched her stride. He sensed Stella fall in at his side. Stealing a glance, he admired Shutterbug's determination. Either she was ignoring him, or she'd become oblivious to her surroundings. The rabbit's nose twitched where it peeked from beneath her elbow, but it seemed content tucked there like a football.

The woman made to sidestep a large crab carcass and bumped his side. Not ignoring him then. Their contact careened her into the pile of debris. She tripped and he lurched to steady her lest she end up in the sand for the second time in two days.

His hands spanned her waist, propelling her past the trap before pulling her gently to a stop. She spun, eyes wide, lips rounded in an *O*. He yanked his gaze from the gray windbreaker's rapid rise and fall to scan her face. Man, she had gorgeous eyes. Several shades of brown held intelligence and depth. And shocked recognition.

The rabbit wriggled free and dropped to the sand, dragging their attention along with it. Stella plopped onto her haunches, tail sweeping broad strokes and ears cocked. Stirling still held Shutter-bug's waist. In his haste to retreat, he toppled over the shells behind him and landed hard on his backside.

For a moment, he froze in place, but slowly, a laugh gurgled out from somewhere deep inside.

With a photographer's instincts, Shutterbug drew her phone and aimed his direction. She scanned the screen, a grin emerging.

Once more, he was mesmerized. She thumbed to another shot and her full lips parted, releasing the power of her smile. It turned his limbs to jelly.

"That may have been a Bocourt crab. They're not common in the Panhandle." She showed him the photo.

Stirling's elation fizzled. He wasn't in the shot.

Stella whined and nudged his leg. His first thought was to bat her away, but she never did anything without purpose, so he looked around to see the rabbit hopping toward a strand of seaweed directly into the path of the next approaching wave.

Shutterbug's gaze followed his, hand reaching toward the runaway. "Sable, come back."

"Stella, herd."

The dog bounded around Shutterbug, cutting off the rabbit's trajectory, then nosing the startled animal toward them and away from the apex of the wave.

Shutterbug dropped to her knees and cradled the bunny before stroking Stella's head and murmuring her thanks. When she met Stirling's eyes, their gazes caught long enough for him to read gratitude and an undercurrent of something else before she stood and offered her hand.

He relished her smooth skin on his calloused fingers as she pulled him to his feet. Her retreat wasn't as violent this time, though she didn't linger. Nor did she give him a scolding look. Was that raised brow a hint of curiosity?

"Do you enjoy sneaking up on women and their pets?"

He brushed off his shorts and sent her a crooked grin. "Trust me, no sneaking involved. You were so deep in thought, you didn't realize we'd been beside you for quite some distance."

Glancing around as if finally noticing her surroundings, she frowned. "When did you join us?"

He swiped grains of sand from his palm. "I'm Mac."

She hesitated, forehead scrunched, then shook his hand. "Scuba and snorkeling? That Mac?"

"The same."

"I love your new sign."

"Thank you. A friend of mine rendered the design quite beautifully."

"Your design?"

He nodded.

Silence fell between them, and Stirling chuckled to break it. "It seems every time we meet, one of us is destined for the sand."

Her cheeks pinked beneath the healthy tan, and she averted her gaze, stroking the rabbit's fur as if uncomfortable.

He pulled a breath, then blew it out slowly. "Do you have a name, or should I continue to call you, Shutterbug?"

White teeth worried her top lip.

"I promise I'm not a stalker, nor am I proposing . . . well, anything. I only want to know your name. Please." He added the last in a coaxing tone, hoping to draw the smile back to her lips.

"Olivia," she breathed, a hint of accent in the center *i* sound.

"Olivia." He tried out the name on his tongue. "Not quite as apt as Shutterbug, but I guess I could get used to it." The shadow that dulled her eyes made him wish he hadn't joked about something so personal. "I'm sorry, I––"

"It's fine. I-I need to go. I'm running late." She backed several steps before turning. Three strides later, she glanced over her shoulder.

"You know where to find me." He rooted his feet to the spot to avoid making another fool of himself. What was wrong with him anyway? He hadn't been so fascinated with a woman since Makaya had beguiled him to learn his video techniques. Likely this girl wasn't as innocent as she seemed on the surface, either. He should just forget her.

Unfortunately, following that advice worked no better than it had yesterday, despite a mostly full schedule of lessons and guided adventures.

Chapter Three

Olivia gathered Sable and led the way onto The Summer House's wraparound porch, raising her face to the breeze and inhaling deeply. The act of leaving the home's walled confinement eased the tension in her neck and shoulders, until she remembered she still hadn't solved her problem. She settled into the swing and stroked Sable's plush fur.

She'd had time to sneak in a call to her mother to ask if she knew anyone qualified to be their videographer. Because of the popularity of her restaurant, Carmela Perez knew almost everyone and their stories. Olivia had resisted asking until desperation forced her hand.

"Have you spoken to Mac?" Her mother had asked.

"Mac who?"

"You know." Olivia envisioned her mother swiping at the air, talking with her hands. "The diving instructor. Mac. He operates off the beach between The Summer House and the resorts. Lives in a cottage west of you aways. He's a whiz with a camera. I'll email you the commercial he did for the restaurant. Judge for yourself." A clang had her mother spouting Spanish to a kitchen helper, then saying a quick goodbye. "Come visit us soon, Chiquita. Promise me."

"I'll try, Mamá."

Lauren glided to a spot near the railing, her steps a soothing counterpoint to Viana's marching cadence.

"They'll be here any minute." Via paced to the pounding of the nearby waves, checking her phone every pass.

"Relax Via." Lauren sipped her coffee.

"I love that Ainslie and Lucas are having a December wedding." Olivia's gaping predicament pushed her to study the subtle shades of Sable's fur. "It's sweet they'll be married and on their honeymoon when Christmas rolls around. No one will expect a wedding at this time of the year." Lame and a coward, just like her sister loved to describe her. Olivia peeked upward, but her friends seemed oblivious to her ratcheting tension.

Viana stopped, her stance rigid. "Who knew a guy responsible for making men around the country style themselves after Cary Grant in skinny jeans with a too cool attitude would fall in love with the princess of the best ways to live each day. And then together they'd become a fashion powerhouse." Viana ran her hand up the post, her fingers tracing the hand-carved floral designs, then opened her ever-present device.

"This wedding is so important. We need more than two weddings a month. Anita can't be laid off like the cleaning staff. We need her on the front desk and as my admin assistant. And our kitchen and grounds staff are vital."

"Lucas and Ainslie will do more than put us back in the black, they're going to put The Summer House on the map." Lauren squeezed Via's hand.

Olivia barely registered their banter as her secret twisted her thoughts into a convoluted knot.

Lauren detailed her progress on the cake.

Via turned to her. "What about you, Livvie?"

Her failure rose up, threatening to choke her, but she swallowed it down. These were her friends and business partners. They deserved the truth. "My videographer quit."

The silence made Olivia want to sink into the cushion.

"Did he give a reason?" Viana asked at last.

"He hates the mother of the bride and refuses to work with her."

Via's fingers pressed her temples. "This is not the worst problem we can have. Not by a long shot. It's one videographer. It's not like the bridal party got stranded on the boat the morning of the wedding."

Lauren chimed in with another near disaster and the pair bantered back and forth each one-upping the last. They'd been together for years and Olivia had only been back a few months. This was her first uber-important wedding. She wasn't in their league when it came to qualifications, but they'd insisted she join them when they'd heard she wasn't opening a Nashville studio. She had to make this right. While turning down the funding the Latin American Aid Society had set up for her had been hard, the idea of operating her own business had been overwhelming.

"I'll find someone." She tried to keep the desperation from her eyes, though it clawed at her gut.

Viana patted her ankle, then Sable's head. "I know you will, but you don't have to do this alone. We're in this together."

Lauren called Via out because the wedding planner was the worst at trying to do it all herself. Olivia understood her compulsion because she shared it, in an inverted way.

"Ainslie and Lucas want a private wedding that they can share with all their fans after the fact." Timing didn't negate the need for a quality videographer. They couldn't afford to mess this up, especially with Olivia's own lack of finesse for staging people in still photos. The videographer would carry a majority of the weight when it was all said and done.

Silver's face came to mind. Mac. His name was Mac.

Olivia reached for Sable as he slow-hopped across the porch swing and pulled him backward towards her. "I want to give them the best but now . . ."

"You're worried you're not up to this job?" Viana asked gently. "And you won't find a suitable replacement in time?"

Olivia inhaled and nodded.

"We're *not* up to this."

"What?" Sable squeaked from Olivia's convulsing grip.

"No one is ready for an event like this." Viana offered an encouraging smile, then began one of the we-can-do-it pep talks she'd been making since high school. They were as much to convince herself as the others, but she was usually right.

"You know, if you didn't sound like such a sergeant major, it might have been a more inspiring speech." Lauren's lazy smile broke the tension.

Viana grinned. "I needed that."

Olivia laughed with her friends, already planning how she was going to convince Silver—Mac—to take on the videographer role. As long as he was as good as her mother claimed.

"There is one thing different with this wedding." Lauren raised her mug.

"What?" Viana closed the spreadsheet.

Lauren waggled her eyebrows. "We have an actual security guard with this one."

"I hope he's not some blockhead." Via scanned the road before facing Olivia. "Let me know if you need any help."

Liv forced confidence into her smile. "I'll find someone, but thanks." She looked between Viana and Lauren. "Your support means everything to me."

Lauren crossed the deck and embraced her. "We've had each other's back since high school, that doesn't change now."

Viana nodded. "I know you're worried, but like we said before, this kind of thing happens at weddings all the time. If you haven't found someone soon, let me know and I'll put out some feelers as well."

"Thank you both so much." Knowing her friends didn't plan to abandon her pushed her to attack the problem, but another thought derailed her. "When I was coming home, I saw the city maintenance crew setting up." Olivia adjusted Sable on her lap.

"They're probably doing routine maintenance. It was on the town's social media page last week," Lauren said. "I hope they'll be finished before the wedding. You know how long these jobs take. Sometimes, it's like they're not even working."

Olivia nodded, formulating a conversation with Silver in her head. Could she convince him to help her after her snap judgement yesterday?

"They're here."

Lauren's announcement sliced through Olivia's rehearsal. Two vehicles entered the gate, raising the stakes. Her heartbeat thundered, blocking all sound as her vision fuzzed. With a forced effort, she gulped in air as doors opened and a couple wearing trendy hairstyles and runway-ready attire exited. How could she presume to pose this high-fashion duo? She rose with Sable tucked beneath her arm, feet dragging down the stairs behind her friends, mind flashing back to that first day of high school when she'd been the oddball who didn't fit.

With dark glasses hiding half her face, Ainslie was nearly unrecognizable, except her personality shone through. She rushed up the steps and gave each of them a bubbly hug which only served to freeze Liv's responses even more. Thankfully, Lucas only embraced his fiancée, an act which removed the seemingly permanent scowl from his face.

Viana greeted the pair, then stared at the man who approached from the second vehicle. Olivia clutched Sable to her chest as she recognized him--Via's former college crush, Camden Mayfield. Her gaze flew to her friend, compassion welling within her. This couldn't be good.

Less than fifteen minutes later Olivia escaped the house and carried Sable to his shaded, fenced enclosure in the back yard. When her phone had vibrated with her mother's evidence, she'd excused herself. The video seemed to endorse her chosen course of action. She could be completely wrong, of course, as she'd been more times than she could count, but maybe this once, things would work out in her favor.

Since he'd trekked an angry path across the state of Florida four years ago, Stirling had never once wanted to hold another video camera. Until today. He blamed it on Shutterbug--er--Olivia, and her superb photographs--even the desiccated crab carcass had looked good. Though perhaps the urge to design a sign for his business had been his creativity-starved self seeking an outlet.

On his final guided dive of the day, the sun had broken through the cloud ceiling at the perfect angle to send slanted rays slicing all the way to the artificial reef his three divers were exploring. Gramps called the phenomena a "promise ring" and had never failed to swim to the center and bask in God's faithfulness.

Stirling had hesitated, afraid the memories would short-circuit his brain, though he was beginning to realize how much he needed the reminder that his identity was tied up in God's promises rather than other people's actions. Another wisdom Gramps had repeated often. He'd checked on his divers but hovered just outside the golden circle. The glittering water seemed to dredge grief to his heart's surface, each of his many losses another layer of silt. First Gramps, then his beloved treasure hunts, his life's work, his family. Even his freedom in a sense. Nearly his faith.

He shook the thought away so it wouldn't derail his positivity. Instead, he'd relished the exuberance with which the divers had detailed their discoveries.

Two short snorkel lessons were left before he could call the day complete. He checked his watch. The first, a family of six vacationing from Indiana, should arrive in a few minutes. Feeling restless, he donned his bucket hat and ventured onto the sand. Stella yawned and made to rise from her shaded nook beside the door, but he waved her down. "Stay."

The dog licked the drool from her chops and settled, eyes alert and watchful.

"Good girl, Stella." Stirling meandered east about a hundred feet to Cap'n Mike's Snack and Souvenir Shack. He'd never met Mike, the absent owner, but was well acquainted with Hueso, the guy who ran the joint. He'd been the one who introduced Stirling to Ana María's Place, his choice whenever he didn't feel like cooking.

"Eh, Señor Mac. Business is up for you, yes?"

"Been keeping busy. What about you? Sold out of empanadas?"

A wide grin smoothed the older man's wrinkled cheeks. He raised two fingers. "I give you a discount, you take them off my hands."

Stirling made a show of patting his pockets. "I seem to have misplaced my wallet. I guess someone else will have the pleasure."

Already bagging the meat pies, Hueso sighed. "Ay, mi mujer would tell me you need flesh on your bones. Take them and be well." He handed the white paper sack to Stirling with a false look of disappointment.

"How is Mrs. Hueso," Stirling asked, accepting the offering and suppressing a grin. They played this game several days a week. He always sneaked back and paid for his food later, trying to deposit it without getting caught. Sometimes it worked and others not, but the camaraderie gave him a connection––a feeling he belonged somewhere.

Hueso jutted his chin westward. "Looks like you've got company."

"It's probably my––" Words failed when he glimpsed the cloud of black hair on the woman bending for Stella to sniff her hand.

"Your?" Hueso prompted.

Stirling swallowed. "I'm not sure." He lost no time retracing his path across the undulating sand.

Olivia straightened when she noticed him and a tentative smile bloomed, then wavered. "Hi."

"Hi." He stopped a few feet away.

Her teeth worried her lip and she seemed unsure what to say.

Stirling gripped the paper bag and scrambled for a way to put her at ease. "Where's your rabbit?"

"Sable doesn't handle the heat well, so I left him at home." She clasped her hands in front of her and looked everywhere but at him.

Brilliant move. Way to make her more uptight.

Stella nosed the woman's hand, then leaned against her leg. Her fingers released and she stroked the lab's head. The rebuke that had risen in Stirling's throat, died. Olivia seemed to draw comfort from the soft fur and pressure of the dog's solid body.

"Why don't we move under the canopy?" He suggested. While the day didn't hold the heat of summer, the sun's presence had elevated the temperature to the mid-seventies. He didn't wait, but lead the way into the shade, then extracted a bottle from his cooler and handed it to her, still puzzling over her sudden appearance.

"Thanks."

"What can I do for you?" Maybe keeping things professional was the best course.

She fidgeted, her fingers finding the dog's back. "I, uh. I need your help." Her gaze flirted with his before darting away.

He breathed through the surge of adrenaline. "Okay. Snorkel or dive lessons?" She hadn't given him much to go on.

"Yes. But that's not the kind of help I need right now."

Stirling waited for her to continue, but when she gazed out to sea instead, he circled into her line of sight and leaned down to connect with her gorgeous eyes. "Olivia, I want to help, but I can't unless you tell me what it is you need. And I'm a horrible guesser. In fact, my second guess would be that you need me to . . ." He tapped his finger on his chin and looked around. "Throw you in the ocean." He sent her an exaggerated grin. "Is that it?" He pretended to reach for her, then chuckled when she backed away mouth agape.

Her eyes narrowed. "You're teasing me."

His nod was solemn, or as solemn as he could make it while fighting back laughter. He waited a beat, then cocked his head, eyeing her. "Shall I go for guess number three?"

This time she rolled her eyes, making the gesture appear more attractive than it should have.

"Ah," he said, "you have siblings."

"How do you know?"

"Older siblings."

"You get older siblings from an eye roll?"

He raised his index finger and pursed his lips. "That eye roll was obviously perfected from the need to react to older sibling bossiness."

"You know this from experience?"

He shrugged. "Now, how may I help you?" He raised his eyebrows dramatically. "And I suggest you tell me this time or I will think of something even more ridiculous." He winked and was rewarded with a flush of pink in her cheeks.

She wet her full lips, then rushed into an explanation, words tumbling over each other in a tumultuous cascade.

An odd tension gripped his insides as he waited for her to pause for breath. He held up his palm before she could resume her gushing. "Let me be clear. You are a wedding photographer with LOVElegant which is housed in The Summer House just west of here. Your videographer quit and you have a wedding in five days. The couple are social media stars who want to stream their wedding after the fact, and you want me to be your new videographer. Does that about sum it up?"

Olivia nodded, the bounce of her dark hair endearing. Her offer tempting. But . . . "Who told you I was a videographer?" Few here knew that about him. His heart thumped faster despite his attempt to stay calm. Likely a product of years spent looking over his shoulder. Olivia seemed too sweet to be in league with his parents. But he thought he'd known Makaya and she'd betrayed him, hadn't she? His own family had hidden things from him.

"My mother gave me your name and sent me a clip you did for her restaurant."

"Restaurant? I never––"

She extracted her phone and showed him the screen. Familiar footage played along with a Latin rhythm and scrolling text.

"Your mother owns Ana María's Place?"

She nodded.

"I see." He remembered the night. Hueso had insisted Stirling celebrate Cinco de Mayo with him since his wife was out of town caring for her sister. They'd arrived to some guy trying to shoot video for an advertisement the restaurant planned to air on the local Latino channel and bungling the job. Stirling had tried to ignore the awful lighting and angles, but in the end, he couldn't sit by and let Carmela spend good money on such horrific work. Instead, he offered to shoot and edit the footage for the price of his and Hueso's meals. He'd been proud of how well it had turned out, especially since he'd done it all on his phone.

He faced Olivia. "You're Carmela's daughter?"

"I am."

"The one who recently returned home from Tennessee."

Her lips tightened in response.

He took in her apricot blouse, white cotton capris, and fancy sandals. Not typical beachwear. Had she come dressed to impress?

"You sound as if you're desperate. Is that right?"

Her teeth caught her lip before she answered. "We are. This wedding is make or break for the business. The couple arrived today and if they find out we don't have a full staff . . .The bride's mother can be difficult. Please, Mac. You're my only hope."

Even if his creative side wasn't itching to say yes, the pleading in her brown eyes would have done him in. "I'll need more details and some time to rearrange things here before I can agree." He had at least one adventure or lesson booked every day for the next two weeks.

"But you'll think about it?"

"I'll think about it."

"And let me know . . . when?"

She wrinkled her petite nose, looking so cute, it made Stirling want to plant a kiss there. He mentally stomped on the brakes. He literally knew next to nothing about this woman. How could he be thinking about kissing her––even if it was on her nose? His thoughts confirmed his body's suspicious reactions. He liked Olivia.

Several figures rounded the shack carrying towels and dressed in swimsuits. "Are you Mac?" The speaker appeared to be in his forties with a bit of a paunch and a receding hairline.

Olivia retreated to the edge of the canopy. "I'll get out of your way."

"Can we meet tomorrow morning? Dawn?"

She smiled and nodded. "See you then."

Stirling couldn't tear his eyes away from her retreat. What was it about her that fascinated him so thoroughly? Only when she'd passed out of sight did he shake himself back to reality and the family patiently awaiting his attention. In the back of his mind, he began a countdown for dawn.

Could he really do this and put himself at risk again?

Chapter Four
Four Days before the Wedding

Olivia awoke before her alarm, having spent most of the night in nervous anticipation of her next meeting with Mac. What if he said no? What if he said yes? She didn't know which one scared her more.

She crawled from the bed, stomach in knots, and peered out the window at the swatch of star-speckled sky visible above the treetops. *Help, Lord!*

LOVElegant needed him. Her mother had been right. His skills were above par, bordering on brilliant. Working with others wasn't her strong suit, however. What if her fizzy feelings turned her into even more of a disaster than normal? Failing on her own was one thing, but if she scared him away, they would all lose their livelihood. She couldn't be the cause of that.

She changed into black leggings and a pink, LOVElegant tee––the only bright-colored shirt she owned––and pulled Sable from his cage, lifting him to peer into his dark brown eyes. His sweet nose wiggled, setting his whiskers in motion. "Do you think I can hide it?"

The rabbit kicked in protest of his midair suspension. Olivia set him on the bed and pulled her windbreaker over the tee, then secured his harness and leash. "At least my hands will be occupied with you along."

Early as it was, she didn't expect Mac for at least twenty minutes, but walking alone for a bit might help center her thoughts. Calm her down. Maybe she could toss her attraction out to sea. Her luck, it would float back in on the next tide. Her worn but comfortable sneakers made little sound as she carried Sable down the porch steps toward the gate. Soon sand rolled beneath her feet.

Her thoughts jumped from Silver to the wedding poses she'd Googled last night when sleep had refused to come. When the path straightened to a view of the beach, she stopped short. The silhouette of a man sat outlined against the ocean on a washed-up tree stump. Broad at the shoulder, with a tapered waist and long legs anchored into the deep sand, it was unmistakably him. The dog padding toward him confirmed her notion.

An ethereal shimmer drew the breath from her lungs. His hair's translucent strands seemed to catch every pinprick of predawn light and reflect it back into the air.

Motioning for the dog to sit, he shifted her way. Oh, professional detachment wasn't going to be easy. She swallowed and moved forward. Pulse pounding in her temples, she willed her tension to ease.

He rose to meet her, and she had to tilt her head to see his face when she stopped a few feet away. Stella's tail thumped a greeting.

"Good morning." His voice was smooth and pleasantly deep.

"Good morning," she echoed, and they fell into step walking toward the water.

His hands were in the pockets of his board shorts, a jacket looped through one elbow, but he appeared relaxed. Completely opposite of her. If her muscles tightened any more, she feared something would snap, exactly like when she'd moved to her new school or when she met new people. A shiver spasmed through her. She hid behind Sable burying her cheek in his velvety fur.

Fabric draped across her shoulders. Her head snapped toward Silver, who shrugged. "You seemed cold."

The gesture warmed her physically and emotionally, thawing the ice and loosening her unease. "Thank you."

"My pleasure."

They reached the hard sand and paused, peering over the expanse of opaque water. A gull screeched and wheeled overhead. A pelican dove, returning to the surface with a glittering fish.

"You have a preference?"

Olivia gazed each way, overwhelmed by this simple decision.

After a few seconds, he took her elbow and tugged her gently to the right. "This way's usually quiet, and we shouldn't run into resort workers or other early risers."

She acquiesced to his lead and suddenly, she was walking in a new direction. If only she had the confidence to make such choices on her own. But that had always been her problem, hadn't it?

"I wanted to go west, yesterday." Heat rose at her blurted confession, and she was glad for the murky grayness that covered her shame. "If I let Sable down, will your dog try to carry her?"

"Why don't we introduce them, then Stella will know she's yours and belongs here."

They stopped walking to let the animals sniff one another. Sable didn't seem to fear the canine and Stella appeared more curious than hungry, so Olivia trusted she would behave.

She placed Sable on the sand and he hopped to investigate a half-submerged stick.

"Stella, heel." The dog halted mid-stride and returned to Silver's side, gazing with adoration and attention at her owner.

"She's so well-behaved. Did you train her?"

He shook his head. "She was an emotional support dog before I got her. Lived with a little girl who had cancer. Not long after I moved here, I found her wandering the beach, bedraggled and wet. Lost. I posted flyers, trying to find the owners. I'd given up, but eventually, someone contacted me. Told me the story and asked if I would keep her. The little girl passed, and the parents couldn't stand having Stella without their daughter. Too painful, so they gave her to a friend, but Stella kept running away. We've been together ever since."

Tears pricked Olivia's eyes. "What a horrible ordeal for the parents."

Silver nodded. "I couldn't imagine going through such a thing. Stella was depressed for some time. She'd look out the window as if waiting for the girl to find her. It never failed to choke me up."

"My father died not long after I was born. But losing my mother or any of my siblings." She shook her head. "Not sure how I'd get over it."

"How many siblings do you have?"

"I'm the youngest of five. Almendra, Rosmarina, Tomillo, Cereza, and me." Normally she resisted telling family details, mainly because she was such an outsider. But something about his mixture of curiosity and gentleness invited her into his confidence.

"All food names except yours."

She averted her gaze and he didn't push.

They passed several generously spaced cottages fronting the beach, but back a hundred yards or more. Tropical trees decorated their front yards and most had a hammock or porch swing somewhere. The lack of conversation wasn't uncomfortable.

Sable found the remnant of a slender stem and began to devour it. Silver looked on until it disappeared then grinned at her. "I've never watched a rabbit eat before. How long have you had him?"

"Six months. Since I moved back from Nashville."

Sable ambled forward along the footpath, sometimes hopping, others stopping to raise up on his haunches and sample the scents with a wiggle of his nose. A quick glance at Silver––she still struggled calling him Mac––revealed a relaxed expression. Perhaps he didn't mind the meandering pace.

He caught her looking and smiled. "You lived in Tennessee? I thought you were a native Floridian."

"I am. Originally from Miami, but I graduated with the other members of LOVElegant from Summer Shore High. We moved here my freshman year."

"So you've known each other since high school."

"We were best friends then kept in touch while attending separate colleges. Now we're business partners, though Viana owns the house."

"And this wedding is in four days?"

"Yes. At The Summer House."

He peered at the path, scooting pebbles aside with his boat shoe. The bridge of his nose creased.

Olivia's breaths shallowed. Would he turn her down? "I-is that a problem?" She loathed the squeak in her voice. He refocused as if he'd forgotten she was beside him, his continued hesitation driving her heartrate into the red zone. She found herself leaning toward him as if her proximity might prompt him to speak.

At last, he cleared his throat. "Sorry. I'm considering how best to reschedule my clients."

A sparse line of trees separated the next set of cottages from the public beach and fractured the dawn light rising at their backs, yet the cut-glass quality of his eyes still had a mesmerizing effect. She blinked to break their connection, and gripped Sable's leash to steady the dizziness threatening to topple her. Working daily with this man might prove a horrible idea. His hand closed on her arm, the strength of it solid, steadying.

"You okay?"

She managed a nod, then pulled in an expanding breath of sea air. "You wouldn't be needed tomorrow, but we should probably tour the venue so you can choose the best places to record from and check out the lighting."

"Your shots are planned?"

At her hesitance, he pursed his mouth. "If you send me your shot list, I can coordinate the video around your stills. Be sure I'm not in your way. That sort of thing."

She hadn't even considered that. The former videographer had quit before they'd done any collaborating. What other things would show her incompetence? "You obviously know your way around this stuff." She nearly groaned aloud. *This stuff?* He was going to guess she was a fraud even before he saw her fumbling when staging humans for portraits.

So caught up in her own commiserating, she nearly missed the look of pain that crossed his face. The sadness that clouded his brilliant eyes snapped her self-pity. Despite her fears, she met his gaze. "Are you okay?"

He seemed taken aback by her question. His Adam's apple bobbed, and he stopped to face her. Stella nosed his palm and he stroked her head.

Olivia recognized the offer and receipt of comfort from her experiences with Sable. A desire to add her own gesture rocked her toward him until the memory of her younger prom date using his puppy-dog eyes to get her to invite him, only to ditch her once they arrived for a different crowd halted her sway. She steeled herself against Silver's almost visceral attraction. She could not--would not--be made vulnerable by sympathy again. No matter how much his eyes challenged her to bare her soul.

"Thank you."

His words, spoken softly, nearly unraveled her control. But then he resumed walking, posture and expression relaxed once more, and she envied his ability to shake things off so easily.

Several cottages farther on, they came to a freshly-painted white one with cheerful trim the color of his eyes. It boasted a screened-in porch perfect for viewing the shore, a stone-lined firepit framed by inviting benches, and tidy flowerbeds edging each side of the curving patio paver walk with bright blossoms. He stopped and she realized it must be his. Not at all what she'd pictured, though as much as he'd fixed up his surf shack, she shouldn't be surprised.

"Would you join me for some OJ and eggs?" His quirky smile tugged the sun above the horizon. "We could finalize our meeting tomorrow and work through a few of the details regarding the ceremony. If you have time, of course."

"As long as I'm back before eight." She agreed to his invitation despite her head's insistence she turn him down.

"No problem. My first lesson arrives in an hour, but since I can't teach on an empty stomach, I may as well whip something up for both of us." He sent a lazy grin her way.

"Then run it off on a nice jog to work." Her smirk came out of nowhere. She never smirked. But if he noticed the shock following on its heels, he was too polite to make anything of it, and led the way along the single-file walkway. She scooped Sable into her arms and buried her flaming face in his fur until Stella's warm body pressed against her leg.

She cradled the rabbit and stroked the dog's head. Peering into the luminous eyes, she accepted the doom her brain insisted dropping her guard would bring.

Stirling was doomed. If he couldn't handle a walk and meal with the woman, how was he to work closely with her for several days without losing his head? Or his heart?

He chugged his water and peered over the glaring sand toward a flock of gulls squawking over a pilfered bag of chips. Olivia had seemed to enjoy his eggs, and he was glad he'd nixed the salsa when she commented how her mother's Cuban food was always too spicy.

Between appointments, he'd contacted his clients and rearranged them to leave time for him to dust off his video camera and meet Olivia for a tour. An unusual burst of nervous energy had him fussing with his equipment. He liked her too much and despite his push for a creative outlet, he wasn't sure how he felt about being on the back end of a camera again.

During a break Hueso sauntered over. "No empanadas today, amigo?" He placed both hands over his heart. "I am crushed, señor."

He raised his sandwich. "Leftover fish."

"Ah, well, in that case, I forgive you."

Stirling straightened from checking a tank and eyed his friend. "What brings you to my humble hut during your peak hours? You've a sly look about you."

Feigning innocence, Hueso spread his hands wide, palms up. "How could you ask such a thing?" Then he winked and added, "Is the pretty lady coming by today?"

"Sorry to disappoint, my friend. Not today."

Up the beach several people broke away from a group and headed toward Mike's. Stirling inclined his head. "Looks like you've customers coming."

Hueso scanned behind him then reached into his shirt pocket. Extending his hand, he said, "Thought perhaps the lady might enjoy a ride on the beach with a handsome gentleman. Since Mrs. Hueso has me booked, I'll give these to you."

Accepting the offering, Stirling glanced at the tickets. "Barbara offers the best horseback riding in the Panhandle. But these are costly. You should take Mrs. Hueso." He tried to hand them back, but Hueso had already moved away waving his hand.

"She won't go near the beasts. Besides, a customer gave them to me. Said his flight was moved up and he couldn't use them. Asked me to give them to a couple in love." With a raise of his bushy brows and a smirk on his lips, Hueso turned and jogged toward his stand where a half dozen people approached.

Despite his friend being out of earshot, Stirling spluttered, "But we're not . . ." He threw up his hands. Heaving a breath, he studied the photo of a couple riding two sleek horses along the edge of the surf, their eyes glued on each other as they rode along. Professional and inviting. Evoking emotion.

The photo he'd seen on Olivia's phone played across his mind. That sun-streaked rabbit hadn't been an easy shot to make.

Such a gift shouldn't be squandered.

The thought hit him out of nowhere and burrowed deep. He wanted to deny he was ignoring his own gift. Tell the Creator he was teaching others to enjoy creation, something he loved. While that was true, Stirling knew part of him longed for more. Stella laid her head in his lap, always aware of his emotional needs and ready to step in to meet them.

Could he do that for Olivia? Be the support she needed to pursue her dreams?

First, he'd have to discover what those dreams were. Giving his dog a final ear rub and pat, he stood and tucked the tickets in his cash box. They were for Saturday. Probably wouldn't work out with the wedding, but maybe he could purchase tickets for another day. He smiled at the image of Olivia galloping along the sand with her hair haloing her face. Definitely a picture he'd like to capture.

A twinge clenched his gut. Could he open up and let her into his past first? He swallowed and reached for Stella, blowing out a breath.

Gramps' ideas about discomfort growing strength didn't ease his mind concerning opening up, but they did underscore his need to do so. Perhaps it was time.

Resigned, he set about preparing for his next group. "If this is what you want, Lord. I'm willing, but you'll have to supply the words." He whispered the prayer to the open rafters of his hut, pausing a moment with his eyes closed. Nothing happened. Smiling, he gazed upward. "Okay, Lord. I guess that's fair. How long did you speak to me before I deigned to answer? But, I'm here now. Whenever you've something to say. I'm listening."

Even with the one-sided conversation, Stirling felt a measure of peace--maybe even healing, though the anger that had driven him to leave the Keys still simmered deep in his soul. Until he found a way to cool it, *if* he found a way to cool it, he'd likely be stuck, so not the best person to help Shutterbug after all. But as it didn't seem she had many others leaping at the chance, he'd do his best while trying to keep his heart from becoming hopelessly entangled.

Chapter Five
Four days before the Wedding

Olivia opened the gate security-conscious Camden kept closing, then waved as Lauren drove away. Liv climbed into her compact and followed, basking in the camaraderie and sincerity of her friends' words. "You're the peacemaker," Viana had said. Lauren chimed in. "We need you, Liv."

Turning toward Summer Shore's quaint downtown, she sighed as she took in the miles of seafront sand, her favorite part of living on a barrier island. Unfortunately, visitors also enjoyed said sand as well as diving the over five hundred artificial reefs the sunken decommissioned navy vessels, concrete debris, and other recycled materials created.

She longed to be among those taking stunning photographs of the abundant sea life, but she'd never even snorkeled. The latest issue of *Floridian Wildlife* discussed the new SNUBA——a combination of scuba and snorkeling——technique, but the article hadn't said whether it was more or less affordable. After navigating the two turns, she parked behind a brightly painted storefront with an unlit neon marquee announcing Ana María's Place.

Her mother's text, received after parting with Silver and walking the short distance to The Summer House, couldn't be ignored. Time to bite the bullet and visit. She opened her door to a swirl of spice that clenched her sensitive stomach. Even this early, Mamá and her chefs prepared Cuban-style pork and chicken for use in today's dishes. Lunch and dinner overran each other regardless of the day.

Spanish chatter spilled from the open kitchen door. Good natured ribbing and the clatter of pans rose above a lowkey Latin beat. Despite her never feeling authentically Cuban, the familiarity of the organized chaos put a smile on her face. The restaurant was always bustling. Never lonely. That much she remembered––maybe even missed.

Tuned to the local Latino channel, a wall-mounted T.V. played Silver's Ana María's Place ad. Seeing it on a larger screen made her appreciate its subtle quality even more. Her videographer was a genius when it came to angles and presentation.

Arms tightened around her waist before the gardenia fragrance her mother preferred reached her nose through the spices.

"Ah, mi Chiquita! Aquí at last."

She turned into warm hands covering her cheeks, pulling her in to plant a kiss on her forehead. Mamá gripped her arm and led her to a small wooden table in the employee alcove. The air was cooler and less oppressive thanks to several high-powered fans repelling the kitchen's heat.

"Ramon, agua con fresa, por favor."

"Por supuesto, Carmela." Ramon's reply hinted at his long history at the restaurant.

Her mother always remembered her penchant for strawberries. The fruit-infused water was a house specialty along with the Cuban sandwiches. The T.V. switched to a local feature concerning turtle migrations, the image of a rare Kemp's ridley capturing Olivia's attention as she read the scrolling caption.

"Local diver spots rare species near Freehold Pass."

She pressed a hand to her heart. If only that were her.

Ice clinked as Ramon delivered her water with a flourish. "Nice to see you, Oliva."

Sending him a shy smile, she lifted the water to her lips. No one in the restaurant or her family had ever used her anglicized name. They stuck with Oliva despite everyone else adding the I. She'd grown used to the idea they'd never change. Just as she'd grown used to the idea she'd never fit in.

Compassion softened her mother's time-creased eyes. "How are you, child?"

Wiping her lips with a napkin, she met her mother's gaze. "I'm fine."

"Were you able to convince Mac to work with you?"

"Yes. We're hoping to meet tomorrow to go over the shots."

"He's very skilled." She gestured to the T.V. "You saw his work. And he'll handle the bride's mama just fine, difficult or no. He's the most laidback guy I've ever met."

Olivia nodded. "That's saying something."

"Nothing seems to fluster him." Carmela gave her a sly look. "Handsome, too."

Olivia leaned back. "Now, Mamá, don't get any ideas. We've just met." She allowed a tiny smile. "Though he seems Heaven-sent."

"You see, I knew you'd recognize how perfect he is."

"I barely know him." Her denial stirred memories of the tingles his touch and kind looks had elicited.

"But you will." The glint in her mother's eye meant trouble. "And what of the photography contest? The one you enter every year?"

Taking another long swallow, Olivia slowly returned the drink to the table. "Not this year." She tracked the rivulets of sweat sliding along the glass.

Carmela joined their hands. "You're giving up?"

An uncommon clenching of her gut cut through Olivia, pushing her to speak. "Am I not allowed to give up? When does it become obvious that I'm not meant to be a nature photographer? Is five failures enough? What about ten? Well, I've officially failed fifteen times submitting to that contest. My professors saw through my dream. I must have agreed deep down or I would have tried harder to stay with what I loved. But I didn't. I am not *giving* up. I've already *given* up. It's just that now everyone will know, and I'll have to admit it to myself."

"Oh, Chiquita, I'm so proud of you." The fingers holding hers squeezed three times then released. Carmela ran a hand over her still-dark hair, smoothing several strands that had escaped her bun.

Mamá's words stung. "This is what makes you proud?" Her throat closed over a sob she refused to release.

Brown eyes pierced hers. "I have always been proud of you, Mija. But always you were the meek one. Too sweet and gracious to contradict. Too polite to insert your own ideas. Too nice to insist others see or hear you. That you were able to speak as you just did gives my heart hope that you will also find the spark to pursue your passion––whatever that might be."

Olivia blinked, then released her held breath. Not the words she'd expected from the woman who'd always stood tall in Olivia's sight. But though unexpected, they held a kind of balm for her soul. An approval she'd needed, but feared never to receive. Something within her loosened and began to unravel, allowing her to breathe a bit easier.

"Besides," her mother flicked her expressive eyebrows, "Perhaps it isn't your dream that's defective as much as how you chose to chase it."

Olivia's phone vibrated in her back pocket, bringing back the noise and bustle of the kitchen. She pressed her lips together, uncertain how to respond, then extracted the device. "It's Viana."

Carmela stood and straightened her apron. "Don't leave without saying goodbye and taking the food we've boxed up for you and your friends."

Fifteen minutes later, Olivia navigated her car into her standard parking place, her mind occupied by her mother's words and the handsome and charming videographer. *Please don't let him change his mind.*

Summer Shore's maintenance truck had passed by when she entered their neighborhood, but she hadn't thought anything about it. Nor had Via's frantic call prepared her for the flood that greeted her foot when she stepped from her car.

After the initial shock and the conversation with Viana and Lauren on the porch where Lauren had suggested moving the wedding indoors as the only option, they'd gotten to work on sorting through the damage. Tension had radiated off Viana when Lauren mentioned Camden's superhero efforts and how well he and Via had worked to mitigate the damage, but Olivia sensed the connection that remained between them despite their falling out. Via's hurt over not knowing where Camden had gone tweaked Liv's compassion. Confrontations and disagreements had always made her cringe––probably why she was so awful at telling people what to do even when it came to staging photos.

Her hands kept busy sorting waterlogged decorations, but her focus flitted between her work and today's surprises. Silver's cooking had delighted her––flavorful, but without spice––raising her already high opinion of him another notch. Her next older sister Cereza often cited her lack of tolerance for spicy foods as evidence for her "un-Cuban-ness" and provided yet another excuse to push Olivia away, something she'd always accepted without challenge.

A car's motor and the opening and closing of the gate yanked Olivia from her reverie. Camden appeared with two men in tow laden with crates of decorations. A strong spicy scent emanated from the bags Cam deposited on the porch table. She hid her smile at Via's loss of words in the face of such a compassionate gesture. Normally, her friend was the one saving the day. How fun to see the roles reversed. Viana deserved to have someone who cared for her, and it was obvious Cam still cared despite their breakup and the lost years between them.

Of course, Via couldn't accept quietly, but Lauren stepped in and smoothed the situation over. As Cam retreated to install security cameras, Olivia gave a low whistle. "I didn't see that coming."

Sharing a look with Lauren, she grabbed a slider marked mild and retreated with Sable to her room. Best create a shot list for Silver's impending site tour tomorrow, providing he could clear his schedule. Would Ainslie and Lucas agree to move the wedding indoors? What an incredible blessing. If the venue changed, he might not discover how incompetent she was when it came to staging. At each of the weddings she'd done, one or more of the standard shots--cake cutting, rings, even the kiss--had held up the flow due to her allowing the parties to arrange themselves. Thankfully, either Via or Lauren had stepped in before any of the guests noticed. Heat shot up her neck.

Her hand froze on the knob. What if Ainslie and Lucas cancelled the wedding? Her biggest sense of disappointment came from not having an excuse to see the handsome videographer again instead of the thought of having to return to the restaurant to work. She was a horrible friend. And how had that man wiggled his way into her life after so few encounters? The danger of her attraction sank her onto an ottoman, Sable on her lap. She dropped the sandwich on a nearby end table and buried her face in the rabbit's fur.

Lord, protect my heart.

She remained there, head bowed through the grating of the gate's opening, the crunching of gravel, and the gate's closing. Doors opened and shut. Some minutes later, a sharp cry pulled Olivia out of her prayer. Still cuddling Sable, she stood to face whatever new disaster had arisen. If she were in a cartoon, a rain cloud would be positioned over her head. When no more shouts sounded, she placed Sable in his indoor pen, got him fresh water, then slipped into her room to change out of her filthy clothes. Her mind churned as she pulled on gray leggings and a simple navy top.

When Silver asked for her number so they could coordinate their plans, her emotions had been all in a jumble. But, he'd yet to call. She stepped into the bathroom and corralled her unruly hair into a ponytail, splashed water on her face, then stared into the mirror, arms braced on the sink. Why couldn't she be strong like the rest of her family?

An incoming text buzzed. Pulse jumping in her throat, she raced to read the message, then flopped onto her bed in relief.

Silver:

> I've cleared a window between eleven and one tomorrow to tour the site with you. Please let me know if this works.

Maybe she wouldn't be the reason their business failed after all. At least, not yet. She sat up, glancing once more at the phone to make certain she hadn't been dreaming, then straightened her spine. "*Fake it till you feel it*" had been her mother's favorite phrase while she taught herself to cook. Olivia had had plenty of practice over the past several years pretending to enjoy portrait photography. What was a bit more piled on top?

Olivia:

The three dots blinked.

Silver:

Not like any wildlife opportunities were falling into her lap. A do-geared issue of *National Geographic* lay abandoned on her nightstand. She rose and crossed to the window. Her bare feet made no noise on the hardwood, just as her photographs had made no impact on her magazine of choice: *Floridian Wildlife*. As she'd told her mother, after fifteen failures, she could feel the breeze from the door slamming in her face. The deadline for this year's contest was only a few days away. Even if she'd wanted to enter, which she didn't, she had no worthy image to submit. Besides, a girl could only take so much failure in her life before it squashed her.

She tossed her notes on the desk and crossed to Sable's pen. As always, the rabbit hopped forward to greet her and she picked him up, careful to support his belly and hindquarters so he didn't kick. Moving to her partially opened window, she let the breeze caress her face, watching

Sable's nose wiggle at the influx of scents. "How do I make these feelings go away, Sable? We have to work together and all I can think about is how enticing his eyes are and how much I enjoy his company."

She nuzzled her cheek on the soft fur of his side, letting him peer over her shoulder. "What if he's just like Emil? What if he's using me?" Sighing, she grabbed the abandoned sandwich and placed the rabbit on his special carpet. One bite had her stomach lurching. The restaurant's idea of mild was not in tune with hers. Tossing the food, she opened her laptop. Best get busy checking that shot list. Besides, who would Mac be trying to use her to get close to? She was letting her past cloud her present.

Three days before the Wedding

The first half of Stirling's day seemed never-ending. The lessons dragged. The older couples on the guided adventure dive were sweet, but chatted incessantly about their vacation, about their grandchildren at home in Tennessee, about their favorite authors and books they'd read on the boat ride to the reef. Then they pried into his private life, and his best efforts at deflection didn't faze them.

"Anyone as charming and good-looking as you needs a wife, young man," the longer-haired sister said.

The other one bobbed her head in agreement, her trendy salt-and-pepper hair spiked stoically against the stiff wind. "Indeed, he does. A shame to let someone so eligible remain single."

He spent the rest of the dive near their husbands or observing from afar while they smirked past their regulators. The thing was, a few days ago, he'd have had no trouble heading off their comments. After meeting Olivia, he might be edging closer to their point of view. The realization dumped him into a deepening pit he might not have the strength to climb out of.

After securing his boat and the equipment, he locked the door and jogged across the sand to Hueso's. "One beef, one chicken and one veggie empanada, por favor."

"Unsure of your señorita's tastes?" Hueso winked when he handed over the packaged pies.

Stirling shook his head and tucked them into the insulated lunch sack he kept for food runs, then secured that in his messenger bag beside his iPad and camera case. The shot list he'd received had been thorough, but still his head rattled with dark thoughts of Makaya. Drawing a deep breath to reset his emotions, he faced westward.

"Stella, heel." The dog trotted to his side and together they set off for The Summer House.

Scenery he normally savored, even though he passed it at least twice a day, went unnoticed as his thoughts spiraled out of control. In a blink, he'd turned onto the drive and stood outside an imposing black iron gate set in the sandstone perimeter wall. Through the bars, the house rose an imposing three stories in its Georgian style with wraparound porches and tall white columns. From the footpath, only the roofline was briefly visible, shrouded by ancient trees. He'd often wondered who lived here but had never investigated. His need to remain hidden trumping his innate sense of curiosity.

The gate wasn't latched, so he slipped inside and patted his leg for Stella to follow. He felt a little like an interloper or a naughty schoolboy and worried he'd meet a burly bodyguard or worse, a snarling guard dog.

"I'll be right down."

The familiar voice drew his gaze to a third-floor porch where Shutterbug stood with Sable. The sight of her elevated his heart rate a notch. He raised a hand. "Take your time. I'm admiring the view." Heat surged up his neck. Had he actually said that? "Of the house." Lame. Her shoulders shook and a laugh filtered down. The low timber shot awareness through him. He closed his eyes as she disappeared into the house.

Lord, give me strength and a functioning brain. The silent prayer grounded him somewhat. She and her friends needed this wedding to work. He was determined to help, not sabotage their efforts. *Peace, patience, goodness, kindness, self-control.* He recalled the fruits of the Spirit, knowing he'd left out a few, but since he most needed the last one, he'd search for the rest later.

One side of the black entrance door swung inward, revealing a professional looking Olivia in a peach top and black slacks. He pursed his lips at the missing cloud of hair. Her body stiffened, and he realized she'd taken his pinched expression for disapproval. Who'd taught her to read reactions as personal criticism?

He approached, taking the steps in two strides. Stella's nails clicked on the wood as the traitor bounded past him to reach Olivia first.

When she bent robotically to scratch the dog's ears, the tight bun at her nape explained where her lovely hair had disappeared to. It had to be a crime to restrict the natural springiness in those curls.

She glanced up at him, straightened, and pulled her expression to one of professional detachment. How Stirling longed to know her story.

Was her expertise in blocking emotions related to how she read them in others?

Widening the ornate door's opening, she gestured to the structure. "Welcome to The Summer House."

"Stella, stay."

Olivia frowned. "She's allowed in."

"I don't want her nails scratching the finish on your hardwood."

"Shouldn't she at least be in the shade?"

The concerned tone caught Stirling by surprise, though he wasn't sure why. He surveyed the yard. "What about beneath that Magnolia over there."

"Perfect. I'll get her some water."

With Stella settled, they entered the house. Stirling appreciated the large opening from the porch that led into a grand foyer. "That sweeping staircase really draws the eye with its curved design and polished wood banisters. The wedding will be inside, I assume, since the yard appears to have recently imitated a fish pond?"

She sent him a wry smile. "The couple agreed moving indoors would be prudent. The ceremony will take place here in front of the stairs."

"There's an abundance of natural light."

"Right? If the couple stands here, they'll look as if they're wearing halos during much of midday. Still, an umbrella lens works best, and in late afternoon it becomes a bit much. Washes out their faces. I know from experience." She grimaced. "We had to make a last-minute staging move my first wedding here."

"Let's see your new shot list so we can coordinate the video."

She withdrew a printed paper from her pocket and unfolded it with shaking fingers. "This should be everything we need. I worked on it yesterday after the venue change, but I'm open to suggestions, additions or changes."

Stirling accepted her list, chest tight. Makaya had used similar words while duping him. He walked the room checking angles with his camera until he could breathe. "What time on Saturday?" The question was more a demand.

Her face blanched. "Two o'clock."

Olivia is not Makaya. The grip on his chest loosened. He found her eyes and cocked his head. "Walk the staircase for me, please."

She frowned, but climbed, turned at the top, and came back down. He stopped filming and watched the replay. Olivia's stilted ascent became a floating descent as she relaxed, though the rosy hue brightening her cheeks made it clear she wasn't used to being on the receiving end of a lens. Her innocence touched a part of him he'd lost after Makaya's betrayal. She watched him, small and biting her lip, and he sent her his jauntiest grin. "My turn." He started for the stairs.

"Wait. What?" Her flustered tone endeared her even more.

"Your turn to check the light, though I'm certain your images won't be as stunning as mine since crustaceans––even dead ones––make more interesting subjects than beach bums." He glanced over his shoulder, turning quickly so she wouldn't glimpse the amusement her horrified expression brought.

He ignored her fumbling fingers as she snapped shots and checked the results, but only a few steps in, her epic unease pinched his gut. When he stuck out his tongue hoping to erase the palpable tension, she nearly dropped the camera. Despite reining in his goofiness for the final few steps so as not to find himself outside with Stella, the giddy lightness coursing through him refused to disappear. A throwback to times spent with Gramps he hadn't realized he'd been missing.

When he reached her side, he restrained his urge to hoist and twirl her. Instead, he asked, "May I see?"

Her brows drew together and he feared she might refuse until she handed over the Canon. Stirling scrolled through her photos––some truly terrible and others only so-so. Keeping his expression neutral, he reversed direction until he encountered the images of turtles, birds, her bunny, and a pair of squirrels so clear and lifelike he could almost hear them quarreling over the ear of corn between them.

Deep furrows carved her brows when he tore himself away. "How many weddings have you done?"

"This will be my sixth. My second indoors."

"Are there proofs I could view?"

She gave a meek nod and walked head down through an adjacent hallway. A woman in a LOVElegant polo emerged from a side door with a sandwich in one hand and a water bottle in the other.

"Oh, I didn't realize anyone else was here," the woman said. "I'm taking my lunch."

"No worries, Anita. Mac, the videographer and I wanted to look over the last few portfolios. Do you know where Viana keeps them?"

"They're on the bookshelf to your right as you enter her office. We keep the latest ones there for clients to browse."

"Thank you. We'll return them when we're through."

"Welcome to the team, Mac." With a smile and a wave of her sandwich, Anita continued on to the office beside the one Olivia entered. She handed him two albums and grabbed two herself before retreating to the hall.

"Want to sit on the porch?" Olivia pointed past the foyer to a large room. "There's an exit through there."

They sat in relative silence while he perused Olivia's photos. Technically, they were fine, but as portraits, they lacked finesse. Movement pulled his gaze to Olivia's hands grasping the table as if her life depended on that anchor. Was she so worried about his judgement? "Find me a nature shot." At her stricken look, he continued, "I want to show you something. Humor me, please."

She accessed her camera and scrolled for a bit, then rotated the viewfinder toward him.

The photo portrayed a grouping of pelicans, several young ones in the center, floating in gently rippling water. "This is . . ." He found her eyes and shook his head, at a loss for words. Tears welled before he realized she'd misinterpreted his hesitation. Quickly, he reached for her hand. "I'm overwhelmed with emotion. So much so I'm having trouble expressing my thoughts." He pointed to the light reflecting off the water and onto the feathers. "There's an ethereal quality to this shot. It evokes beauty. Peace. Communicates the quiet co-existence of the birds and their environment."

She pulled her hand from his grip, swallowed, and swiped at her eyes. "Thank you." Her gaze slid to the wedding shots. She gestured. "How terrible are they? Be honest."

"It's obvious you're more comfortable outdoors. Your technical understanding and sense of composition are impeccable. I'm not sure what makes––" He peered at her face, watched the amber in her irises darken and swirl. "It's people. That's the difference, isn't it?"

At her nod, he pursed his lips, considering. Making a decision, he closed the albums. "I think I can help––if you want. But you'll have to trust me."

Her nostrils flared. Her lips pulled tight. "Trust you with what?"

"Do you have a swimsuit?"

"What does that have to do with photography?"

He studied her, working through his idea. "You mentioned wanting to learn to dive. What about learning to snorkel?"

She leaned toward him. "Are you serious?"

"Be at my hut in an hour. Bring a towel and wear your suit." He pushed to his feet, anxious to move on his plan. "Let's return these, and I'll be off."

At the door, Stirling put a hand on each of Olivia's shoulders. "You have a natural eye and tons of talent. Trust me. See you soon."

He supposed her tight nod was the most he could hope for.

Chapter Six

Olivia wasn't what Stirling had expected, but he couldn't keep his thoughts off what he'd witnessed as he gathered equipment under the canopy for this afternoon's impromptu lesson in people management. If he hadn't seen her rabbit and wildlife photos, he wouldn't have believed she had any experience behind the camera. As soon as he'd coaxed her to turn her lens on him in the wedding venue, her shaking hands prevented a single focused shot.

Stella's ears perked and she rose to her haunches. Stirling followed her line of sight and sucked in a breath. Polished and professional was attractive, but blue jean shorts and a "Save the Turtles" tee made his blood run faster. Olivia's natural look revealed her beauty in a new way. With an effort, he pulled himself together and jogged across the sand to greet her.

He resisted the impulse to intertwine their fingers, falling into step beside her instead. Stella padded on her other side, leaning into an ear rub. His dog was as smitten as he. Adrenaline surged, and he barely contained his urge to run.

"I'm so excited to learn to snorkel. It's something I've always wanted to do." Her face flushed and her gaze fell to the sand.

The honesty seemed under laden with something heavy, rousing the protective instincts that had tucked Tian and Hai under his wing and reminding him why he'd invited her. "Then it's my pleasure to be the one to teach you. But first, I thought I'd have you take some publicity photos of the lesson group. Since I have a sign, I should probably advertise. You'll be compensated, of course." He sent her his most welcoming smile.

The pink drained from Olivia's cheeks, and her gaze flitted about like a little bird seeking an escape. "I'm not the right person to ask." Her voice shook.

"You're exactly the right person. Your grasp of light and shadow is among the best I've seen."

She tried to conceal her reaction by lavishing more attention on Stella, but Stirling caught the shimmer of tears and the quivering lips. His fists clenched against whoever had wounded her so deeply. With an extreme effort, he kept his expression neutral, his words light. "It's a small group, and they're very friendly. Not a disguised shark in the bunch."

His humor was rewarded when a tiny wrinkle creased the corner of her mouth. Stirling pointed to a table beneath the canopy. "Ready your camera there. After the shoot, we'll lock everything away inside the hut and Stella will guard it for you."

Her tentative glance revealed a pinched expression and unshed tears. She sniffed. "How'd you know I'd bring my camera?"

"You're a photographer. The camera's your window to the world. You probably feel naked without it. I guessed you'd not want to meet new people naked." He winked. "But I brought mine in case I was wrong." He grinned at her exaggerated eye roll, then gave her space while he greeted his friends, the "students" he'd hand-picked.

A few minutes later, she joined them, camera in hand, her steps stilted. He introduced her to Hai and Tian, Linda and Barry who'd taken an hour away from their fish market, and Armando, a waiter at one of the hotel restaurants, then waited to see how she would handle setting up the shot.

She surveyed the area, shoulders rising and falling rapidly, then turned glassy eyes on him. "Do you think your new sign should be in the photo, or the hut with the equipment?" She bit her lip. "Or maybe the ocean as a backdrop?"

Her hesitance almost prompted Stirling to take charge, but he settled for encouragement. "I want you to see the shot in that photographer's mind of yours and set it up to maximize the appeal."

Glancing between the options, then at the people waiting patiently for her direction, she swallowed. "Maybe you two stand on each side of the sign?" She indicated Tian and Hai, who sent Stirling a grin before moving to the places she showed them.

"Um, you others fill in behind the sign, please."

When they'd done as she asked, Stirling cleared his throat. "What about me?" Her stricken expression told him she'd forgotten or not realized he wished to be included.

"You can, maybe, crouch down in front?"

That she'd asked rather than told him proved her hesitance. Stirling had pity on her. "What if we include some of the equipment to give everyone something to do with their hands?" He glanced at her to gauge her reaction. At her nod, he continued. "Then, if we switch the order so the tallest is in the middle." He physically moved each of the three behind the sign into the spots he preferred and distributed snorkel and scuba equipment to each person, then sat cross-legged directly below the sign and between the Korean siblings with his Ipad tucked beneath one arm. "What do you think?"

Olivia's face illuminated. Almost as if her creative spark had visibly ignited. She peered through her camera, then adjusted a setting and did another check. "Something's missing." She turned in a small circle. Spying Stella lying in the canopy's shade, she patted her leg. "Here, girl."

The dog cocked an ear. Stirling released her with a hand gesture, and she sprang up and bounded to Olivia, then sat at her feet with her tail sculpting sand angel wings and tongue lolling.

Olivia rewarded her with a vigorous neck scratch, then brought her to their group. "Have her lay with her head on your lap if she will. Put her body in front of this girl." She smiled at Tian, who beamed.

Once Stirling maneuvered Stella into place, Olivia called for smiles and snapped several shots. She checked them and frowned, then called to Tian. "Could you crouch down and put a hand on Stella's back?"

The girl repositioned, and Olivia checked her viewfinder. "Sir, Barry, could you take half a step forward. Yes, perfect. Now, you Armando, move a bit to your right. Exactly. And Linda, hold the mask a bit higher. Great! Now, act like you're enjoying yourselves." Clicks sounded from the camera as Olivia operated the shutter. She moved to several locations and took more shots, both with them looking at her and focusing into the distance. Letting them relax, she scrolled through the images.

Tian grinned and squeezed his shoulder, whispering, "She's pretty, Mr. Mac."

He caught the glint in the teen's eyes as he met her gaze, but he couldn't deny the truth. "That she is."

Clicking pulled his attention forward to where Olivia had resumed shooting. He raised his brows and shook his head, then held up his hand.

"Okay, surely you've got enough for several ads stored away in there." He pushed himself off the sand. "Let's go snorkeling."

Olivia tucked her camera into her bag and removed her shorts and t-shirt. Had she ever had so much fun photographing people? The closest had been the engagement photos she'd done at Casa Vargas in Nashville right before returning to Summer Shore. Quinn and Tiago were a delightful couple and so photogenic they'd managed to make every pose they'd affected look amazing.

"Coming, slow poke?"

She emerged with her towel wrapped around her modest one-piece suit and shielding her face from the water's glare and Silver's scrutiny. "Ready."

Tian reached for her hand. "Mac's the best teacher. You'll see." She led Olivia to her mask and flippers then into the surf, demonstrating the "stingray shuffle" Silver advised everyone to adopt while wading in the shallows.

After twenty minutes of practice fitting the mask and the flippers and clearing water from the short tube, Silver, er Mac, indicated a boat moored a short way off. "Is everyone ready to go out and view some sea life?"

Olivia's stomach clenched. Was she? While he'd been thorough and patient as he explained each step and worked with all the learners until they had no more questions, Olivia had no confidence in her abilities once her feet could no longer touch the bottom.

Mac must have noticed her hesitation because he fell into step with her on the way to his boat. "You okay?"

She scanned the sand, unwilling to view the likely disappointment lurking in his eyes. A look she'd received so often from her siblings, she could sense it coming with the keen abilities of a hound to a scent.

"Hey? What's wrong?" Mac stepped in front of her and placed both hands on her bare shoulders.

Her skin sizzled where he touched and she instinctively retreated. His arms dropped to his sides, but he didn't move. Voice pitched low, he said, "I won't force you to go out. But I thought this was something you wanted to do. Was I wrong?"

She gave a quick shake of her head, not meeting his eyes.

"Talk to me. I can't help unless I know what you need."

She flicked her gaze to his face and read concern in his creased forehead, earnestness in his eyes. "I'm not a good swimmer." She crossed her arms over her stomach.

"Okay. And?"

Sucking air through her nose, she noted the sand on her flip-flops. A finger slowly raised her chin until their eyes met.

"I won't let you get hurt. I promise."

Behind him, the others stared at them from the pier, and her cheeks began to burn. "Let's go." She tried to brush past him, but he caught her arm and halted her beside him, so close she could feel the heat from his burnished skin. His mouth closed in on her ear.

"Will you tell me once the others are in the water."

She shrugged, unable to commit. He let her go and she speed-walked to the steps and onto the pier, feeling as if she were about to implode.

Climbing into the final seat which happened to be beside Mac, she exhaled a long breath. "What have you gotten me into, Lord?" The breeze whisked her words away unanswered.

Chapter Seven
Two days before the Wedding

Olivia cooked her eggs in the third-floor kitchen she shared with Lauren and Viana, a Latin rhythm accompanying the kaleidoscope of images swirling through her head. Loggerheads, Greens, and several smaller species of turtles, an array of fish whose names she didn't know, two stingrays, and several sand dollars, not to mention the corals, starfish, and a school of Lined seahorses with their tails anchored to undulating seagrass so they appeared to dance in the underwater currents.

Her fears had almost denied her yesterday's snorkeling adventure and the whole new world it had opened. She imagined God chuckling and sent Him silent thanks.

Lauren slipped behind her for coffee as Viana came stretching from her room. "Any new drama overnight?" Via retrieved a bowl and snagged her Lucky Charms from the cabinet.

A breeze fluttered sheer curtains as Olivia crossed to one of two recliners in the open concept living room with her plate.

Lauren shook her head. "None that I know of. I'm meeting an outside client for a cake today."

Viana scooped a bite into her mouth. "Ainslie tried on the dresses last night. We're going to do another session when her mother gets here."

"Florence is coming today?" Olivia's eggs turned to chalk.

"Yes." Viana gave her a reassuring smile. "We can handle Florence."

Lauren snorted. "You have Florence on do not disturb mode most of the time."

Viana raised her brows and grinned. "And you both should do the same if you want any peace."

Liv's stomach clenched as Via's grin disappeared as if it sensed a blow coming.

"With everything going wrong, we are not going to have much peace until the wedding is over."

Olivia could only nod while attempting to swallow her bite. Eventually, she jutted her chin toward Viana's cereal bowl, renewing an old argument to distract them all. "Aren't you ever going to eat anything else for breakfast. You've been eating that stuff since high school." She wrinkled her nose. "You know it's full of sugar."

Lauren's laugh cut Olivia's tension. She loved the easy camaraderie they shared. It made coming home seem less like failure.

"Longer actually." Viana took another defiant mouthful. "It's my thing, okay? I eat Lucky Charms for breakfast."

Laughter filled the room.

Olivia put down her fork. "I've found a videographer." Memories of Mac's touch while he showed her how to navigate the mouthpiece or pointed out some new sight under the water sent heat racing up her chest and neck. "We met a few days ago."

"Who is he?" Viana's body visibly relaxed and Liv was sorry she'd caused her friend so much stress.

"Sil--uh, Mac." She studied her plate's subtle design. "He's a scuba and snorkel instructor with a kiosk down by the pier. I've never seen such skill with a camera. Way better than the last guy." Her ears had to be turning red. Could she blame it on the sun?

"Oh, you have a crush!" Lauren's smile widened. "How'd you meet him? And why haven't you told us anything?"

"There's nothing to tell." Olivia's gaze strayed to the window. "I didn't want to say anything until I was sure he'd work out." She paused. "We met on the beach when his black lab thought Sable was her new toy."

"Ooh, enemies to lovers, all those sparks." Lauren raised her eyebrows.

"Don't you talk," Viana pointed her spoon at Lauren. "Who's that guy I saw you with yesterday? When I was leaving town. You were out front of Castaways."

Lauren's face slipped into nonchalance. "No one you know."

Viana rolled her eyes but her smile teased. "Keep your secrets then."

"Speaking of sparks—" Lauren nodded at Viana. "How are you and Cam getting along?"

Viana stood and washed her bowl in the sink, ignoring the loud stares of her friends. "Camden and I are fine. We're professionals."

Olivia followed Viana and cleaned her plate and fork. "There's sparks, we can all see it." She gave her friend a quick hug. "I'll be back later."

Scooping up her pet, she crossed to retrieve her stuffed beach bag from her room. "Sorry you have to stay in today with your outdoor area still waterlogged. I'll be learning about diving and taking more publicity shots, and you wouldn't like Mac's boat." She twirled the way she'd done as a girl. "Look at me calling him Mac." She kissed Sable's nose and set him gently inside his pen. "Not that I'll be diving, mind you, but I promise I'll report every creature I see when I'm back."

Sable raised onto his hind legs and twitched his nose as if reminding her of her promise, then hopped to his carpet and stretched out.

Olivia tried to sneak across the common room without attracting attention.

"Have fun!" Lauren laughed at her lame glare.

She zipped down the stairs to escape the heat climbing her neck.

Her vigorous pace brought her to Mac's hut in record time, but he was nowhere in sight. Stella rose from her spot in the shade and padded over to inspect Olivia's bag and receive her pets and scratches. "Where's your owner, girl?"

"He had to get a few tanks refilled."

She jumped at the gruff voice with a light Hispanic undertone. Spinning, she faced a fixture from her past. The man who'd eased her family's transition to Summer Shore. "Hueso?"

His beard-scruffed chin dipped. "Soy yo, Oliva."

She rushed to embrace him. "I haven't seen you since I left for college."

"Such a little thing you were. Look at you. Tan linda."

The sound of a motor droned near, then shut off.

Shaking her head, she began to deny she was beautiful, but another voice chimed in from behind her.

"I concur. You, Miss Shutterbug, are outvoted." Mac waggled his expressive eyebrows, and flicked her nose. "I officially declare you pretty. There'll be no more denying it." Before she could voice words of protest, he jerked his head toward some tanks in the back of an ATV. "Wanna help me get those into the hut before our first group arrives?"

The tanks had her sweating and feeling grimy by the time the vacationing family of five arrived for their guided adventure. Olivia dragged a hand across her forehead to unstick the hair plastered there. See, so *not* pretty.

"Ready, Shutterbug?" Mac called from outside the hut.

She rolled her eyes, though no one could see her, grabbed her bag and headed out only to run smack into a firm body. An involuntary shriek escaped as strong arms came around her waist to keep her upright. She inhaled the scent of sea, salt, and something distinctly Mac that added speed to her already racing pulse.

"I've got you, darlin'." His voice rumbled deep and for just a moment, she rested her cheek on that firm chest, sinking into the security he offered. Feeling the thump of his own beating heart. Her arms snugged his trim waist and his heat melded them together. When he rested his head atop hers, a strand of gossamer hair tickled her nose. She freed one hand to run along the strand relishing its salt-roughened texture against her fingers.

Mac caught her hand and brought the palm to his lips, loosening his hold and finding her eyes. When his gaze moved to her mouth, she sucked in a short breath, her stomach tightening in anticipation. His irises darkened from summer sky to sapphire as he leaned toward her.

A sudden pressure on her leg diverted Olivia's attention away from the impending kiss. Stella gazed up, her body pressed against both of their legs. When Olivia returned her focus to Mac, he grinned and pressed a quick kiss to her forehead before releasing her.

His brows quirked as he stepped away. "Rain check." He gathered her discarded bag and removed her camera, replacing it with another in a watertight plastic case. "I'm loaning you my underwater camera for today. No sense chancing yours getting ruined by exposure." He handed her the heavy bag then cocked his head toward the door. "After you."

His grin rivaled the sparkle in his eyes, flooding her body with sensations as Olivia preceded him from the hut and across the sand to the waiting family. They moved to the boat, lugging the diving equipment and a picnic lunch Mac had packed. Stella padded alongside.

"Is the dog going too?" one of the teen brothers asked.

"Yep," Mac answered. "She loves Freehold Pass. Lots to see, even from the surface."

Olivia honed in on their destination. "Isn't that where a diver spotted a Kemp's ridley turtle earlier this week?"

Mac's lips pursed. "I hadn't heard that."

"It was on the local channel when I visited my mother at the restaurant."

His expression turned thoughtful as he directed the placement of equipment and seating, called for Stella to jump aboard, then released the mooring ropes and stepped across to the front deck. Once they'd navigated away from the pier and out to open water, he addressed Olivia who was again in the co-pilot's seat.

"You're wearing your suit, right?"

"Yes, but I don't dive." She lifted the camera. "Promo shots, remember?"

He nodded, altering course and edging the throttle upward. His arm swept an arc around the left side of the boat and he spoke over his shoulder so the family could hear. "The tide's fairly low, so you can see the tops of a few of the shallower artificial reefs peeking above the waves." Two large, long-legged birds landed near one of the mounds. "Those are Great Blue Herons." He indicated a pair of shapes bobbing off to the boat's opposite side. "The white ones are Egrets."

The wife and daughter brought their cell phones to bear on the birds, smiling as they captured photos. Chatter sounded from circling gulls as several brown pelicans dive-bombed the water. Some surfaced with fish secured in their expandable pouches and returned to the sky. Others popped up to float on the water's surface.

An urge to capture the images pulled Olivia's gaze to Mac. She pointed to the camera and quirked a brow.

He nodded with a grin while continuing to point out and name the surrounding fauna.

Nervous energy fumbled her fingers as she freed the camera from its outer case. Relief loosened her breath. A Canon. The settings should be similar even though it was a much higher-end model than her own. She glanced over to see Mac smirking at her. To retaliate, she turned the lens on him, capturing several shots of his cut-glass eyes lit with a reflection of the brilliant sky as he laughed. His silver hair lent him a look of otherworldly power and mystical attraction that sent tingles down her spine.

She blinked and shifted in her seat to frame the mother and daughter, still with phones raised and huge smiles on their faces, then caught the twin sons high-fiving, the father with a relaxed posture, arm on the side of the boat, face tilted into the wind. Maybe photographing people wasn't all that different from the animal life she'd always preferred. At least, in this informal setting. The weightiness of weddings was another matter altogether.

Several minutes later, the boat slowed and changed course. Olivia peered ahead when the top of an artificial reef came into view, a thrill tightening her chest. Numerous other boats were anchored at various distances from the reef, some occupied and others empty.

The mom leaned toward Olivia. "Popular spot."

"Seems so." More people reduced the likelihood of sighting any rare species. Her hidden hope faltered.

"This is one of the best reefs for inexperienced divers," Mac said, surveying the surrounding craft. "And, actually, the crowd is lighter than normal. Good for us." He killed the engine and let down the anchor, keeping them equidistant from a small speedy-looking red-and-white boat and another larger charter craft.

He stood, rubbing his palms together. "You all ready?" At their enthusiastic nods, he grinned. "Let's get your equipment on and go diving."

Olivia snapped some shots of the preparation process and of Stella, lounging in the bow. A tiny pop sounded in the open water beyond. She stood, bringing the camera up to click rapid fire as a pod of dolphins breached the surface in arcing leaps.

"Look, dolphins," the daughter exclaimed from behind Olivia.

She swung the camera around in time to catch awe flooding the girl's face. When she shared the shot, the girl's smile filled Liv with a buoyant exuberance she hadn't felt in years. When had photography lost its ability to put her on top of the world? She straightened and Mac's gaze locked on her conveying approval and something else she wasn't ready to examine. She used the camera as a barrier, framing and preserving the look until such time as her courage grew bold enough to face what her heart begged her to latch onto.

The father asked a question, redirecting Mac's attention and releasing Olivia from his hypnotizing eyes. She pretended interest in the expansive, cloud-free sky but Mac's kindness and compassion blinded her to the gorgeous view. Had anyone besides her mother ever looked at her like that?

A touch on her arm startled her and she pressed a hand to her chest as Mac chuckled.

"You take pride in scaring the wits out of me, don't you?"

His lips pulled sideways as he contained a grin. "I'm just glad the camera's waterproof."

"Eres un pícaro."

"¿Qué? Don't believe I've heard that one."

"You're a rascal––with charm." She tore her gaze away.

"Ah. Glad I've moved up on your charm gauge." He blocked her attempt to swat him with a life jacket and snorkeling mask. "In case you're interested in trying out my camera in its preferred environment." He indicated a set of flippers at her feet. "I've got to go get the others started and supervise their dive, but I'll be back to check on you in fifteen minutes or so. Stay in the area between our boat and the reef and you should be good."

She framed shots of the six of them in the water preparing for their dive. Once they'd disappeared below the surface, she set the camera down and stared at the snorkeling equipment Mac had left for her. How considerate he was. She'd planned to wait on the boat for everyone to return and share their adventure. Not that she minded, but yesterday's taste of the underwater world compelled her to remove her current life jacket, strip down to her swimsuit, and don the equipment. Securing the camera's strap to her wrist, she said goodbye to Stella who raised her head long enough to blink acknowledgment before returning to her siesta. Gingerly, she stepped over the side onto the ladder, descending into the turquoise water.

Remembering Mac's lessons, she checked the set of her mouthpiece and spread her body horizontally along the water's surface, the life jacket keeping her afloat without any effort on her part. She purged the breathing tube, and pressed her face below the surface, then opened her eyes.

Oh, Lord! It's so beautiful!

Olivia struggled to keep her mouth clamped around the breathing apparatus. Her jaw kept wanting to sag with every new discovery, the camera bringing even the more remote finds into focus. Vibrant colors on both fish and plants urged her heart into a faster rhythm. She propelled herself closer to the reef, enjoying the caress of the water on her skin.

A few smaller turtles glided among schools of tiny fish who zigged and zagged among the anemones and coral and darted in and out of the reef's various crevices. A screeching pulled her eyes from the water as gulls quarreled over a meal.

A smiling Mac approached.

She gave him a thumbs up, and he sank below the surface. Above, a few clouds had gathered, but they were the fair-weather variety.

Exploring a while longer, she found several Lined seahorses anchored in a natural trough where they could feed continuously on the organisms caught in the small eddy it created. Liv admired their delicate structure and incredible will to live. She wouldn't enjoy an existence that consisted of breathing in food while anchoring herself against strong currents that wanted to wash her ashore and away from her life mate.

She preferred the idea of the Kemp's ridley. Swimming free in the entire Gulf. Nesting in Mexico. Following the currents wherever she wished to go the rest of the year. She aspired to be as tough and tenacious as the turtles.

Breathing a silent sigh, she focused on a dark recess where an invasive lionfish with brilliant stripes and venomous spines chased several tiny orange and purple fish through a maze of underwater flora. A pair of striped shrimps scuttled out of the way. Liv snapped several shots before retreating from the threat of painful lionfish stings. Her stomach growled. Perhaps she should ready their lunch. She kicked for Mac's boat, surprised how far she'd drifted.

When she neared, Stella stood and stretched, then panted a welcome, crossing to greet Olivia when she emerged atop the ladder. More clouds had gathered, blocking the sun. The breeze brought a chatter to her teeth, so she retrieved her towel and draped it around her before opening the cooler and half-grimacing, half-smiling to herself. Ana María's Place wrappers greeted her along with sides in plastic tubs.

Mac relaxed into the appreciative smile Olivia sent him when she discovered not all the sandwiches contained spice. He grinned as he surveyed the family, chatting between bites and an occasional groan of enjoyment. *"Time in the water adds satisfaction to a meal."* Another of Gramps' wisdoms. One he'd taken to heart that had become a major recommendation for his services.

"What was your favorite discovery?" Olivia addressed the family. "I've never been diving, so I'd like to know what I can look forward to."

Mac observed Olivia while the others described their sightings: an eel, several Manta Rays, a Clown Fish, with comments about the vibrant colors and being immersed in the undersea world. Olivia's delight seemed entirely genuine. She laughed at the brothers' antics as they one-upped each other's finds, encouraged the sister when her brothers teased her interpretation of the reef, and sent friendly smiles to the parents who held hands and soaked in their children's impressions.

Was anyone that transparent? Olivia seemed too good to be true. Past experience dictated that anything––or anyone––so perfect usually proved false.

Still, her shy glance when the mom pressed her to share her own discoveries said she was what she appeared to be. Nothing more. Nothing less.

Throughout lunch the clouds had warred with the sun. As they corralled the final wrapper in a bag and tossed everything back in the cooler, the sun burst through in triumph. The resulting promise circle grabbed Mac's attention and he hurried to point it out. "I'm not sure what your spiritual beliefs are, but my Gramps always used to say if you swam to the center of one of those, you'd be in a direct line-of-sight to God on His throne in Heaven. And if you listened hard enough, you'd hear Him speak promises over you." He swallowed hard against the tightening in his throat. "I'm not sure I ever heard voices, but the sensation is a powerful one."

Another ray broke through creating a second ring of light.

"Can we do it, Mom?" The daughter turned beseeching eyes on her mother, who turned to her husband.

"Shall we, Charles?"

"What are we waiting for? All in!"

The family jumped over the sides of the boat, life jackets bobbing them to the surface, and swam for the still vibrant circle.

Olivia connected her gaze to his. Arched one brow.

Mac drew back. "I'm not sure––"

She stood and extended one hand, his camera clutched in the other. "Come on, Silver. Don't miss an opportunity. Your advice, remember?"

He inhaled and released a long breath. Nodded. "Let's go." Their hands connected and they stepped to the dive bridge. "On three."

She didn't wait but tugged him after her. Stella splashed in behind them.

When they reached the outer part of the circle, Olivia treaded water, an expression of awe on her face. Maybe she'd be content outside. Mac's tension ratcheted upward when she plunged forward, crossing the curtain of golden light and emerging within. Her smile stretched ear-to-ear.

She beckoned, but his extremities refused to adjust his position. Stella nudged him from behind. He wrapped an arm behind her life preserver, hugging her as close as he dared while avoiding her churning legs.

A hand reached through the light and tugged, stranding him half in, half out. He peered upward as understanding blinked on. *This is how I've been isn't it? Half in. Half out. I'm so sorry. To you too, Gramps.*

Olivia let go, face upturned, eyes closed, peace in every softened feature. Releasing Stella, he kicked the rest of the way in, and waited. Expectant. Afraid. He closed his eyes and treaded water, listening with his heart and his mind, but hearing nothing.

Hands closed over his forearm, and he opened his eyes to find Olivia close. He stroked her flattened hair, then pulled her to himself. Her body fit perfectly against his despite the awkwardness of their flotation devices. He pressed his lips to hers. Quick and chaste. A fire ignited in his belly, and he wanted nothing more than to devour her lips here in the middle of the ocean. The light pulsed, then faded. Stella barked. Mac felt eyes on them and released Olivia to arm's length, retaining a hold on her hand.

With a squeeze, he released her completely, though his heart pinched at the loss. From the wistfulness in her expression, she hadn't wanted the moment to end. Her peace leached in reminding him of God's promise never to forsake His children.

I'm sorry I ran away, Lord. I'll stop. As of now.

"Look!"

Olivia's whisper cut through his promise. He followed her line of sight to a grayish-green shape moving toward them. Panic gave way to recognition as a hooked beak on a triangularly-shaped head emerged for a second from the waves. He signaled Stella to heel, and she swam obediently to his side.

Clicks sounded as Olivia took shot after shot of the rare sea turtle. Grasping her around the waist, Mac hoisted her so she could get a better angle. Amazingly, the creature continued to swim nearer. It passed only an arm's length away, headed for the now-submerged reef. He switched the camera to video mode, and they followed it until it dove beneath the surface.

Olivia twisted in his hold and grasped his shoulders. Her wide eyes were dark, pupils dilated. She swooped in and planted a kiss on his lips, murmuring her thanks against his mouth and rousing new and dangerous sensations in his belly. Then she released him and swam a bit awkwardly toward his boat. He followed in her wake, needing time to compose himself before rejoining the others.

Once on shore, gear piled outside the hut, Olivia used her own camera for shots of the family in various poses. The growth in confidence puffed Mac's chest. She'd freed some abilities from the prison of self-doubt and fear. He had a few that needed rescuing from the same jail, but today's revelations had moved him forward.

"A leap forward today. A step back tomorrow. But never quitting. That's how progress is made." Gramps again.

He, like everyone, loved those leaps forward, but oh, how he dreaded those inevitable steps back.

82

Chapter Eight
One day before the Wedding

"Who did you say the bride was?"

Olivia pulled the phone away from her ear and frowned at Mac's uncharacteristically sharp voice. "It doesn't matter who. It matters when."

"No. It matters very much who, if the who is who I think it is."

She tried to picture angry Mac. Was he a pacer? Perhaps he ran his fingers through that exquisite white-blond hair of his. Maybe––

"Olivia!"

Him barking her name didn't bode well. He couldn't back out now. Not with the wedding so close. She stepped from her room into the empty living space. "Mac, calm down, okay? I just need to know if you can be here tomorrow afternoon instead of Saturday. There's been a snaffoo because the bride's mother may have let the wedding cat out of the bag, so to speak. The security guy's worried crazed fans will show up if we wait, so everything's been moved to Friday. We're the final obstacle to a green light."

Mac went quiet, but she thought she heard a door open and close. She walked onto the third-floor porch and peered at the sky. A shiver from an ocean gust wrapped her free arm around herself as she moved to her left where a few twinkles of starlight shone through.

At last, he cleared his throat. "I can work it out to be there, but Liv, I need to know the bride's name. Please. I'll keep the secret. It's important."

She blew out a breath. He wasn't ditching them. Her. "Ainslie. She's got some viral social media following. So does Lucas, her fiancé. That's why they're worried about rabid fans."

"Ainslie Tucker?"

"Uh, yeah, that's right. Do you know her?" An odd unease swept through Olivia at the prospect.

"Not well."

"Mac? Are you okay?"

There was such a long pause, Olivia wasn't sure he planned to answer. She strode inside and grabbed an oversized sweater from her closet, put the phone on speaker and slid it over her head. Just as she grabbed the phone again, he said, "It's in the past. I'll be fine."

Liv slid on the first pair of shoes she could find, a ratty old pair of sneakers, and exited to the stairs. Taking the phone off speaker, she spoke quietly so as not to disturb anyone who might be trying to sleep, though it wasn't quite nine. "Are you trying to convince me, or yourself?"

His long inhale sounded loud in the stairwell. "I'm not sure."

"I'm coming over. Do you want to meet on the beach or at your house?"

"No. Shutterbug, it's okay. You don't have to--"

"I know I don't have to. But we're friends. At least, I think we're friends. And friends are there when other friends need them. You need me." Wow. Where had that backbone come from? A tiny smile spread for her own bravado.

His chuckle sent more chills rippling through her--ones that had nothing to do with air temperature. She stepped out of the house, avoiding the wettest patches of lawn until she came to the newly locked gate. Darn it all! How was she supposed to get out?

"Livvie? Is that you?"

Camden's deep voice spun her to face him. She felt like a teen sneaking out of her parents' house. "Yes, it's me. I'm not used to having to unlock the gate."

His scowl said she should be.

She shrugged. "Sorry. Did I wake you?"

"Nah. Too wired to sleep. Trying to think of all the possible problems and block them before they happen." He ran a hand across his stubbled jaw.

"Sounds exhausting."

He dipped his chin. "I want it all to be perfect for--"

She raised her brows. "For Viana?"

"Yeah. Ainslie and Lucas, too. For all of us, really." His hands found his pockets.

"She never got over you, you know? Don't give up on her. She's had a hard go."

He strode to the gate and unlocked it, then slid it open so Olivia could slip out. "Text me when you want back in. I'll be up."

Olivia patted his arm on her way out. "I believe in the two of you, if it means anything."

The gate grated as it slid closed. Before it latched, Camden said, "Thanks. It means a lot."

Despite the concern for Mac's situation her feet seemed to bounce as she hurried to the cottage road. Spying the washed-up trunk where he'd waited for her two, or was that, three–– "Oh, no!" She stared at her phone, her blood rushing faster, bit her lip and raised it to her ear. "I'm so sorry, Mac. Forgive me."

"Who was that man you were talking to?"

Olivia jumped and peered into the darkness. Slowly lowered her phone. "Where are you?"

Mac stepped from the tree-shrouded lane, Stella at his heel. In his dark, form-fitting tee and dark jeans, he'd blended into the shadows. "Who was he?"

The growl in his voice halted her approach. "Whoa there! He's a friend." She softened her tone. No sense throwing gas on his blaze. "Security. For the high-profile couple's wedding." She tilted her head and stepped closer. "The one with the bride you kind of know, but that's got you all worked up despite it being 'in the past'." She air-quoted the final phrase and closed the rest of the distance. Stella fitted her head beneath Olivia's hand.

Mac shook his head. "I can see I'm out-numbered." He gestured toward the deserted beach. "Come on. Might as well walk."

They navigated the transition from pavement to sand in silence, where the uneven footing shoved them close then yanked them apart. At last, they made it to the packed foreshore. Olivia grabbed Mac's arm and emptied her shoes. "Sorry, they weighed a ton."

He stood there scowling down at her, arms crossed and feet apart.

She took a step back and eyed him then wrinkled her nose. "Lance or sword?"

"Excuse me?"

"You're a disapproving knight, but to finish the look, you need a weapon. I'm asking if you have a preference."

He slowly shook his head the way her mother had done when her imagination ran overtime.

"Some armor might work too. Or a horse." She put her finger to her lips. "You know, I've always longed to ride a horse on the beach." She raised her arms to the side. "How free it must feel, galloping across the sand, the mane flying, hooves splashing as the waves break and drain back into the sea." Her gaze roved the shoreline and she could almost hear the rhythmic pounding of hooves in her mind. Mac's exasperated sigh broke apart her image.

"If you're trying to wear me down with nonsense, it's not working."

"Hmm. Too bad. Mamá always said if I hadn't taken to photography, I'd have become an author." She dropped her arms and wiped the amusement from her face. "Look, I'm--"

"Before I bare my past, I need something from you."

Mac erased the distance between them in a single step, standing as close as possible without actually touching her. She swallowed. Heat from his body seeped through her thin clothing. If she touched him, she was certain she'd melt. She pushed words past dry lips. "What--" Her voice cracked. She cleared her throat and changed tacks. "I'll give what I can."

He closed his eyes as if offering a prayer, then reached for her hand. Moonlight caught in the fractured blue of his irises. A dazzling effect. When she didn't move, he brushed the back of her fingers with his. "May I?"

At her nod, he joined their hands and led her closer to the surging waves until the leading edges of frothy lace almost touched the toes of their shoes.

Liv relished the security of his hand around hers, the brush of their shoulders, the play of light on his elven locks. Being together felt right, even with so much unsaid between them. A supernatural peace fell over her and gave her the inner calm to hear the truth behind his words. She prayed she wouldn't mess this up.

"Have you ever wanted something so badly you refused to let it go until it nearly crushed you?"

A crab scuttled sideways out of the path of the next incoming wave, his movements both graceful and comical.

"For years, I prayed my photographs would gain the notice of a wildlife magazine. I entered their contest fifteen years running. Not one of my entries made even the semi-finals. Winning the contest became my standard of highest achievement." She gave a wry laugh and locked onto Mac's eyes. "You know what I just realized?"

He shook his head.

"When I was little, I came across that contest in my quest to find somewhere I could combine my love of wildlife preservation with my love of photography. In my all-consuming quest to win, I lost sight of my original goal--species and habitat conservation."

"That's why you were so eager to see and photograph the Kemp's ridley."

"I've always wanted to see one in the wild." She covered a snorting laugh with her free hand. "Do you know what I thought when I was a girl in Miami?"

"Tell me."

"I thought I was going to be some well-known YouTuber with a channel dedicated to showcasing the endangered species of the world. Crazy, huh?" Her smile froze at Mac's flinch. "What did I say?"

He waved her off. "Keep going. It's part of my rather long story. I want to hear about you first."

Ahead something scuttled across the wrack, the area where the seaweed and debris piled up at the high tide line. Mac tugged her to a stop and pointed. "Ghost crab."

"It's so fast."

"That's because they only use three of their legs to run."

"Wow, I didn't know that."

"My gramps taught me about many of the creatures who live in or near the ocean. Said if I was going to coexist with them, I should understand something of their habits."

"That's very wise."

"He had a hundred sayings like that. Wisdoms, he called them."

"Sounds like you two are close."

Mac squeezed her hand and resumed walking. "We were. He passed away when I was eighteen."

"That had to be hard." They sidestepped a hunk of driftwood. "I never knew my father and my grandmother moved away when I was a preteen. After my aunt and uncle were killed in a car crash, Mamá packed us up and moved us from Miami to Summer Shore. If not for Viana and Lauren, I'd never have survived high school. They made me feel welcomed for the first time in my life." She sent him a half smile. "I never fit in with my family. Was never Cuban enough. In fact, before we walked into Summer Shore High, my sister told me to stay away from her and not tell anyone we were sisters so I wouldn't embarrass her."

Strong arms wrapped her in an embrace. "Oh, Shutterbug. How awful."

She let herself lean into him, drawing comfort from his compassion, before pushing free. Swiping at her eyes, she blinked to clear them. "It turned out God had the situation under control. When he brought Viana and Lauren into my life, he gave me what I'd been lacking."

"He has a way of doing that, doesn't He?"

Liv was drawn back into his orbit, her gaze captured by the tenderness in his expression, the gentle way he brushed the unruly curls from her face. His fingertips lingered on her cheek, then caressed the line of her jaw, his touch setting her skin ablaze. How could she stand to be near this man? But how could she stand to be away? His other hand found the small of her back and tucked her tighter against him so his lean muscles melded with her curves. She lifted her face, and he cupped the back of her head. Never loosing eye contact, he lowered his mouth until it hovered tantalizingly close to hers. Painfully close.

"May I kiss you?"

The husk in his voice was her undoing. She raised on her tiptoes, traversing the remaining distance, and pressed her lips to his. Warm and soft, they tasted of sea salt and spice and something fruity. The intimacy of his touch had grown a bubble inside her chest. The caress of his lips, so sweet and gentle, filled the bubble to bursting and coated her soul with a contented heat. She'd never felt more at home than in the arms of this man.

Stirling's heart was lost the moment their lips met. He breathed in her fresh scent, something intoxicating in the combination of wind and waves and starlight. He wound his fingers in the exquisite texture of her curls and deepened the kiss.

When her mouth yielded to his exploration, an involuntary groan escaped. If he'd understood the soul-deep pleasure that would come from holding this woman––kissing her––he'd have done it long ago. That peck in the ocean hadn't been a fair preview. When little mewling noises came from her throat, the pressure in his chest nearly snapped his heart in two.

How could he love her when they'd only just met?

Not the puppy love of a besotted teen, but something that could grow into the mature love God ordained for a man to a woman. The forever kind.

A yelp followed by a bark, froze his growing passion. He pulled away and looked down at the receding wave. Chuffing a laugh, he swept Olivia into his arms and raced to higher ground, their shoes thoroughly drenched in saltwater. Stella's paws pounded alongside.

"That's proof God pays close attention," he said, lowering her feet to dryer sand.

She looked at him, eyes reflecting the moonlight, so he couldn't see inside. "How so?"

Grasping her hand, he raised it to his lips and kissed her knuckles. "Your sweetness was driving me over the edge of rational thought. He knew I respect you too much to let our kisses get out of hand. I guess cold water really does quench the fires of passion." He unfurled her fingers and placed a lingering kiss on her palm. "At least temporarily."

Her sharp inhale melted his core, and he made to pull her close.

"Perhaps we'd better walk." She danced out of his embrace, tugging gently as she skipped backward. "Stella's tired of being still."

That her smile wobbled, reassured him she was as affected by him as he by her. "Good plan."

"Besides," she said, "you promised to share your story."

He slanted a glance her way. "Not letting me off the hook, eh?"

"Not a chance."

Her grin set his heart racing. He peered down the beach, gathering his scattered thoughts. The smoky shapes of pelicans roosting on the pier pilings and the rhythmic slap and whoosh of the waves calmed him enough he could sort through his past. Seek the points where choice and circumstance had collided to alter his life's trajectory.

Olivia tightened her grip on his hand, raising her other to squeeze his shoulder. A move that was both encouraging and distracting.

They exchanged soft looks.

"I already told you Gramps was a key person in my early life. He got me started snorkeling, then diving. Taught me to operate watercraft and respect the animal and plant life we share the planet with. He was a history buff--knew all the wrecks in and around the Keys--and instilled his love of treasure hunting in me."

They reached the pier and climbed the steps. The click of the dog's nails caused several pelicans to ruffle their feathers before settling back into sleep. Tiptoeing past the birds, they reached the center of the pier where the fishermen cleaned their catch on wooden tables attached to the pier's railing. A lingering fishy odor permeated the place, though scavengers had cleaned every scrap from the wood.

Olivia wrinkled her nose, then grinned. "Stella likes this place."

Sure enough, the lab scampered back and forth, nose to the ground, tail wagging. "She's never been on the pier, for obvious reasons."

Olivia shared his laugh. "The fishermen's frowns would reach epic proportions." She flopped onto a bench and pulled her knees to her chest. "You were telling me about your amazing Gramps."

He nodded, memories flooding in. Pacing along the rail, he told about the time they dove a wreck after a hurricane had swept through. "We'd been down for about fifteen minutes when I entered what may have been the captain's quarters––a larger room near the forecastle. When my light hit it, the Manta Ray resting in there retreated in a swirl of silt. I caught a glint of something through the muddy cloud and reached for it, though it wasn't the brightest thing to do. My hand closed on something round with a bit of weight to it. I put it in my dive pouch without really looking and moved farther into the room to explore. When we surfaced, I took the object out and showed it to Gramps. He got really excited, saying it looked authentic. Some sort of gold coin."

"Was it?" She leaned forward.

He turned away from the distraction of her parted lips. Nodded. "It was authenticated as a Spanish ocho escudos coin from the treasure fleet sunk in 1715 by a hurricane."

"Amazing. And your pronunciation was pretty good there."

"Gramps insisted I study Spanish as part of my homeschool curriculum." He shrugged. "My pronunciation might be good, but don't ask me to converse beyond basic responses to 'how are you' and 'what's your name'."

"Most students have the same struggle. What happened to your discovery?"

"We sold it to a museum for their collection."

"Nice."

"It sparked my dream of treasure hunting. Brought it to a new level. The next year I suggested we start a YouTube channel where we videoed our treasure-hunting efforts."

"This was with your family?"

He nodded, hands clenched.

Her face scrunched. "How old were you?"

"Seven." He turned his anger toward the ocean where a chilly wind blew across the water. "My parents weren't great with money management and when my dad lost his job, we were pretty strapped for cash. He and Gramps argued about the proceeds from the sale of my coin, but Gramps insisted the money be invested in a long-term fund. He refused to let Dad touch it. The YouTube idea was my way of smoothing the waters."

"Did it work?"

Her fingers rubbed the tension from his neck and back, and he grabbed the railing for support. Swallowed. "For a time."

"What about the Ainslie connection?"

He heaved a sigh. "With the success of our show came public recognition. We were nominated for a few awards and gained some national exposure. I was eighteen. Gramps had just passed away. I met a girl named Makaya who was a couple years older than me. She was easy to talk to and frankly, I needed a distraction. When she showed an interest, I taught her some of the video techniques I'd perfected. Let her in. She and Ainslie were cousins or something, so I met her once or twice and showed her a couple of things as well. Helped her start her first YouTube channel." Olivia's hands stopped moving and he turned to face her. "Yeah. So, this could be a bit awkward. Or, she might not remember me. Who knows?"

A shiver ran the length of Olivia's body. "You're freezing." He wrapped an arm around her shoulders and rubbed his other hand along the length of her thin sleeve. "Let's get you home."

She put a hand flat on his chest. "No. There's more."

He looked away. "Once Makaya learned all I could teach her, she broke it off with me. I'd fancied myself in love. Turns out, it was one-sided." He steered Olivia toward the beach and patted his leg for Stella. Smiled when her wet nose found his palm.

A few steps passed in silence, then Olivia looked over at him, finding his eyes. "She used you."

"Seems so."

"I get it. My junior year, a freshman boy began flirting with me. I thought I was finally learning to fit in, but it turned out he had a crush on an older girl and I was his ticket. After we arrived, he ditched me to hang out with her crowd. When I tried to join them, he told me to quit whining and get lost."

Stirling stopped and turned Liv to face him, resting his hands lightly on her waist. "I'm so sorry." That some guy had hammered in her sister's barb engulfed him in swirling emotions. He wished he could absorb her pain, but appreciated Viana and Lauren for not relegating her to the background, despite her hesitance with people. He tucked a stray curl behind her ear. "And yet, you're the gentlest, kindest, most understanding woman I've ever met. The hurt didn't change you."

She gave a quick shake of her head and captured his hand against her cheek, turning into it slightly and closing her eyes. Her lips parted. "You're wrong. It made me shrink inside myself until I focused solely on my photography. I became obsessed with the *Floridian Wildlife* contest and poured all my efforts into that single pursuit. Then, in college, when my professors steered me toward portrait work, I didn't have the strength or the passion to stand my ground. Those years of losses told me I wasn't good enough, and I believed it to be true. So much that I had no will of my own."

She released his hand, resuming their walk. Two steps later, she sent him a crooked smile. "It wasn't until you brought back my love of the camera and the amazing images it's made to capture, that I remembered the joy of photography itself. It helps others see themselves or the subject of the picture in a new light. That's what I always loved about it, but in my warped focus on winning, I forgot." She pressed her head against his arm for a brief second, then straightened. "Thank you."

They descended the steps to the sand. Stirling found a driftwood stick and chucked it ahead of them. "Stella fetch."

The dog became a black blur as she chased the flying object.

"I haven't seen or spoken to my family in four years." Stirling waited for Olivia's response, a strange tightness across his chest.

Stella galloped back, planting her hindquarters at his feet in a spray of wet sand, the driftwood in her mouth.

"Release."

The dog dropped it across his toes.

"Ow!"

Olivia laughed and ruffled the lab's fur. "Good girl."

He sent her a pained look, picked up the stick and handed it to her. "You throw it." She did, and he sent Stella bounding away.

Expression serious, Olivia asked, "Were you hiding here in Summer Shore?"

"I guess. Yes."

She cocked her head as Stella returned. "Does your new sign mean you're ready to stop hiding?"

"Maybe."

She thought a moment, then nodded. "Me too. I think." Pulling away, she did a few shuffling steps. "Race you to the stump." Without waiting for his answer, she sprinted off.

Stella whined, and Stirling sent her after Olivia, who imitated a Ghost Crab, flying over the sand.

He watched the two of them for a moment, feeling lighter than he remembered since the moment his family had told him Gramps had planted the coin for him to find, then admitted to planting treasure for their hunts. Maybe he had to confront them before forgiveness could come. And if so, he needed to do it soon, because he was ready to rid himself of the dark cloud hanging over his past and move on.

He took off, pounding toward what he hoped would be his brighter future.

Chapter Nine
Wedding Day

Even after his late night, seeing Olivia to her gate where burly Camden let her in, then locked him out with a firm click barely slept. Rising at dawn, he'd organized his video equipment, laid out his tux, and cooked himself a sausage scramble. As he meandered his cottage, plate in hand, his vision snagged on the underwater camera he'd loaned Shutterbug.

Abandoning his half-finished breakfast, he panned through the shots. The video of the Kemp's ridley played, the quality only so-so with the lens receiving constant splashes from the waves. Still, it lent itself to a kind of in-the-moment realism, a sense of "being there," many nature-lovers would likely find appealing. A promising start to that YouTube channel she wanted to create, and something he could easily help with if she was serious.

Stella wandered over and nudged his leg, casting forlorn glances at his plate. He rubbed her ears and shook his head. "Sorry, girl. You'll have to stick to kibble." He grabbed another forkful while he skipped back to Olivia's underwater shots, instantly struck by her focus and shot composition. Clearly, her training hadn't been wasted. She had a masterful eye, each succeeding photo bringing a new swell of emotion.

Until he came to one of several Lined seahorses. They leaped out of the shot, vibrantly alive. So much so he could imagine their tiny noses fluctuating as they sucked in a constant supply of nutrients. He blew out a breath to slow his pulse. Hit the button for the next photo.

And stared. He could not be the only person to view this scene. He linked the camera to his computer and began the download, already thinking on how to best frame the print.

Fifteen minutes later, dressed in jeans and a button-down beneath his leather jacket and armed with his phone and an SD card, he fired up his little-used motorcycle. While normally, he'd make this trip via bicycle, today's errand required more speed. With empty city streets, he arrived at Ana María's Place in short order, then worried he may have beaten Carmela there.

"Who bangs on my door before even my help arrives, hmm?" Olivia's mother answered his knock with her customary bright smile. "Ah," she said upon seeing him. "It's my favorite videographer beach dude." She waved him inside and placed a hot mug of Cuban coffee in front of him.

Stirling took a sip of the strong, sweet and frothy drink and swallowed appreciatively. "I needed that this morning, Mrs. Perez."

She swatted his arm with her newspaper and sat across from him. "I've told you none of that Mrs. stuff. Carmela or," ––she batted her lashes over widened eyes–– "Mamá if you prefer."

The swig of coffee became a gulp, burning his throat as he swallowed, then coughed. When he'd stopped sputtering and wiped his tearing eyes with a napkin Carmela thrust his way, he took a large, cleansing breath and exhaled slowly, nodding.

"While I'm not sure we're ready for that step, Carmela." He enunciated her name deliberately, dipping his chin for her approval which she gave with a smirk. "This does have something to do with Olivia."

Carmela's sigh made him frown.

She gave a sad shake of her head. "Every time I hear her called by that name, it pains me. Here." She pressed a work-worn palm to her heart. "To me, she will always be Oliva. Named for the beautiful, bountiful Olive tree which our blessed Lord Jesús used for shade and oil in his days on Earth. It is a good name. A wholesome name with ties to the fertile soil. But my daughter rejects her heritage and her connection to our family. I do not know how to bring her back while making her understand she is free to soar in her own way. She thinks I want to tether her to this restaurant when I only want to give her wings to follow her own passion." Carmela patted Stirling's hand. "But you didn't come to listen to an old woman's ranting. How can I help you?"

Stirling grasped her fingers before she could pull away. "She loves you and I don't believe the name change means she's rejecting her heritage. In fact, I wouldn't be surprised if it wasn't intentional at all." He smiled. "It isn't my story to tell, but I would ask her about her sister and the start of high school."

Carmela straightened. "Cereza?" Her expression clouded. "That girl has always been a bit high and mighty. Never understood why Oliva didn't like wearing flashy clothes or disliked spicy food."

He leaned toward Carmela. "Olivia––Oliva––mentioned a contest she used to enter sponsored by some magazine. Would you happen to know which one and when the deadline to enter might be?"

Her eyes widened. "Of course. I urged her to try again, but she refused. Stubborn. Like her father. I'm sure there's a copy in her old room. Let's go see."

Stirling followed Carmela's colorful skirt up the tiny back stairs. "I forgot you used to live above the restaurant."

"Moved two years ago. But only two blocks over. I still walk to work." She pushed open a door at the head of the stairs. "In here."

The room was a time capsule, a frozen moment from Olivia's past. An almost eerie feeling flowed over him as he perused the things a younger Olivia had obsessed over. One bookshelf overflowed with nature and photography magazines, another with novels––*Charlotte's Web* and *The Black Stallion* among the titles. His heart beat a little faster when he spied *Treasure Island* and *Robinson Crusoe* with worn covers a bit farther down.

Carmela crossed to the nightstand and extracted several magazines from the drawer. A piece of paper fell from one when she handed them over. He bent to retrieve it, reading the first line. *We regret to inform you that your entry was not chosen . . .* His gaze scanned to the date. Sixteen years ago.

"Was this her first rejection?" He held the smudged paper out for Carmela.

She pursed her lips. "Must be. I didn't know she kept it all this time."

He pointed to the magazines. "*Floridian Wildlife* sponsors the contest?"

Nodding, she glanced at her watch. "This year's deadline is today."

"I best get busy then. Thank you for your help, Carmela."

"It's my pleasure, Mac. Or should I call you Stirling?"

"You're a sly one, aren't you?" He moved to let her descend the stairs. "How'd you find out?"

"No one is that good with video by accident. I did a little digging. Turns out one of my customers used to live in the Keys." She glanced back with a grin. "He remembered a little whippersnapper whose family had some kind of treasure-hunting show. Told me he met the brains behind the whole thing once. A kid named Stirling MacAllister."

They exited the stairwell, spice and Spanish chatter enveloping them. Carmela stirred a pot of bubbling pork, nodded at the worker and moved on, speaking over her shoulder. "He wondered what happened to you. Said he'd been an acquaintance with your grandpa, and the man had bragged about your commitment to the Lord and enthusiasm when it came to discovering the truth. He loved that about you. That coin was a prize your grandpa always wanted to find, but he was glad you were the one who found it. Said it made him proud the way you handled the fame and fortune. Wasn't sure he'd have done as well."

Stirling swallowed. "Did he say if it was real or if Gramps planted it for me?" He almost didn't want to hear her answer, but prayed he could handle whichever it turned out to be.

"He didn't mention that. But why does it matter."

"What do you mean? It matters a lot."

"Not the way I look at it." They'd exited the spacious kitchen, and Carmela faced Stirling. "Whether your grandpa left it for you to find or whether the Lord made it possible for you to find it, you're the one who gave it to the world. You released the power of the coin to enliven the imaginations of others. You didn't hoard it for yourself. If your grandpa found it at some earlier site, do you think he'd have kept it hidden from you all that time? That's the question you have to answer for yourself, but in my opinion, it's a moot point. Sometimes you just have to let things go."

Her words shattered Stirling's argument like a ship on rocks and he didn't try to gather the broken pieces. Instead, he let it slip beneath the waves and breathed.

Carmela squeezed his shoulder. "You take care of Olivia for me. And remind her to come see her family once in a while, sí?"

"Sí." He smiled at her use of the anglicized version of her daughter's name. Grabbing his helmet from the table, he tucked a magazine and the letter into the inside pocket of his leather jacket. "Gracias. For everything."

"You come back and bring my daughter." She pointed to a newer line painted below the menu on one wall. "She can taste some of our new options."

Low spice, no heat? Order any item a la Oliva

"She'll love that." On impulse, he stepped forward and gave Carmela a hug. Her response was warm and welcoming, and he realized Olivia's personality reflected her mother in a big way. He anticipated the feel of her arms. But first, he had some loose ends to tie up.

Olivia paced her room. Sable perched on his carpet head synched to her movement like a fan at a tennis match. She wrung her hands then glanced in the full-length mirror. The black silk flowed to mid-calf. Black satin slippers encased her feet. Her hair was subdued in braids tied with tiny ribbons Lauren had added before pinning everything into a neat bun at her nape. With light makeup, she'd transformed into an exotic-looking version of her natural self.

Though if she were truthful, she wasn't super solid on who that self was anymore. Or what she should strive to be. Too much caffeine after her late night and way too early morning had her nerves tangled in bunches. In fact, if it wasn't for the sand-encrusted tennis shoes, she might wonder if she'd dreamed the entire encounter.

She'd kept busy all morning helping with decorations, last minute additions and changes, a tweak here or there. With the flurry of activity, she'd had no time to dwell on last night's serious sharing between her and Mac. The fact he was half an hour late made her wonder if she'd managed to misjudge yet again. Had he decided she was too much of a mess to take a chance on? Too needy or pushy or weird?

Her phone buzzed and she answered without looking at who called.

"Livvie, you dressed?" Viana sounded as anxious as she felt. "The guests are ready for greeting photos. Can you come downstairs, please? And do you know where your very handsome videographer is?"

"Be right down." She clicked off. If she knew Mac's location, she wouldn't be the nervous wreck she was right now.

Stomach threatening to rebel, Olivia wrapped a towel around Sable and moved him to his pen. She grabbed the handles to her camera bag in one hand and her "Justin Case" bag in the other. It held all the extra things she shouldn't need, but didn't want to be without. Just in case. She hurried down the narrow stairs, grateful no one had insisted on heels.

"Stay away from me. I don't want people to know we're sisters." Cereza's long-ago declaration jangled like a siren in her mind. Maybe Mac had decided she'd be bad for business. Or worse, maybe he thought she was

like Makaya, Ainslie's friend——using him for his knowledge and what he could teach her.

That thought hollowed her out so she nearly missed the last step and faceplanted in front of a startled Ainslie and her mother. They reached out to steady her, and she regained her balance without taking anyone down. A minor miracle.

"Thank you," she breathed.

"Are you okay?" Ainslie put a hand on her shoulder. "I know Via made it sound like we were in a rush, but really, there's plenty of time." She glanced at her mother, who found a nearby flower arrangement worth closer inspection.

"Oh no. It's fine. I was just . . . We can do some still shots if you like. I'm uh, I'm waiting——"

The front door opened and in swept a version of Mac that Olivia had never seen. Dressed in a black tuxedo with a sky-blue shirt that matched his eyes, blond hair secured in a man-bun, and armed with two leather cases, he looked as if he could be a big-time executive or

. . .

Her brain couldn't come up with an "or" due to lack of oxygen. She had stopped breathing the second his gaze locked onto her.

"There you are." His voice was low as if speaking only to her, despite the guests and wedding party milling about the room. He crossed to her, put an arm around her waist, and squeezed once, then faced the crowd, putting them shoulder-to-shoulder.

Thus anchored, Olivia found her breath and her voice. "Mac, meet Ainslie Tucker, bride-to-be, and her mother Florence."

He took half a step forward, hand outstretched.

Ainslie met him, a furrow lining her forehead. "Do I know you?"

"Yes, ma'am, but it was a long time ago. No reason you should remember." Mac released her hand and shook Florence's.

Lucas joined them and Olivia introduced him to Mac, then requested they gather in the foyer to photograph an official wedding party greeting of the guests. The strength of her own voice surprised her, but she wasn't about to question.

Mac stopped her from following with a tug on her hand. "I'm sorry I was late. I didn't mean to make you worry."

"Why would I be worried?" She tried for nonchalance, but failed miserably when her voice cracked on the last word.

He pulled her close and rested his chin on the top of her head. "Oh, Shutterbug."

The nickname calmed the stress that had dogged her all morning. He released her too soon, but locked onto her eyes long enough to reassure her memories were real and promise something more. "Let's do this." With a smile, she stepped away and moved to set up the first shot of many on her list.

Chapter Ten
Day after the Wedding

Exhaustion had sent Olivia straight to dreamland when the festivities finally wound down after the ceremony and reception. Her head still on the pillow, she lifted a hand to her lips. Fire surged through her at the memory of Mac's lingering kiss before he disappeared into the shadows beyond the gate. She'd stayed until his jaunty whistle had been whisked away by the ocean winds, then gathered her equipment and lugged it upstairs to her room. She'd planned to download the photos before bed, but her drooping eyes hadn't cooperated. Her camera sat beside her laptop. The job left for later that day.

With a stretch and a yawn, she roused herself and padded to the bathroom. Judging by the closed doors, her friends' days hadn't yet begun. She scooped Sable from his pen and planted a kiss on his nose. "Want to see the pictures?"

She circled to her desk her stomach a battleground of winged creatures. What if her work wasn't good enough? What if she thought it was good, but it turned out her judgement was lacking as it had been each of the fifteen times she'd submitted an entry to the contest? If she downloaded them, she could view them on the larger screen. After moving Sable to his carpet, she connected the two devices, then navigated to the file transfer screen.

The bar indicated several minutes. A brief reprieve. Surely at least some of the thousands of photos would be acceptable.

Opening her email, she scanned the subject lines for ones requiring immediate attention. Mostly the usual newsletters and alerts until one received Friday morning caught her eye. She wrinkled her nose in confusion. Clicked and read.

Entry Receipt from *Floridian Wildlife*

Fee paid. 1 entry. Annual "Get into Nature" Photography Contest

Category: Professional

Entry Title: Maze Swimmer

She stared, slack-jawed, at her screen. Shook her head and blinked. "What? Who? How?" Her gaze bounced from the screen to Sable as if he knew the answer.

A ping indicated her download was complete. Tucking her questions away, she opened the folder.

The winged creatures grew into Pegasi as Olivia opened the file. Lifting Sable onto her lap, she squeezed her eyes tight. Clicking the mouse to load the first picture, she lifted the rabbit toward the screen. "Is it good?" Realizing how ridiculous she sounded, she screwed up her courage and opened her eyes, then clicked to the next picture, and the next, and the next.

With critical eyes, she took in the color composition, the lighting, the focus. Ainslie's radiance as she and Lucas clasped hands beneath the arbor. Even the guests looked good.

The daisies popped against the white frosting on Lauren's cake, and the edible crystals added a fairytale quality. The surprise on Viana's face as the bouquet fell into her hands was priceless. As was the wistful look on Camden's later when Olivia had caught him gazing at Via.

She'd captured the dancers' joy, a smirking Lucas wiping smeared cake from his face, and Mac behind the video camera looking absolutely breathtaking in his tux. What would it be like to be held tight in his embrace, dancing the night away? Likely she'd never know, but a girl could dream.

There were throwaway photos too. Lauren's Cake Guy holding a spatula in front of his face. Ones where someone had inadvertently stepped into a shot. But all the prime moments were there, perfectly framed. Or at least they would be after a bit of editing.

Unable to stop herself from taking another look, Olivia returned to her email tab. The message from *Floridian Wildlife* hadn't disappeared. In black and white it declared her entry into the contest.

"I don't get it, Sable. Who would enter, pay the fifty-dollar fee, and credit me with their photo?" She chewed on her bottom lip. "I didn't have a shot good enough. I looked. And even if I did, how would someone have downloaded and sent it without my knowledge?"

She speed-dialed the restaurant. After several rings, Ramon picked up. "Ana María's Place, how may we help you?"

"Ramon, can I talk to Mamá?"

"Of course, Oliva. I will get her. Un momentito."

Her hand hurt from gripping the phone as she waited for her mother to answer.

"Olivia, what's wrong?"

She almost fell out of her chair when her mother added the *i* to her name. "Mamá! Are you all right?"

"I'm fine, Chiquita. You're giving me gray hairs. Tell me what's going on."

Right. "Did you enter one of my photos in *Floridian Wildlife's* contest?"

"How would I do that, mija? I have none of your photographs. Even though I've asked for some to display and you continue to refuse me." The wheedling tone transported her to her teen years when stubbornness and fear had kept her from obeying or sharing. Feeling convicted, she said, "I'm sorry for being so difficult, Mamá. I'm going to do better."

"Querida, I love you the way you are, but sometimes you do not see with open eyes."

"You're right. Another thing I'm working to correct."

"You're very agreeable today. The wedding must have been a success."

"A huge success." The thought of Mac encouraging her from behind his camera. Sending a wink or a thumb's up or a crooked grin popped her to her feet. "I need to go. We'll talk soon."

Olivia ended the call and dialed Mac's number, needing to hear his voice. When the call went to voicemail, she grabbed her rabbit and strapped on his harness, then changed out of her pajamas and ran to the bathroom, nearly plowing over a sleepy-eyed Viana who was exiting. "Sorry." She slipped past and in less than five minutes was headed to the stairs.

Lauren stood in the kitchen staring at the coffee pot.

"We're headed to the beach."

Though she lifted her mug, Lauren didn't turn around. Olivia paused, one foot on the top stair. "What's wrong?"

Lauren shook her head.

Reversing direction, Olivia set Sable in his pen and put an arm around her friend's shoulders. "Talk to me."

Her smile trembled. "I think I'm falling in love."

Liv's brows rose. "With the cake guy, Duke or whatever?"

A snort of laughter doubled Lauren over. "You call him the cake guy?"

"You wouldn't tell us his name. So . . ." She shrugged.

Lauren cocked her head toward the stairs. "Go on. I'll be fine." When Olivia hesitated, she gave her a little shove. "Really."

Liv retrieved Sable and when she looked back, Lauren was pouring coffee. She jogged half the distance down the beach, then slowed to regain control of her puffing breaths before she reached Mac's hut. From a hundred feet away, the place looked deserted. "Oliva, idiota! You knew he cancelled all his Saturday clients." She glanced around, but it seemed no one had heard her talking to herself.

A black streak came at her, skidding to a stop in a spray of sand. She squeezed her eyes closed and ducked her head to avoid the worst of it. Sable squeaked and wriggled free, digging his claws into her arm as he jumped away from the barrage.

"Stella, heel." The command wasn't issued in Mac's deep voice, but in a familiar accented one.

With a lick of apology to Olivia's hand, the dog stood and padded over to the voice's owner. Sable tugged on the leash. Olivia snatched a piece of dried seaweed from his mouth then moved him to a clear patch of sand.

She squinted into the sun until a shape solidified. "Hueso? Where's Mac?"

"Gone. He was supposed to text you." Hueso removed his cap, scratched his forehead, then replaced it. "I don't think he slept last night. Called me at one this morning, dropped Stella off, then roared away on that motorcycle of his."

A terrible feeling began to claw its way from Olivia's past. "Did he say where he was going?"

"The Keys, I think." Hueso shifted his weight, and cleared his throat. "He said you'd take Stella." Creases formed on his forehead. "Will you. Mi mujer is allergic and, well, she don't look good with hives. And it don't put her in too good a mood either, if you get my meaning." Patting Stella's head, he sent her a sheepish grin. "Bringing this dog home tonight means I'll be sleeping in the dog house."

Olivia slid her phone from her pocket and opened her texts. Nothing. She swallowed, her teeth finding her lip. Stella whined.

Hueso pursed his lips. "You're bleeding."

She glanced at the scratch. "It's fine."

He grabbed some napkins from his stand and handed them to her. "Better than nothing."

Half an hour later, Olivia sat across from her mother at a patio table outside the restaurant with a bowl of fluffy eggs and roast pork "a la Oliva." Stella lay with her head on Olivia's feet. Sable occupied her lap. She forked a bite and chewed, enjoying the perfect blend of flavors sans spice. Then she recalled the eggs Mac had served her and her throat tightened. She pushed the food away.

Her mother frowned. "I've asked Hank to add the *i* to Oliva. I'm sorry I've been so reluctant to accept the change."

"No, Mamá. Oliva is my name. I only use Olivia because my friends say it that way. It just became easier. I'm flattered--honored--by the new menu. I just can't eat right now." Tears stung her eyes. "What if he doesn't come back?"

Her mother came around the table and drew her into a hug. Stella whined. Sable shifted. Olivia's shoulders shook and hot tears soaked into Mamá's apron. Eventually, Olivia straightened and blew her nose. Met

Mamá's gentle eyes. "What if he decides he doesn't want to be associated with me?"

"Oh, Chiquita, that first boy was a scoundrel and you let yourself hope his spots would change. And you were a victim of your sister's fear. This one is different."

"If he reconciles with his family he might not want to come back."

"Perhaps."

Olivia bit her lip.

"You love him?"

"I might be falling for him." It was all she could admit, though her heart called her a liar.

"Well, I guess you'll have to decide if he's worth waiting for. Or relocating for. We often want things to fall into our laps. But sometimes, the Lord wants us to fight for them. Sometimes we're called to stand our ground, pursue our own passion, and wait on the Lord's timing to bring everything to fruition. Not an easy thing for the girl who tends to retreat from the battle." She rose, patting Olivia on the back. "I have food to prepare. Call if you need me." She bustled toward the door, then looked over her shoulder. "So you know, I believe love is worth fighting for, but maybe God's giving you time to figure out your own path before you tie it to another person's journey."

Stella's golden gaze added another plea to Mamá's words. Olivia scooted the laptop nearer and opened it to the webpage she was creating. If Lauren could have outside clients, she could too. She envisioned it as a place to offer prints of her wildlife photos along with hints on how to aid conservation and preservation efforts. Fingers poised above the keys, she glanced upward into the cloudless sky. *Lord, lend me the strength to wait and the courage to pursue the love you've given me.*

Chapter Eleven
Three days after the Wedding

"**C**ome on Stella, want to join Sable and me on the beach?"

The dog stood from the blanket at the foot of Olivia's bed, tail wagging. Olivia glanced at her still-silent phone before she tucked it into her leggings. "He's coming back. Right, Stella?" The oversized sweater she slid over her head fell past her hips in soft lavender drapes, something new she'd picked up at Castaways. "No news is good news." She pushed a perky brightness into her tone, but questions bombarded her nonetheless, her new knowledge of who Mac really was creating a cloud of doubt.

She'd been a fling. A temporary distraction. Or worse, a charity case. Why would wealthy Stirling MacAllister want to associate with stubborn, oddball Oliva Perez, champion avoider and runner from difficulty?

She tucked a harnessed Sable beneath her arm and was met with golden eyes. She ruffled the dog's fur. "I guess if you love him, he can't be all bad."

They found their way downstairs and outside without setting off any of Camden's alarms. An image of Viana and Cam sitting with heads together made Olivia smile. At least they seemed to be getting closer. And Lauren had been unusually upbeat yesterday. Driving off wearing boots and a Stetson, saying something about horses and a cowboy. What had Stirling MacAllister thought of her silly horseback riding dream?

Unlocking the gate with the code Camden had shared and made them all memorize, she directed her montage through, then closed it behind her. Funny how their habits had changed.

Stella's bark pulled Olivia out of her head. The dog bounded forward, nearly tackling a man who rose from the driftwood stump backlit by the first taste of dawn.

"Mac. You're back." She ran two steps before she stopped. "You left. Without telling me."

"I texted."

"No. You didn't." She backed away, tears threatening.

He dug out his phone, scrolled, and stared. Swallowed. Pushed a button.

Olivia's phone pinged. She narrowed her eyes but refused to reach for it. "Here's Stella." She turned on her heel and retreated toward the gate.

He got in front of her, palms out. "I'm sorry. I thought it sent."

She dodged and kept walking, not meeting his eyes. Stella barked.

"Olivia, please." He caught her hand.

She jerked it away, breathing hard. "Three days. You didn't try to call or send another text. For three days. If I'm that forgettable, that expendable, then you don't truly want me. I refuse to be with someone who doesn't choose me."

"As you should."

His voice was so soft. And he was looking at her with those spectacular eyes. That tender expression. She yanked her gaze from his. Made to step around, but found her way blocked by a large black dog. She sighed.

"I don't expect you to trust me, but I meant to send that text, not to leave you hanging. Do me one last favor and read it."

She wanted to hurl some angry retort. Instead, she snagged her phone then bit back a cry when it refused to cooperate.

"Easy, Shutterbug. Let me."

She shoved the phone at him in a final act of defiance. He handed it back a few seconds later with another soft smile that tugged at her heart despite its bruises.

Silver:

> I didn't want to call and wake you, but don't want you to worry. My mother called, asking me to come home. Said it was urgent but wouldn't tell me more. I feel God is behind this. Please do me and Stella a favor. Go and rescue her from Hueso. If you can, keep her company until I return. Not sure when that will be.

Her doubts persisted. Still. "I'm glad you came back."

"If you'll walk me home, I have something for you."

Olivia hesitated, indecision pressing against her new sense of accomplishment. *Stop. Lord, show me Your way.* She looked at Mac. At his disheveled appearance, the bags under his eyes. What had he been through the last three days? Whether they were friends or more than friends, this was the man who'd rearranged his life to help her save a wedding and remind her to love. "Okay." The relief that flooded his face made her heart sing though she tried to restrain it.

They walked in silence until Mac's cottage came into view. Once inside, Stella raced around sniffing each room, lapped some water, then circled her bed three times and flopped down with a large doggie sigh.

"Tired of sleepovers, eh, girl."

"I could tell she missed you."

"Did you miss me?"

Olivia clung to Sable and studied the floor.

"I didn't mean to push. See if this works for the rabbit." He indicated a corner of his kitchen, blocked off with pet panels, a litter box on one side and empty food and water bowls on the other. He lifted a bag. "The right kind, yes?"

"How did you know?"

"I pay attention to what matters to you."

The words caused a flutter in her midsection. She released Sable from the harness while Mac added fresh water and set the bowl beside the food.

Mac looked her up and down.

"What?"

"You might want to change into the clothes your mother sent. They're in the bag on the table."

She narrowed her eyes, but marched to the table and pulled out jeans and her riding boots, then stalked to the bathroom.

When she emerged, the sheepish grin Mac sent her eased a bit of the irritation over her mother's collusion with Mac behind her back.

"I wouldn't have thought you the boot-wearing kind," Mac said as he ushered her from the house.

"I used to live in Tennessee. Of course, I wear boots."

Holding up both hands in surrender, he led the way to a small outbuilding. Raising the garage-style door revealed a medium-sized motorcycle.

"Where are we going?" Olivia asked as she strapped on the helmet Mac handed her.

He stowed the lunch bags he'd been carrying in the motorcycle's saddlebags then peered deep into her eyes. "Can you trust me?"

"I guess I don't have a choice since you virtually kidnapped me." Her attempt at sternness fell flat.

"Not really." His smug look released her laugh, adding to the sense of freedom that Friday's wedding successes had initiated. When his deep chuckle joined in, her heart seemed to expand despite her inner voice urging caution. He backed the bike from the shed, threw a leg over, and waited for her to climb on behind him.

"This better be good. I'm missing my morning walk and breakfast."

"Don't worry. I've got you covered." The engine rumbled to life.

She leaned forward, prepared to yell, but he tapped the helmet and his voice sounded near her ear. "We have comms. Just speak normally. I'll hear you."

"Oh. Okay." She secured her arms around his waist enjoying the tingly sensations being so near created a bit too much.

"Were you going to say something?"

"I've decided to enjoy the moment."

Another deep chuckle tickled her chest where it touched his back. She inhaled deeply, breathing in the crisp morning air, the hint of sea, musk, and leather from Mac's jacket. Closing her eyes, she offered a prayer for peace. She'd had few moments like this in the past. Perhaps her future could hold more. Just thinking the thought unsettled her, re-cinched the recently loosened band around her heart.

"Were you satisfied with the photos from the wedding?"

Genuine interest came through in the gentle tone of Mac's voice. It soothed her as no one had been able to do before. Welling emotion clogged her throat and she nodded, then wanted to bop herself on the forehead. "I think they'll do." The thrill from when she'd viewed the raw frames in her room days earlier had faded to doubt.

The emailed receipt edged into her thoughts. It had to have been sent in error, right?

Mac steered the motorcycle into an unfamiliar part of Summer Shore——one that had expanded since she'd gone away to college. "You didn't think they were good?"

She swallowed to clear the lump that her uncertainty had formed. "I'm not the best person to ask."

They stopped at a four-way stop. No vehicles waited at the other points of the intersection, but rather than move forward, Mac swiveled around. "Why not?"

His gentle question penetrated deep, all the way to her bones. She stared at the pavement, unable to handle his intense scrutiny. Refusing to examine the source of her answer.

A car rolled up behind them, and he returned his attention to the bike, accelerating away from the town parallel to the shore. A short ride later, the route veered away from the beachfront, climbing several hills until they were on an elevated bluff set back half a mile or so from the water. A sign pointed the way to Beach's Best Stable, and Olivia's thoughts and desires crashed together.

They parked in a deserted lot that fronted a neat wooden barn painted white with black trim. Several horses grazed in fields and still others poked heads from short runs. Mac removed his helmet and she followed his lead.

"You remembered."

He extended his hand. "The entire time I was away, I considered how best to bring a smile to your eyes. This topped the list."

Stirling checked the time. "They should be out soon."

Olivia faced the clopping hooves with emotions buzzing. Two stable hands wearing T-shirts in the blue and white colors of Beach's Best Stables each led a saddled horse towards them. The girl stopped in front of Olivia with a beautiful gray. "This is Mystery. She loves the ocean, and from what Mr. MacAllister described of your experience and preferences, will be perfect for you."

The other animal, a dark bay with two white feet and a star nuzzled Mac's hand. The teenaged boy leading him chuckled. "He's looking for a treat."

"I wish I had one for him. What's his name?"

"Charger. He's gentler than his name suggests."

"That's good because I haven't ridden since I was a teen."

Olivia's face scrunched. "I've only ridden in Tennessee. I joined a horseback riding club in college to get out of my dorm and into nature. I still have photos from some of those rides. In fact, I think I submitted one of them to the *Floridian Wildlife* contest, even though the wildlife wasn't Floridian. Probably why I didn't win that year." She pursed her lips. "I bet if I revisited my past entries, I could figure out why each of those photographs didn't capture a judge's attention."

Stirling squeezed her shoulder. "You've come a long way since those early shots, I'm betting."

She had, hadn't she. A stray thought had her side eying Mac. But that was crazy.

An odd look crossed Olivia's face. For a second. Stirling wondered if she suspected him. Surely by now she'd seen the entry receipt. Yet, she hadn't said anything.

"Let's get you in the saddle. We'll give you the safety talk and a few laps around the arena before we turn you loose on the trail." The girl smiled at Olivia. "Ready?"

Olivia's face brightened. This time Stirling felt her excitement to his toes. He was beyond thrilled to gift her this experience.

Twenty minutes later, they emerged from a well-worn track onto a sandy beach populated only by creatures of the sea and sand. The briny smell increased as a breeze shoved the hair from Stirling's face. A glance at Olivia showed her familiar cloud of black curls streaming behind her ears, a sight he absolutely loved. He snapped a picture with his phone.

Olivia urged her horse forward until they reached the packed sand, reined in and peered out at the horizon.

Stirling snapped half a dozen more pictures then tucked his phone away. "Are you going to stand here all day? Or are we going to ride?"

She lifted her reins, accepting his challenge, and urged her mare to the edge of the breaking waves. Then she faced Mystery westward and took off at a gallop. Her musical laugh floated back to where Stirling remained on his big bay.

"You certainly are the patient sort, aren't you?" He patted his mount's neck, then followed Olivia's example, whooping in sheer delight as Charger's hooves pounded the sand.

His mount slowed as they approached a line of trees. Olivia's mare stood ankle deep facing the ocean as she watched his approach. The serious lines on her face hollowed his gut. The big gelding edged close to the gray and Stirling took Liv's hand.

"Mom called as I was walking through my door after I left you at the gate. She wouldn't tell me how she got my number or how long she'd known where I was, but she begged me to come home." His mind recalled his doubts and nausea forced him to breathe deep.

Olivia inclined her head toward the beach. "Let's walk."

She offered her hand and a small smile once they'd dismounted. Hope bloomed in his chest. "I almost didn't go. Then, an urgency hit that pushed me to act. I can't explain it." Her squeeze encouraged him to go on. "I called Hueso, met him on the beach with Stella, then flew to Key West."

Olivia let go and selected a shell. "Angel wings." She passed it to him.

He balanced the fragile connected ovals on his open palm. "Before I left four years ago, Dad and I argued. We weren't speaking––haven't spoken since that day. When I arrived, he was in the hospital and so weak. If I'd waited, we may not have had the opportunity to build even the fragile bridge we managed in the hours we had." His voice broke and Olivia's arms came around him.

"I'm so sorry, Silver."

He clung to her, accepting her comfort. Soaking in the feel of her, the sense of belonging he hadn't known since his grandpa passed. He inhaled the hint of salt on her clothes, admired how the tips of her tresses teased her shoulders, and spoke into the black cloud of curls. "I was able to reconnect with Mom and my siblings. God knew I couldn't handle the regret of losing Dad without apologizing."

Only his need to read her reaction pushed him from her embrace. "I never meant to ignore you. I could give you a ton of excuses, but the truth is, I was afraid you'd find out I'm not Mac, beach bum and diving instructor."

Her growing smile sent a prickle across his scalp. When she winked and mounted her horse, he feared the worst. Following her lead, he climbed into the saddle, sending a prayer for mercy.

Olivia gripped Stirling's waist as they motored away from the stable. "It's much easier to think of you as Stirling than Mac." His abs tensed beneath her hand. "I came so close to your real name that first day when I called you Silver." Laughing at the memory, she noticed his building tension and gentled her voice. "Stirling fits so much better. You are like precious metal amid the world's dross. What you did for me today was amazing. Thank you so much for remembering."

Stirling freed one hand from the handlebar and clasped hers where they connected around his waist. "Only the first of many dreams I want to help become reality."

She rotated her hand so it joined his palm to palm, the connection sending a shock to her heart. "Tell me who you really are."

"You sure you want to know?"

She squeezed his hand three times, the signal she and her mother used for I love you, though she wasn't ready to admit the truth.

He pulled his hand from hers and inhaled.

Deciding she could wait, she said, "I'm working on a website. I want to pursue the passion I'd forgotten when I got so caught up in winning the contest. Your help could make another dream come true."

"What about that YouTube channel? I already have an idea for the first episode."

"Oh yeah? What is it?"

Stirling seem to hesitate before answering. "I'd rather you see it for yourself. Wait till we get to our next stop and I'll show you."

"I'm going to hate it when this fairytale vacation ends, and we both have to get back to work."

"I have some ideas there, too. But they'll need to wait until I've sorted the details."

Olivia's stomach growled as she stepped off the motorcycle and removed her helmet.

"I heard that. Good thing lunch is next on the agenda."

This secluded part of the beach featured a jetty of giant rocks perpendicular to the shore. Stirling handed one of the insulated bags to Olivia, then extracted two bottles.

"Let's head there." He pointed to a large flat rock about halfway along. "It should have a fantastic view."

Together they navigated the climb then picked their way to the rock. They settled down to eat, feet dangling above crashing surf. Overhead, wispy clouds floated in robin's egg blue. They munched on Cuban sandwiches, one regular and one a la Oliva, and drank aguas frescas.

"You asked who I am." Stirling wove his fingers with Olivia's. "In the past, people have treated me differently when they discovered my name. I don't think I could bear it if you did that. I like who I am as Mac. Stirling gave up and lived in fear. Though maybe I'm coming to realize God has used my self-imposed exile to draw me to Himself." He caressed the back of her hand with his thumb. "And maybe to lead me to you."

Olivia peered deep into his gem-stone eyes. "You are Stirling MacAllister, former member of the Treasure Hunting MacAllisters, and current owner/operator of Scuba and Snorkeling by Mac. You also own a small private island not far from here."

"I'm impressed. Guess I'm not the only one with some skills. You left off proud dog-dad, boycotter of cars opting instead for motorcycles, bicycles, or legs on land and boats on the water, videographer, and techy geek with a penchant for YouTube and video editing." Her laughter prompted him to continue. "I am quite fond of a certain dark-haired, dark-eyed girl who has an amazing photographic eye and a fondness for taking fluffballs on early morning walks on semi-deserted beaches. I hope to be able to build her confidence in her own abilities by––"

"Okay. Okay." Olivia hugged her knees. "I get the gist." Certain her ears had pinked she gazed out to sea.

"Look!"

Olivia pointed to a pair of ospreys soaring near the end of the jetty. Below them a silver fish jumped, flipping into the water and creating ripples that radiated outward. Several tiny turtles sunbathed on the lower rock.

Stirling packed away the trash and retrieved his phone. He searched for a moment then offered it to Olivia. "Here's the video I want to put in our first YouTube episode."

Olivia accepted the device and raised a brow. "Our?"

He blinked. "Unless you don't want me involved."

She pressed play. Images came to life on the screen initiating a tremor that worked its way through her body. Words rushed from her mouth.

"It's from the diving adventure. When we saw the Kemp's ridley." She gripped the edge of the rock and found Stirling watching her, something like pride shining in his eyes. Biting her lip, she returned her attention to the screen. As if living the scene again, water seemed to caress her skin, splash her face. The grayish-green turtle swam past her toward the submerged reef. Powerful flippers propelled the two-foot round carapace through the waves until it vanished from sight.

"Even with such poor quality, it's a powerful video. It's perfect and we can showcase the protected status." She handed the phone back.

"Olivia, I have a confession. I took one of the photos from the day you saw the Kemp's ridley and I ent––"

A noise drew Olivia's gaze across the water. "That's your boat. Mamá and Ramon are on it. Is that Hueso? Who else?"

Stirling chuckled at her excited flow of words. "Tian and Hai. I didn't realize it would take so many people."

"It was you! I never even considered you." She tapped her finger to her lips, rewinding her memories. Her wide eyes roved Stirling's face. "The pictures from snorkeling? You used one of those. They were on your camera."

"Took you long enough." He gestured to the group clambering over the rocks toward them.

Carmela held a covered package in her arm as Ramon guided her over the uneven surface. Olivia eyed them. Perhaps something was brewing in the restaurant besides coffee.

Her mother reached Olivia and gave her a one-armed hug. "Chiquita, I'm so excited to see you two together. What a beautiful couple you make."

Pulling away, she protested. "Mamá, we're not––"

Stirling wrapped his arms around her waist from behind and whispered so only she could hear. "I'm willing if you're willing."

His warm breath on her neck shot shivers through her body, and the feel of his arms seemed to bring comfort and peace. Ignoring the presence of the others, she pivoted to face him, twining her hands behind his head.

"I choose you, Olivia, and I want everyone to know." No longer a whisper, Stirling's declaration reached those gathered on the jetty. "And I want you to know that no matter what happens, I'm never going to tell you to stay away. I'll never deny our relationship whether we're arguing or at peace. I want you by my side from now to forever.

Heat rushed to Olivia's face, turning her mouth to sand. "Are you asking?"

Stirling shook his head. "Not yet. For that, I'd prefer no audience, but I do have a gift. It's a promise really. A down payment that I plan to replace with a ring very soon if you'll have me." One of his hands left her back. Paper crinkled.

Reluctantly, she released her hold, facing those who'd come to witness his promise gift.

Stirling presented her the package, and she meant to untie the string, but his hand gripped hers. When their eyes met, a sense of coming home flooded her being.

"I hope this offering reinforces the new confidence I sense in you. It's not only because I love you that I tell you how talented a photographer you really are. When I saw this photograph, it told a story. I believe that's your gift. You tell stories with pictures."

His broad smile amplified the intense blue in the startling cut-glass eyes she loved.

He caressed her cheek. "You have become that author you mentioned. Your medium is color--light and shadow--rather than words." He dipped his chin to the package. "Open it, but forgive me while I capture this reaction for our children's benefit." He released her, raising his phone with a wink.

Fingers trembling and stomach dancing at his words with deeper meanings that unleashed heat in her core, Olivia unwrapped a framed photograph. She removed the protective cardboard, and the image of two striped lionfish chasing five juvenile red snappers through the reef maze stared back at her. The vibrant colors belied the danger inherent in the situation, reflecting how life sometimes hid danger in daylight but also beauty in shadow. She swiped a tear from her cheek and faced the man she loved. The man who knew her well enough to identify her passion and gift it to her as a symbol framed with love.

"I find words an inadequate thank you, so let me show you how accepted your gift makes me feel and how loved." She closed the distance between them, gripped his jacket with both hands, and tilted her head upward in invitation.

He obliged, pressing his lips to hers in a kiss both tantalizing and sweet that held the promise of more to come.

SURPRISED BY *Love*

Jessica Wakefield

Chapter One
Five days before the Wedding

"They'll be here any minute." Viana Lawson checked her phone for the umpteenth time as nerves jangled up and down her body. She paced the width of the inn's porch. It was now or never. This was the moment when the rest of her life started or fell into disarray.

The moment to bring her parents' dream—and hers—into full reality.

"Relax, Via," Lauren Stewart, one of her best friends, said as she stood against the porch railing, cradling a mug of coffee. Waves sounded at the beach nearby. Their rhythmic pounding normally soothed Viana, but not today.

"Easy for you to say," she responded. How did Lauren, former model and now exquisite wedding cake baker, always look so effortless? She exuded a peace that Viana never felt. She couldn't, though, could she? She had to be on top of everything all the time.

Olivia Perez, their team wedding photographer, sat on the porch swing, her pet rabbit, Sable, resting in her lap. Viana had never seen a rabbit so domesticated and relaxed as Sable. Great, even the pet was more chill than she was.

She looked at both girls, all of them best friends since high school, and took a steadying breath. She and Lauren had started the business—LOVElegant—five years ago and Olivia had joined this year. New to wedding photography and the wedding business in general, she was still finding her feet, and this wedding was making Olivia nervous.

"I love that Ainslie and Lucas are having a December wedding," Olivia piped up. "It's sweet that they'll be married and, on their honeymoon, when Christmas rolls around. And the best part is, no one will expect a wedding at this time of year."

Lauren grinned. "Who knew a guy responsible for making men around the country style themselves after Cary Grant in skinny jeans with a too-cool attitude would fall in love with the princess of the best ways to live each day? And then, together, they've become a fashion powerhouse."

Viana ran her hand up the post, tracing the floral hand-carved engravings. Each post bore a different design. Just like everything in The Summer House, her parents' fingerprints were all over it. In a way, Viana was glad they weren't here to see her fail and lose their legacy all in one fell swoop. She hadn't told the girls on her team that the house itself was at risk too. The one mortgage payment she missed was like a pesky online ad that kept popping up, and the bank wanted it repaid by the end of the year. On top of the upkeep on the house, the pressure kept building. Lauren and Olivia's disappointment in her would be too much to bear on top of everything else. So, she stayed silent and kept pushing forward.

And the only way forward was to thrive. The thought sunk deep, giving her pause. Maybe that wasn't the best route, after all. Losing her parents' legacy would be devastating, sure, but at least there would be nothing more to lose if that happened. She'd learned the hard way that people leave when she succeeded.

And ever since *him*, she'd made sure her heart couldn't get broken.

After all, if there wasn't anyone to leave her, then she could fly as high as the gulls that soared over the ocean.

Still, Viana's heart ached at missing Mom and Dad. She wished more than anything for their guidance, for Mom's hugs, and Dad's will power to see something through. He would believe in her. He always had.

"This wedding is so important." Viana shook off the heavy thoughts. "Obviously, we need more than two weddings a month, and we already had to lay off the cleaning staff. We can't let Anita go, too, since we need her on the front desk and as my admin assistant. And we really need to keep our kitchen and grounds staff."

She opened her laptop and pulled up the spreadsheet on the wedding.

"Between Ainslie and Lucas, they're going to more than put us back in the black...they're going to put The Summer House on the map." Lauren squeezed her hand, her other one still holding a mug.

Lauren's loose-fitting jeans and black t-shirt was such a Lauren outfit. It was as if she was trying to not be the high-fashion girl she used to be. Her floral kerchief holding her hair back sent out the relaxed vibe that she wanted to project into the world. But Viana knew underneath, Lauren was sharp, quick-witted and professional. She just preferred life to go at her own pace without people telling her where to be and what to wear.

"Lauren's right." Viana glanced at the screen. The spreadsheet displayed everything that needed to happen over the next five days. "I know you're nervous about this wedding Livvie." She glanced at Olivia and Sable on the porch swing. "And Ainslie's mother is a pain, but that just comes with wedding territory."

"Oh yeah," Lauren echoed. "Remember when that bride changed the cake design five times before the wedding?"

Viana laughed. Doing so eased the tightness in her chest. "You almost tore your hair out dealing with her."

Lauren took another sip of her coffee and wrinkled her nose. "I still get stressed when I think about that particular event but thank the Lord you handled the lion's share of that wedding party." She tipped her cup in Viana's direction.

As wedding planner, Viana dealt with everyone and brought it all together. When things got too tense, she was often the only one keeping the world from tilting off its axis.

But who looks after you when there's a crisis? The thought came unbidden, unwelcome. She pressed her lips together and carried on. "We're all ready?" She looked at Lauren.

Lauren raised her mug. "All the preliminary design has been done. And I had the final meeting with Ainslie and Lucas and they're happy."

"What about you, Livvie?" Viana asked.

She rolled in her lower lip, wincing as she waited a beat before answering. "My videographer quit."

Silence met her bombshell.

"Did he give a reason?" Viana finally asked, her brain running ahead a million miles, working out scenario after scenario and potential solution after solution.

"He hates the mother of the bride. He won't work with her."

Viana pressed her fingertips to her temple as she mentally regrouped. "This isn't the worst problem we can have. It's just one videographer. It's not like when the bridal party got stranded on the boat the morning of the wedding."

"Or like when the groom arrived late after getting a speeding ticket on his way to the wedding," Lauren added.

"Or when that hurricane broke the bridge, separating the wedding parties," Viana added.

"Panhandle living," Lauren laughed.

"I'll find someone." A mixture of hope and desperation filled Olivia's eyes.

Viana reached over and squeezed her friend's arm, then gave Sable a pat. She let her fingers sink into Sable's soft fur, allowing the little bunny to lend her some peace. The rabbit twitched its nose. "I know you will, but you don't have to do this alone. We're in this together."

"Pot calling the kettle black there, Via?" Lauren's smile softened her words. "I love you, but, woman, you are the most independent of the three of us." She stretched and repositioned herself against the railing. "We're here to help you just as much as you're here to help us."

Heck, this wedding was stretching Viana's nerves tighter than an expanded rubber band.

"We've never done a wedding with so much riding on it." A flicker of panic flashed across Lauren's face, before her trademark calm returned. Sometimes, Viana wondered why Lauren wasn't the wedding planner instead, as she was more chill, but then again, Lauren hated dealing with people—her life as a former model spoke to that. She much preferred life in the background, and baking stunning cakes was her happy place.

"Ainslie and Lucas want a private wedding that they can share with all their fans after the fact," Viana added.

Olivia reached for Sable as he slow-hopped across the porch swing and pulled him backward towards her. "I want to give them the best, but now..."

"You're worried you're not up to this job?" Viana asked gently. "And you won't find a suitable replacement in time?"

Olivia inhaled and nodded.

"We're *not* up to this."

"What?" Olivia's eyes grew wide.

"No one is ready for an event like this." Viana offered an encouraging smile, wanting to allay her fears. "But we *can* do it. It's twenty people max. We handle that all the time. We also handle difficult brides, difficult family members, hurricanes." Viana looked at her friends, passion rising in her chest. "It's just last-minute jitters. It happens with every wedding. And it should. Because we care about giving the bride and groom an amazing day with a lifetime of memories that make them smile every time they think of it."

"You know, if you didn't sound like such a sergeant major, it might have been a more inspiring speech." Lauren's lazy smile broke the tension.

Viana broke out into a hearty laugh. "I needed that."

Olivia joined in, but Viana could tell the newest member of their team was still struggling.

"But there is one thing different with this wedding." Lauren grabbed her mug.

"What's different?" Viana closed the spreadsheet.

Lauren raised her eyebrows. "We have an actual security guard with this one."

Viana scanned the road that led to The Summer House. No vehicles turned onto the paved drive. She checked her watch and glanced back to the street. "We've never worked with security before. I hope he's not some block-headed guy with no sense of what's needed." Instinctively, Viana reached for the shell necklace that hung low around her throat. It was the habit she'd formed when she was little, using the shell necklaces her Gramma made. Ever since her parents...she gripped it tighter...and Camden...The necklace lay flat against her skin. She ran her hand over the grooves, feeling the comfort of the familiar lines on her fingers. Her heartbeat slowed, and the tension in her shoulders eased.

And the recollection of walking along a North Carolina beach with Camden rolled through her memory...

"Here." Cam had bent down and retrieved a scalloped shaped shell. "I think this is perfect." He held it up, his eyes bright in the morning sun. His gaze was only for her.

Viana's heart trilled at knowing this man was hers. She took the shell and ran her fingers over the rough surface. "This is perfect. Now I have one for each of you—Dad, Mom and you." Her voice cracked on the last word.

Cam pulled her into a bear hug. "I'm not going anywhere, Viva." She loved it when he called her Viva, no one else did. It was his name for her. "You won't lose me." He whispered against her temple.

Except he had. Three months later Camden had walked out of her life to pursue a dream that wasn't even his.

Viana allowed the memory to fade, and she turned to Olivia. "Let me know if you need any help getting a videographer."

A tremulous smiled touched Olivia's lips. "I'll find someone. Your support—both of you—" she looked between Viana and Lauren. "Means everything to me."

Lauren sat down and hugged Olivia. "We've had each other's back since high school, that doesn't change now."

Viana nodded. "I know you're worried, but like we said before, this kind of thing happens at weddings all the time." The words stuck to Viana's throat, but she kept her smile generous. There was no point in sharing just how much was riding on this event. "If you haven't found someone soon, let me know and I'll put out some feelers as well."

"Thanks." Olivia's smile had gained some confidence. "When I was coming home, I saw the city maintenance crew setting up." Olivia adjusted Sable on her lap. The three of them lived together on the third floor of The Summer House.

"They're probably doing routine maintenance. It was on the town's social media page last week," Lauren said. "I hope they'll be finished before the wedding. You know how long these jobs take. Sometimes, it's like they're not even working."

They all laughed.

Summer Shore, population four thousand, sat on the barrier island on the Florida Gulf Coast, about a two-hour drive from Pensacola.

"It's funny how we all came home," Olivia mused. "Life's best laid plans."

Viana laughed, but pain pierced her heart. The dream to run the wedding venue in the house built by her parents was a family dream—hers and theirs. Running it without them still hurt, but at least she had Lauren and Olivia. They wouldn't leave. Her success meant their success. They were a team.

But still, the hollowness of her parents' absence clung to her like sea spray from the ocean.

Lauren looked towards the road. "Ainslie and Lucas are here."

A slate-grey Range Rover navigated the L-shaped driveway, turning to pull up out front. All three of them stood, Olivia keeping Sable firmly in her arms. A second car, a black SUV, pulled up behind them.

"We're here!" Ainslie squealed as she climbed out, sunglasses covering half her face, her smile huge.

Lucas climbed out of the driver's side, sunglasses also adorning his face, his hair in some newfangled style that Viana could never understand why it was popular.

But that didn't matter. They were here and everything was going to go perfectly.

Another man exited the second car, his back to them as he went to the trunk and opened it. Viana noticed his wide shoulders and her gaze rested on the weapon holstered under his bomber jacket. She gulped. Things had just gotten serious.

But the security guy wasn't her problem.

"Welcome!" She descended the steps and greeted Ainslie and Lucas. "I'm so excited you guys are here. I want you to use the next four days to just relax. No one knows you're here and we will keep it that way."

"I knew why I wanted you three to do this wedding." Ainslie hugged Viana, Lauren and Olivia in turn. She whirled around taking in the property. "I love this place so much. I can't believe your parents built this. It's the perfect hideaway."

"Have you met our security man?" Lucas said, indicating the second car.

The man walked around the trunk, holding a black duffel bag and then stopped mid-stride, his gaze landing on Viana.

Viana gasped. "Camden?"

It wasn't possible. But truth was stranger than fiction. Viana Lawson was standing in front of him, along with her two high school best friends,

Lauren and Olivia. But to him, Viana had always been the beauty in the room, even next to former model Lauren. His opinion hadn't changed in eight years.

"You two know each other?" Lucas looked between the two of them.

Cam and Viana continued to gaze at each other. He could sense everyone's gaze on them.

"Yes—" Viana started.

"We went to college together," Cam broke in.

Lucas kept swivelling his gaze between them. "Right," he said slowly. "As in, dated in college?"

"Yes," they said in unison.

Lucas kept watching them. Cam felt like he was back in boot camp minus the yelling of his training officers. Lucas's gaze was sharp. The guy might act all cool and chill, like the fame thing was nothing, but Lucas Milner liked things to go according to plan—particularly his wedding. Cam didn't blame him one bit. He'd want his wedding to go as planned as well.

Unbidden, his gaze swung to Viana, and his heart thumped. Her long dark brown hair still hung well past her shoulders and her brown eyes were as astute as ever. She'd grown up more, though. The soft lines around her lips and eyes spoke of experience and a life he knew nothing about.

"Is that going to be a problem?" Lucas continued to watch them.

Cam looked at Lucas directly, folded his arms across his chest. "It won't be an issue."

Lucas nodded.

Cam caught the flash of anger swipe across her face before she, too, held her ground. "Being caught by surprise isn't the same thing as being unable to work together." Then she smiled at Lucas and Ainslie. "A wedding planner is nothing if not able to handle *anything* that gets thrown at her during wedding week." She tossed Cam a sweet smile that was as false as the veneers on Lucas's teeth.

Ainslie took Lucas's hand and smiled up at her groom. "See? I told you Viana was the perfect person for the job and everything's going to be fine. Camden was a last-minute replacement. Our previous hire had a car accident. Camden comes highly recommended...I mean, he used to look after the Governor of Virgina."

Viana raised an eyebrow at the high praise.

Cam wanted to crawl into a hole at Ainslie's words. Sure, he'd done all that, but he was shadowing, Tobias, the guy actually in charge. Most of Cam's time had been spent outside in a car driving the Governor to and from his house. But Tobias had gone above and beyond to give him a good endorsement.

One he should attempt to live up to by focusing on the job at hand. He tore his gaze away from Viana and transferred his attention to Ainslie and Lucas.

"We need to move inside, ma'am." He directed Ainslie straight to the steps. "You too, sir."

"It's Lucas, man." Lucas grinned.

"I'm here to look after you. It's sir and ma'am." Camden smiled professionally.

Lucas nodded. "Suit yourself."

The group walked inside while Cam strode to the gate and swung it shut. Why wasn't it automatic? It needed to be. He made a note to ask Viana about it.

His phone vibrated in his back pocket. He pulled it out and answered. "Big brother, what's going on?"

"Not much. Where are you these days?" Jay sounded tired, but that was nothing new.

"New job in Summer Shore." Cam watched the front door close behind his clients...and Viana.

Jay, a former Army Air Assault Captain, didn't bother to ask anything more. He knew Cam couldn't tell him. Jay loved the military, but since Amy died, his big brother was lost.

"Alright." Jay paused and Cam knew what was coming. "Dad wants to know if you got his messages."

"I did, but I'm not reenlisting to work under him. And I'm not going home. I took this job to take control of my life—isn't that what Dad always wanted me to do?" Cam bit back all the other things he wanted to say—as long as Dad dictated the terms, he was happy for Cam to be independent. But that wasn't independence, it was control. He thought about Mom, her gentle expression. Home was Nashville—where she was. And all the memories there weren't bad, it just felt like a backwards step. Not to mention Dad was at a new base in Texas. Going back to Nashville felt like Cam was giving up on creating his own life. And reenlisting in the military and working with Dad was the last thing he wanted.

Jay's protracted sigh tunnelled through to Cam. "I know. But it might not be as bad as you think—coming home, I mean. I'm not asking you to reenlist."

Cam walked back to his SUV and shut himself in, his free hand resting on the steering wheel. "I'm not going to work under him just so that he can tell everyone our family is fourth generation career military."

"That's a bit harsh," Jay said quietly.

"That's Dad." Cam massaged his jaw. "I tried it and I didn't like it. End of story. And don't forget, I don't have the same relationship you have with him." Golden Child, that's what Jay was to their father—even after everything that had happened to Jay.

"I'm not in the good books anymore. I left, like you did," Jay said. "He's mad at me too."

"Then that's his loss." Even as he said it, a tiny part of Cam, the part he never liked, flickered with glee. He wasn't the only one being punished anymore. He banished the thought.

But he would never reenlist.

However, if this job didn't do well, he might need to make the trek back to Nashville. Working with Mom might be okay...but no. He needed to prove to all of them that he didn't need their help. He could survive on his own. Like he had that day at the fair. Like he had when Dad walked out on Mom and he helped her keep it together. Instead, he'd focus on making sure this job went off without a hitch.

He'd keep everything together.

But that was him. Something was obviously going on with his brother too. "You okay?" Cam floated the question to Jay, his hand gripping the phone.

Jay's silence was loud, except for the distant chatter of people and the occasional clink of cutlery.

"That good, huh?" Cam supplied.

Jay chuckled, low and throaty. "I'm—" his voice cracked. Cam closed his eyes, thinking of his sister-in-law, Amy. If he missed her, how must Jay feel? The second anniversary of her death had rolled around too quickly. Life shouldn't pass that fast.

"I'm okay." Jay's quiet voice didn't fill Cam with any confidence, but what could he do? Life moved on. It sucked, but there it was. "So, how's Summer Shore? Been a lifetime since you last visited that place."

"Viana's here." Cam dropped his voice, his gaze swinging to the wide, wrap-around porch and the expansive gardens separated by a wide gravel driveway. The Summer House was stunning. His gaze flicked to the porch, where Viana had stood only moments ago.

"You're kidding?"

"Wish I was." Cam stared at the garden—it was easier on his head and his heart.

"Dude—" Jay said.

"I've got this, alright?"

"If you say so." Cam could see, in his mind's eye, Jay sitting at that café he always went to, drinking too much coffee and watching the world pass him by. He was either there or working with Mom at her business—almost never at home. "Are you available to come down in the next few days if I need you?"

"Sure thing. Things are slow at the moment," Jay said.

"How's that going?" Cam asked.

"That is currently undecided," Jay replied. "I'm working things out. Just call and I'll be there."

"Thanks." Cam forced himself to climb out of the vehicle. He had a job to do.

"Later," Jay said.

"Later." Cam pocketed his phone and opened the trunk and pulled out his gear bag. He'd already checked it but doing it again—the rhythmic nature of checking and repacking the bag—soothed him. He opened and began pulling items out.

"You're here."

Cam turned to find Viana standing in front of him.

They looked at each other for long seconds. And memories, one after the other, cascaded through his mind. Their first date on the wild ferry ride they'd taken over the Potomac, the first time he'd kissed her, and the last time he'd seen her—when he walked away—breaking her heart and his.

"I'm here." He matched her gaze and stance.

Viana let out an exasperated breath. "I don't know about you, but this wedding is really important. And I want us to do as Lucas asked and work together." Her tone meant more like stay away from each other.

"I can do that." He dipped his head.

Her gaze slipped to the gun in the holster, then back to his face. "We'll both do our jobs and the past stays in the past." Her eyes shifted to the items laid on the back of his suburban. "Duct tape. Zip ties. CPR mask, first aid kit, cameras, binoculars, pepper spray. Folding shovel. What are you doing? Trying to stop a kidnapping?" The scowl on her face raised his ire.

"I'm doing my job. Which is to be prepared for any and all situations." He jerked his thumb behind him. "That gate should be automatic. It makes good sense to keep anyone from just wandering onto the property."

Viana glared at him. "Let's get one thing straight. I know how to do my job. How about you do yours and I'll do mine? We leave each other alone."

Cam resisted the urge to glare back. *She hadn't changed at all. Success—it was all that mattered to her.* But he let the unkind thought drop. After all, she wasn't the one who walked away—that was on him.

"Yes ma'am." The breeze carried the familiar scent of Viana—daisies and sunshine. Sunshine was a smell, even if no one knew it but him. It was Viana all over. But he didn't move. He wasn't going to give her any ground or betray the fact that his heart thudded every time he looked at her.

But this wedding was imperative for him too.

His future depended on it.

Chapter Two
Four days before the Wedding

Viana waved from the porch as Camden backed the car down the long drive, on his way to take Ainslie and Lucas to the marina for a private boat cruise. Noting the open passenger window, she cupped her hands and hollered for good measure. "Have a great day!"

She would, personally, because she got a break from Camden for a bit. Unfortunately, he'd be back after the tour.

Ainslie stuck her head out the window as they approached the gate. "Don't forget, the dress is coming today by private courier."

"It'll all be taken care of by the time you get back," Viana assured her.

Camden stopped at the gate, made a show of getting out of the car and pulled it open, drove through it, got out again and pulled it shut, giving her a pointed look.

Viana smiled at him and waved them off.

Camden was back in her life. And he didn't dress like a security/bodyguard, whatever he was. No suit and tie. And in the preceding years, he filled out better than ever. Jeans, combat boots and a black and brown bomber jacket—he kind of looked like a taller, modern-day James Dean. It would be easier if he didn't look that good.

And that gun. Though he was raised in a generations-long military family, Viana had never once seen him hold a gun. The sight of one strapped to his side was unnerving. Seeing him in work—no—protector mode burned a hole inside her. Where was this level of dedication when they were together?

"We're heading out on errands." Lauren and Olivia joined her on the porch. "Why is the gate closed?"

Viana's jaw hurt from how hard she was clenching her teeth. "*Camden* thinks it should be automatic to keep people from wandering onto the property."

The girls' unasked questions as they stared at her sounded as loud as the waves crashing on the nearby beach.

"It's fine," Viana said. "We're fine working together."

Lauren huffed. "I'll believe it when I see it." She lowered her voice. "You cried for weeks after he left."

Viana shoved the truth and the awful memories to the back of her mind. "That was eight years ago. I'm over it—over him."

Lauren gave her a long look before she fluttered her eyelashes. "Eight years has been very kind to him."

Viana glared at her.

Lauren laughed. "It's been way more fabulous to you, Via." She gripped Viana's arm. "Just...don't lose your heart to him again."

"Not. Going. To. Happen." Viana declared.

Olivia grinned. "Do you have any idea how alike the two of you are? You come across as cousins half the time."

"You're the peacemaker—" Viana grinned at Olivia.

"Uh yep," Lauren laughed. "We need you Liv, otherwise Viana and I won't make it."

They dissolved into laughter.

"You girls make this business fun. I don't know what I'd do without the two of you," Viana said.

Olivia hugged her. The quietest and gentlest of the three of them, her heart of pure gold was a balm on a weary day. "See you later."

A few moments later, Olivia and Lauren left in their respective vehicles, leaving the gate open.

Viana breathed a sigh of relief. The house was empty, and the peace and quiet meant it was the perfect time to do inventory on the outdoor tables and chairs. And give anything a cleaning that needed it. She walked down the driveway to the storage shed, designed to look like a quaint white cottage, that perched at the end of the gravel drive. It was sectioned off by a small white picket fence. Viana said a hello to Sable in his outdoor pen next to the shed. Inside the shed, one wall was filled with crates full of linen and draperies, floral wire and tape, command hooks, tape and zip ties, candles and lighters, extension cords and power strips, ribbon, extra sashes for chairs, and more odds and ends. She had four whole crates filled with faux flowers—they always came in handy.

The other wall was lined with shelving that held umbrellas, bug spray and citronella candles. Next to them on the floor sat space heaters, cooling towers and fans, tents, canopies and flooring panels. In the middle, up against the wall opposite the door, was stacked tables and chairs and their three arbors—one a classic white, another a beautiful rustic option made of wood, and the third a black metal framed version. She'd used all of them over the five years and each one would be tailored to the bride's wishes with flowers and fabric draping over it.

Over the next half hour, Viana filled the yard with the tables and chairs, and opened boxes of flowers and other decorations. She was checking the white marquee when a low rumble caught her ear. She stopped, looking around for the source of the noise. It continued, a hiss adding to the ominous sound. "What on earth?" Viana walked up the driveway, feet crunching on the gravel. The hissing and rumbling growing louder as she arrived at the main gate.

Suddenly an explosion of water, like a fire hydrant gone rogue, arced high into the air, soaking everything—including Viana—in its path. The icy cold water cascaded down her hair and into her eyes. "No!" She pushed her hair from her eyes and jumped away from the deluge, now shivering in her sopping wet clothes.

The burst water main threw wave upon wave of water onto the property. The water hit the ground and formed a slippery pathway down the slight slope of the property—right in the path of her supplies.

"No, no, no, no," Viana moaned just as Camden pulled up and jumped out of his SUV.

Camden stood staring at the tower of water, getting as wet as Viana was. Then their eyes connected, and it stirred them both into action. He grabbed something from the back of his car and jumped the gate like he was some kind of superhero.

"Make sure the house is closed." Camden shouted above the noise of the cascading water. "Just in case."

Viana didn't need to be asked twice. Her sandaled feet slapped through the cold water as she hopped onto the porch and closed all the windows and doors, leaving wet footprints in her wake.

Panting and trying to keep panic at bay, she rushed outside and joined Camden. "We need to protect the shed from..." But the words died on her lips.

Camden, wet from the water, jeans muddy to his calves, was using a shovel and digging a trench line right in the middle of the garden.

Viana leapt over to him, her ankles now muddy too. "What are you doing? That's where the wedding is going to be held!"

Camden paused, water dripping from his wrists. He pointed to the cottage, where water was now invading her precious supplies. "I'm diverting the water away from your things."

He returned to digging, his arms working hard and fast as he moved across the lawn, dirt and chunks of grass flying behind him as he ripped up her perfect lawn.

Water arced high, and fell gushing down the gravel drive. The air was full of cold mist, sending goosebumps up her arms. Viana glared at his back as she yanked her phone from her pocket. Great, it was wet too. Rushing inside, she grabbed a towel from the ground floor bathroom and wiped her phone dry. Breathing a sigh of relief to see it was still working, she ignored the six text messages and two missed calls from Florence Tucker, called city maintenance and requested assistance. Then she sent a text to Anita, letting their assistant know about the issue and asking her to follow up at the city office while she was in town.

Viana ran back to the yard and found Camden holding Sable in one arm, and the emergency shovel in the other. "I need to keep digging. The trench isn't enough to divert that much water."

"I called city maintenance, they're on their way. I'll take Sable." She reached out for the quivering rabbit and tucked him close. "You're going to keep digging?"

Camden's response was to slosh through now ankle-deep water to her things. "Got any other ideas?" he called over his shoulder.

"I have inflatable sandbags in the shed. I'll put Sable inside." Viana cuddled Sable close as she darted across the lawn, cringing with every squelch of her steps in the muddy, flooded yard. This was the worst thing that could happen. She found a clean towel and dried Sable off and then ran him upstairs to the third floor where she, Lauren and Olivia shared living quarters. She placed him in his indoor pen, made sure he had water and food, and raced back to the disaster.

She began hauling tables and chairs, pristine and white only a few minutes ago, now wet and muddy, onto the porch and away from the flood.

Camden was using the sandbags to create a barrier between the water and the shed door. Maybe it would hold it off, and not everything would be ruined.

He joined her, taking four folded tables at a time.

"I've got this. Keep sand bagging!" she barked.

"We're out of sandbags. We need to move everything out of the spray."

"What did you think I was doing, my hair or something?" It was easier taking out her fear and panic on him. He'd walked away from her, after all.

Camden looked at her, his dark eyes unreadable. "I'm doing my job, and it seems so are you. Which means our jobs are colliding right now."

They worked in silence, both of them soaking wet, and guilt nipped at her. He was being helpful, even if it caused different problems. Viana's hair was plastered to her head and back. Camden had ditched his bomber jacket, his long sleeve t-shirt a second skin. She shivered. Though she wasn't under the spray anymore, the cool air from the ocean kept her from getting warm, but there was no point in changing until everything was safe.

The maintenance crew arrived.

"Finally." Viana exhaled a sigh of relief.

Within minutes, the arc of water stopped as quickly as it started.

Silence thudded in her ears as her heart continued to race.

"There'll be no water for a few hours until we get this sorted." A man dressed in coveralls trooped through the muck that once was her perfectly manicured lawn.

"Thanks," Viana said faintly.

In the silence, she took in the scene in front of her. The yard was waterlogged, the crates of flowers full of water, the chair and table legs muddied. The arbors had met the same fate. She marched to the shed, the water ankle deep as it pooled around the building and sandbags. She peered in through the glass panels in the door. Water had filled the floor of the shed. Viana's heart sank. She'd have to clean the whole shed out and check what on the floor was salvageable.

"What am I going to do?" She pressed her palm to the cold glass, fighting the despair and panic that threatened to rain down on her.

"I think you'll need to have an indoor wedding." Camden's clear, direct voice was too close.

She whirled around to find him standing near her. "Are you kidding me? Ainslie and Lucas wanted a garden wedding." She pointed to the ditch marring her once perfect lawn. "This isn't what anyone had in mind." It was supposed to be the event that saved their business, saved her parents' legacy—saved *her*. A wave of defeat swept over Viana.

But instead of giving in, she marched inside and grabbed more towels and began wiping off what she could. She would thrive in spite of this. Her heart was still intact—no one had breached her defences since Camden walked out.

The irony of him standing in her driveway with a shovel dangling from his hand was not lost on her.

He walked over. Viana turned her back to him, unwilling to face the hit she'd just taken—and maybe, even him.

"I'm being realistic," Camden said quietly, emptying the crate of flowers and laying them out in the sun on the porch.

"I know," Viana said through gritted teeth. "I just need time to take it all in."

He leaned the crate upside down against the railing, letting the water drain out. He repeated it again with the other crate of flowers.

"You're mad." Camden's quiet observation prickled at her. He knew her and that fact irritated her.

Viana dumped the wet towel on the ground. "Yes, I'm mad. At everything— the water, my yard, my ruined supplies." She inhaled. "You. The fact that you're here. In my life."

"I'm sorry." His contrition needled at her.

Was he apologizing for now or for the past? Did she even want him to?

As he moved away, he grabbed a dry towel and draped it over her shoulders, his hands resting there for a nanosecond longer than necessary. His brief eye contact shrank the air between them. His gaze dashed to the shell necklace hanging around her neck. Instinctively she wrapped her hand around its familiar shape.

"You're shivering," he whispered.

And then he was gone.

Viana stood, tugging the towel around her shoulders, watching him round the corner as her emotions jumbled and frayed.

A car sounded in the driveway. Viana walked through the house and out the ornate black front doors. Just like that, Camden had burst into her life with color, irritation and compassion. Why did he care so much now, when he'd left her shattered eight years ago?

The courier was standing by the gate, not getting past Camden. It seemed there was no getting past Camden, was there?

"It's the wedding dress." She walked over to them and signed for the box.

Holding it like a precious jewel, she took the box inside, averting her eyes from the gouge in the lawn.

But an uncomfortable truth wouldn't go away. Without Camden's quick thinking, she'd been in a bigger mess than what was in front of her. His superman leap over the gate kept floating in her mind. Maybe, *maybe* it wasn't so bad that he was here—to save the wedding.

Her heart, however, would remain firmly locked up.

And she would thrive.

Chapter Three

Viana stood on the porch with Lauren and Olivia later that afternoon, checking the time on her phone. They'd be back any minute. "I don't want to know how Ainslie and Lucas will react when they see this."

"What are we going to do?" Olivia hugged Sable as she joined the others in surveying the flooded yard. "We can't have a backyard wedding now. It won't dry in time."

"Indoor wedding," Lauren said simply.

Except it wasn't that simple, no matter how many times she—or Camden—said it. Viana crossed her arms over her chest, fighting the urge to protest again. It was probably stupid to be so stubborn about it. They changed plans like this all the time, it was why The Summer House was such a good option—they literally had a backup plan right next to the outdoor option. Still, it irked her. Maybe because Camden had suggested it first?

"Maybe..." Viana paced along the porch. "We can position the guests in such a way as they don't even have to go near the trench. We can fill it in..."

"It wasn't your fault, Via." Olivia patted Sable. "You don't have to fix everything."

"I know." Viana stopped pacing, her breaths now as fast as her heart rate. "But this was supposed to be our launch into bigger and better things. It has to be, otherwise we have no business—no jobs."

Silence sunk around them, just like the grass drank up the water. And like the lawn, they were flooded and would be overrun if things didn't turn around.

Viana looked at her two friends. "Thanks for coming so quickly."

Lauren smirked. "You didn't need us. You and superman Cam had it all sorted."

Viana rolled her eyes. "More like we worked together, grudgingly, as a team."

Lauren continued to smile. "You worked well, period."

"I'm not listening to this." Viana flipped over the flowers, allowing the sun to dry them. "Let's hope they dry, and we can still use some. We'll have to rebuy so much stuff." A crushing weight settled on her shoulders. Why did this have to happen now? She looked heavenward. Viana trusted God's plans, but in moments like these, that trust felt fragile.

"Did the storage shed get much water?" Olivia piped up.

"More than I'd like. The floor was covered to my ankles. Those emergency sandbags were a lifesaver." But now, that was more things to buy. More things they *shouldn't* have to worry about.

"Then a major crisis was averted." Lauren started stacking the chairs. "The arbors are fine." She ran a hand along them. They'd been moved onto the porch too. "A bit of water never hurts those. But we should go through everything and make a list of what we need to purchase now and what can wait."

"You're doing my job." Viana smiled faintly.

"We share the load," Lauren said. "And besides, I've seen you do this for five years now. I know what to do."

"Where's Cam?" Olivia asked. "His car isn't here."

Viana saw Lauren and Olivia exchange knowing looks from the corner of her eye.

"What? Do you think I keep tabs on him? I have no idea where Camden is," Viana replied. And she didn't.

The girls laughed.

The rest of the afternoon they went through all the wet stuff, dried what still needed drying, tossed the items that were unrecoverable.

"This isn't salvageable." Lauren held up part of the bridal aisle runner. It was still soaking, water now warping it.

"Toss it," Viana sighed, as she dumped flowers on the ever-growing pile of waterlogged rubbish, her dreams slipping away with every slap.

A car sounded. Camden must be back. She could hear his already-familiar ritual of open the gate, drive through, close the gate. Then he rounded the house and came into view.

Viana's jaw dropped.

Cam wasn't alone. Two men armed with crates filled with new faux flowers placed them up against the house, away from the discarded rubbish and the water. Then they tromped back out of sight, the mud getting deeper with every step. They returned with more crates. This time filled with white linen for tables and extra power cords.

Camden was pulling out sacks of food. "We need to eat." He ignored them and made a beeline for the porch table and chairs set up for guests to have breakfast overlooking the garden.

The scent of cajun spices filled the air and Viana's mouth watered as she watched him put Po'boy sliders on the table, cajun chicken tacos, and mac and cheese from her favorite place in town. Her stomach growled at the scent and sight of the food. She hadn't thought to eat for hours.

He placed napkins on the table. "I hope I got things you all like."

He knew she loved mac and cheese.

"Where did you get all this stuff?" Viana stared at the boxes of supplies.

"I went to Hobby Lobby and these two gentlemen were very helpful. When you were inside earlier, I took photos of the flowers. I matched them as best I could."

Viana stared at him. "You did all this for us?" *For me?* Her heart thudded that last thought. But no, it was about the wedding. It had to be.

Camden surveyed the soggy yard. "It sucks that this happened. I wanted to help in some way."

Lauren joined Viana, nudging her.

"Can you give me the receipt, so I can pay you back?" Viana said.

Lauren snorted and stifled a laugh.

Viana shot her a glare.

Olivia looked innocent as she took in the whole scene.

Camden studied Viana for several seconds. "Don't worry about the receipt. Look at this as part of my job to make sure this wedding goes off smoothly."

"That's my job."

"That's everyone's job," Lauren interjected. "We accept your gracious gift, Cam." She nudged Viana again, sending her a pointed look.

Viana pulled herself together. "Thank you. It was very thoughtful." She knew she sounded like a robot, and she *was* grateful, but this was also her job. She was meant to fix it, to thrive, and he'd come in and taken over. Did he think she couldn't do this on her own? Well, she could. She'd been managing fine without Camden or anyone for a long time.

Or had she? Her business was almost in the toilet. She surveyed the ruined yard and suppressed a sob. *It's not supposed to be like this.*

"I'm going to install my security cameras, and then I'm going to pick up Ainslie and Lucas. I suggest, when walking outside, to stick the path we've already tracked, it will keep the rest of the yard for getting pockmarks." He didn't wait for a response, just gave them all a quick nod and walked back to the front of the house.

"Wow," Olivia whistled. "I didn't see that coming."

"He got you mac and cheese," Lauren added, amusement in her voice.

"He got us all lunch." Viana still sounded like a robot.

"Whatever you say," Lauren chirped.

Both girls dived into the food but left her the mac and cheese.

Cam needed to warn Ainslie and Lucas about the flooded yard. It was the only way to keep the disaster from derailing the wedding. The only things he knew for sure about Ainslie and Lucas was they were committed to getting married and not putting it on social media until after the fact. Otherwise, his clients were still a bit of an unknown. He'd trolled through their social media posts, identifying potential credible problems like crazy fans, possible stalkers and inappropriate comments—which there were plenty of—but so far, his search hadn't revealed anything to immediately suggest someone could be following them.

Cam met Ainslie and Lucas at the marina and drove them back to the house. One block before he reached the gate, he stopped the car and faced the couple—sitting in the back, holding hands.

"What's going on?" Ainslie asked, her eyes bright with relaxation and love.

"A burst water main erupted over the house this morning." Cam didn't bother sugar-coating the news. "The house is fine, but the yard is flooded."

Ainslie's face paled. "Really flooded?"

Lucas frowned.

"It took fifteen minutes for city maintenance to come and turn off the water."

"So it's flooded," Lucas stated.

"You've got an indoor option," Cam said. "I'd run with it, if I were you."

"I want to see the yard myself." Ainslie peered out the window.

"Yes ma'am." Cam drove them to the house, performed his now very irritating ritual of opening the gate, driving through, getting out and closing it. They really needed to get it changed to automatic. This was ridiculous.

"Oh no," Ainslie moaned.

Lucas whistled low.

Viana met them on the front porch, her face pinched with stress. Cam wanted to take as much as he could off her shoulders—not just for the success of the wedding but to make up for walking away from her. She might not have had much time for him when they were together, but it was him who broke her heart, and he didn't want to add destroying her business to his list of failures. He needed this wedding to go ahead. His future lay anywhere but the military, and he wouldn't humiliate himself by going home to Nashville.

"Follow the barricades and stick to the already-worn path," Viana called from the steps. "I know it looks bad." She glanced at Cam, but he couldn't read her expression. Was she happy he was helping or mad?

"The good news is your dress arrived!" For the first time since he'd walked back into her life, Viana's smile seemed genuine. He could have stood there drinking her in all day when that smile danced across her gorgeous face. "And we can do an indoor wedding. That's why you picked The Summer House—privacy and unforeseen circumstances. Let me remind you how spectacular we can make an indoor wedding."

Cam watched as she led them inside.

Lucas cast long looks at the destroyed grass, but Ainslie tugged at his arm. "This isn't a big thing. Now, if there was an issue with the dress, then I might start to panic..." Her voice trailed off as they walked inside.

Viana was amazing at organizing people and events. And the past reeled him back to the last time...

"Viva, can I help you?" Cam had sat in the office chair at the university's event coordinator office, opposite Viana, who had her head buried in a laptop, with a notebook open on the desk, her messy handwriting filling the pages. He saw dates, times and people's names with jobs listed beside them. "We've got dinner plans, remember?" He tried to keep the agitation from his voice, but even he could tell it wasn't working.

"I know." She looked up and met his gaze. "I'm sorry, but this can't wait." She reached over and squeezed his hand. "I realize I'm a pain right now but be patient with me. Once this ball is over, everything will be back to normal."

Cam had heard this line for the last three months. "This is your baby, I get that." He gently tapped the notebook. "But you have all these people to help you." He scooted the chair around the table, then tugged Viana's chair towards him. "This is us," he spoke softly, taking hold of her hands before letting them go and running his hands up her arms. Leaning in, he softly kissed her. "Put the work away for tonight and come out to dinner," he whispered, his mouth pressed to her forehead.

Viana leaned into him, her beautiful hair falling like a waterfall down her back. "Give me five minutes to pack up." She kissed him once on the lips, smiling.

Tension eased from Cam's chest. For the first time in so many years, he had let his guard down. Viana saw him for who he was, and he was falling in love with her.

Then her phone rang. Tossing him an apologetic look, she answered it—hanging up thirty minutes later. "We're good now," she announced, a huge smile spreading across her face.

"We missed our dinner reservations." Cam headed to the door, his head and heart tired of the same dance.

Viana walked over to him, pulled him into a hug. "Forgive me? Let's have dinner back in the dorm tonight. We can go to the North Star another time."

Cam stared at her, blinking for long seconds as the realization sunk in. She had no idea what today was. "Viana, it's our six-month anniversary today."

Her eyes widened and then abruptly shut. "I'm sorry, I'm so sorry." The apology came quick, but the truth remained—he wasn't a priority.

"This is a disaster!" Ainslie's cry from inside yanked Cam into the present.

He raced out of the car and into the house.

He found the entire group gathered in the dining room, Ainslie crying and Viana pale and wide eyed.

"What?"

Viana's voice was strangled. "They sent the wrong dress."

Chapter Four
Three days before the Wedding

"**I**'m checking the security cameras." Cam checked the feed from the camera to his laptop, as he talked to his best friend, Declan Collins, through his wireless ear buds. One of the cameras wasn't sending any video. He unhooked it and examined it.

"Are you a one-man show on this one?" Declan asked. "Not happy with driving the Governor around anymore?" He could hear the mirth in his friend's every word.

"Oh, you're real funny." The two of them met in college in Washington D.C. and had become fast friends. "How's Addey?"

"She's good. Are you coming to our wedding?" He could hear rapid typing as Declan talked. "I know it's still six months away, but my soon-to-be mother-in-law is getting antsy already, wanting to know everything now." Declan's grumble was threadbare, but he heard it all the same.

Cam chuckled. "Of course I'm coming. How's thing's with Addey's parents?"

Declan paused, and Cam could imagine his jaw working. "Jonathan and I are solid. Vivien is harder to get to know, but the ice is thawing."

Just then Viana rounded the yard, still walking along the designated path. Her frustrated groan was easy to hear.

"Can I help you with anything, Viana?" Cam called without thinking.

Viana faced him. "Yes, you can keep that gate open! No one is here right now. We don't need it closed all the time."

"Viana?" Declan's voice jumped down the line.

"Uh, yeah, did I forget to mention that?" Cam winced.

At the same time, Declan spoke. "You're working with Viana? *Our* Viana?" Declan's too loud voice continued to hammer Cam.

Cam gritted his teeth. "Yes, the one and the same."

"Oh boy, you're in trouble." Declan laughed.

"I'm fine," Cam snapped.

"Whatever you say. Tell Via I said hi." Declan ended the call, laughing.

Cam pulled out his earphones and looked at her. "Declan says hi."

Viana's eyes widened, and her features softened. "How is he?"

Camden couldn't stop the smile spreading across his face. "He's getting married."

"What?" Viana stood still. "Grumpy, 'I-hate-the-world' Declan is getting married?"

Cam grinned. "Yep. He finally found someone who got him to drop his walls. She's spunky and tough, yet really kind." He glanced at his screen, still nothing. His heart pounded and he kept his gaze on the screen. "You're a lot like her. You guys would get along."

A beat of silence followed.

Cam summoned his courage and glanced at Viana.

Her hand was limp by her side, and her forehead was wrinkled in a frown. "Tell him..." She glanced around the porch before landing her gaze on him. She crossed her arms over her chest. "Tell him I said hi back, and congratulations."

"I will." He'd flustered her, put her off-balance. He hadn't meant to, but Cam liked the idea of reminding her that not everything in their past was tainted with his walking away.

"Now, can we please keep this gate open?" Her in-charge persona was back.

And so was his. "I'm not doing my job if anyone can just access this house. As we're all aware, both Ainslie and Lucas have a high enough public profile that warrants their wedding to be secure. There is a legitimate chance that you'll have fans show up for both of them if they find out they're here—"

Viana leaned forward. "They're keeping it a secret. Only family and select close friends are coming. They won't be broadcasting anything about the wedding until they've returned from their honeymoon."

Cam raised his eyebrows. "Do you really think they'll be able to keep it quiet?"

Viana arched her eyebrows in return. "If everyone—including Lucas and Ainslie—doesn't mention it, then yes."

Cam pressed his jaw tight. "Have you seen how zealous some of these fans are? Have you seen the things they post? Some of them make it a point to stalk them online. I've told Ainslie and Lucas to not post anything that could give away their whereabouts. Nothing in the background that could let people know where they are. My job is to think through the potential problems and plan for any and all disasters."

"Sounds like my job," Viana shot back.

Once again, she wasn't letting him in. Just out there, not caring about him or anything he needed while she was on the job.

He squinted. Not that she owed him anything, now. Man, he better be careful, letting the past creep up on him like that. He might start wanting other parts of it back. "Our jobs are totally different. Are you going to let me do mine?"

Silence stretched between them—for the first time they were touching on the subject they hadn't acknowledged out loud since he showed up.

Viana clutched her shell necklace. "I always let you do your job. You just didn't like me doing mine."

Cam ground his teeth. "Your job came first. Our relationship was a distant second."

Viana flinched. "But I didn't walk away." She took a small step back. "That was all you, and for what? You didn't even stay in the military."

Cam closed his eyes. No, he hadn't. Apparently chasing a dream for someone else was a stupid thing to do. He opened his eyes.

"I remember," he said quietly. "I walked away, but you didn't try and fight for us. I was fighting for us, but you were too busy proving yourself unstoppable."

Viana stepped back, her frown deep and her shoulders stiff. "Our breakup was not my fault. It takes two people to make a relationship work. I might have been busy, but you spent just as much time doing whatever you pleased."

Cam blanched internally. Maybe Viana had a point...not that he would let her know that.

Appearing satisfied that she'd had the last word, Viana continued. "Now, I've got to go and drive around to about a hundred places today to see if I can find Ainslie a new dress. If I text you when I'm almost home, will you please come and open the gate?"

Cam nodded. "But I'd start getting quotes on making it automatic."

"Yes, sir." She touched her hand to her forehead in a salute.

"Very funny," Cam muttered.

"Pleasure working with you, Camden."

She was his vice, and he didn't like it. But he was addicted all the same.

Viana walked out of A Bride's Dream, agitated that there was no dress and that Camden kept walking through her mind like the unwanted intruder that he was. His words had stuck to her like sand on wet skin—itchy and impossible to avoid.

So what if she liked to work, and work hard? There was nothing wrong with putting her best foot forward at all times. Back in college she'd been indispensable to her boss. And now, The Summer House required all her effort to stay alive. Her parents' memory needed it. And she needed it like she needed her next breath.

The main street of Summer Shore was quiet today. Cars rolled by slowly, people strolled along the street checking out the shops. Winter was the low season, after all. She liked the quiet season. Teeming crowds was good for the town, but it did get tiring.

But there was no escaping the niggling effect Camden's words had on her. Had she really been too busy for them? Maybe, but he was the one to walk away.

Viana stopped mid-step. Was that Camden? The man crossed the road, no bomber jacket, no holster with a gun in it but it could be him.

Ugh, stop thinking about him. Focus on the task at hand. Ainslie had texted letting her know that her mother, Florence Tucker, was also trying to source the dress from the designer but was not having any luck. The guy wasn't answering his phone. How had they sent the wrong dress and then disappeared? It was mind boggling.

Florence could be very scary and had so far proved to be a more difficult mother of the bride. The number of calls and texts Viana had fielded from Florence about the wedding, and her ideas that were the complete opposite from Ainslie's vision, had weighed on Viana and made the job harder. But having her attempt to chase down the designer might be the perfect job for her. Florence was delaying her arrival until tomorrow, to try and work out the dress problem from her end. Which was both good and bad. Ainslie had let it slip a few times how much pressure Florence put on her to have the perfect wedding.

A familiar SUV pulled out of a park a few cars down. Aviator sunglasses. It was definitely Camden. Was he following her?

Then it clicked. The day spa was on the same block as the wedding store. He was dropping Ainslie and Lucas there.

He saw her and waved, his elbow stuck out the window. Why did he have to look so good? And why did she have to bring up their relationship like that?

In order to thrive, she had to lock her heart away.

It was dumb, but life had taught her if she wanted to chase her dreams, she couldn't let people in. People left, others died. The memory of watching her Dad's coffin being lowered into the ground panned across her mind. Mom's premature death had left her and Dad on their own, striving for the dream of The Summer House. Then Dad was killed in a car accident—Viana closed her eyes and pushed the unwelcome thoughts aside. Life with Aunt Wendy started when she was thirteen—a good life, but nothing erased the fact she was an orphan. Viana wrestled her mind back to the present.

Camden pulled up beside her. His elbow stuck out the window, his aviator sunglasses on his face—some things still didn't change. "Any luck with the dress?"

Viana shook her head.

He rested his sunglasses on his head. "I'm sorry for bringing up our past earlier. It was unprofessional."

"I brought it up actually," Viana said.

A smiled touched his lips. "I wasn't going to bring *that* up."

What happened to him? He wasn't the same guy she knew back then. He'd found a touch of grace.

"Thanks," she said quietly.

"What can I do to help?" His expression was open, like their argument hadn't even happened.

Viana inhaled, grateful for the reprieve. "Can you help me find a wedding dress today?" She squeaked out the question, unsure if she actually wanted him to say yes or not. "I've got a lot of places to go and your help with the driving and everything will—"

"Tell me where I'm going." The smile he shot sent tingles up and down her body. She remembered that smile. It was there when we she walked into a room, or when they sat on the sofa laughing over a competitive game of Monopoly. "Jump in." He jangled his keys, and like a girl still half in love, she followed him.

"Thanks." She climbed into the front seat, unable to meet his eye. "I can leave my car parked at the back of Summer Shore Sweets, the owner won't mind."

"No problem." He moved into the traffic. "Again, I'm sorry for making this uncomfortable before."

The sincerity she found in his voice was her undoing. There was one thing she knew about Camden Mayfield and that was when he said sorry, he meant it. He didn't back away from his choices and he faced them head on—whatever the consequences were. She'd loved that about him. Loved the steadfastness of it, but she didn't love the way he wasn't there for her—ironically the same complaint he had.

Just as they were driving away from the main street, Viana caught sight of Lauren standing outside Castaways, the trendy second-hand clothing store. She wasn't alone. "Who's that man with Lauren?"

"Maybe Lauren has a boyfriend she hadn't told you about." The car whizzed past and out of town.

"No way. Lauren would tell us if she's involved with someone." *Just like you're telling them you're with Camden right now?* But she wasn't. This was business.

"You know her best," Camden said casually.

She did. They fell into silence as Viana glanced out the window, taking a second to drink in the blue water and enjoy the sun shining. Florida in winter was always lovely. Camden drove along the coastal road, the Gulf of Mexico on one side, towns on the other. While he drove, she called every bridal store in a three-hour radius of Summer Shore. And found several able to help—she just had to get to them.

"Can we get to these five stores today?"

Camden slowed down for traffic and glanced at the tablet she held up with her list of locations.

He raised his eyebrows. "You want to go from Pensacola to Mobile to Montgomery and back to Summer Shore in one day?"

"Yes," she winced.

He checked his watch, and to her amazement, simply nodded. "Let's get this done. Give me the addresses of the shops we need to go to."

Watching Camden work out the most efficient route as they drove filled her with the first ray of hope since Ainslie opened the box and realized the mistake.

"Anyone find out how the wrong dress was sent?" Camden asked as they entered Pensacola.

Despite the panic and the fatigue that nipped at her heels, being in the car with him brought back memories. Riding on long country drives when they wanted to escape the hustle of Washington D.C., blaring country music as the miles rolled under them. Or the times they'd park at the top of one of the parking lots and sit on the hood of the car, watching the sun set over D.C., drinking soda and eating pretzels. The inside of the car still smelled like oranges and Coca-Cola—his two favorite things.

What happened to that? To them? Those questions hadn't left her, but now, faced with Camden in her space all the time, the questions came renewed with a force she wasn't prepared for.

"Viana?" Camden's voice pulled her into the present.

"Sorry." Viana looked out the window to hide her reddening cheeks. What would he say if he knew she was thinking about them? Or how she loved the smell of oranges? Her phone buzzed with an incoming text. She grabbed it and scanned the message. "Ainslie just texted. Her mom went by the designer's store, and it's closed. Like, there's nothing there."

Camden whistled. "So, the guy just ghosted her?"

Viana glanced across at him, dread filling her stomach "If you can ghost someone, you can send the wrong dress."

Camden drummed his fingers on the wheel. "Can anything else go wrong with this wedding?"

"Don't—" Viana held up a hand. "We don't think things like this. We fix and we solve."

Camden glanced at her, a tiny grin touching his mouth. "Yes, ma'am."

Viana laughed, but inside, Camden's words burrowed deep, like a tick on a dog, slowly spreading poison through the body

What else was going to hit them next?

Chapter Five

"This isn't going to work. We can't find a close enough match." Viana sat on the floor and buried her head in her knees. They were in the last store in Montgomery. The owner, a lovely lady named Nora, who Viana had crossed paths with several times over the years, had moved out the front to begin closing up. Which only served to tighten Viana's already-overstrung nerves. "I have to give Ainslie some options when we get back. It's four in the afternoon. We're running out of time." Desperation scraped out of every word.

"What about this one?" Camden was holding up a dress that looked nothing like the one they needed.

Frustration bubbled. This whole situation was impossible. And just staring at Camden, back in her world, was sending her crazy. "Seriously? That's a totally different style." Viana massaged her temples with her knuckles. Her headache would balloon into a migraine if she wasn't careful.

"Viana, I'm trying to help you." He spread his arms wide. "I'm in this jungle of white dresses listening to really bad Christmas music, trying to help you save this wedding. And I don't want you to get a migraine. They leave you exhausted for days."

Viana looked at him.

Camden cocked his head, his mouth tipped into a knowing smile. "You always rub your head with your knuckles when a migraine is coming on."

"Why are you here?" Viana stared at him, hating that he knew her so well, yet somehow, also loving it. But she could never let him know that.

Camden put the dress back, where it bunched and fell to the floor. He picked up and hung it carefully. "I've been hired to keep Ainslie and Lucas safe. That's my job. And if this wedding doesn't go ahead, I don't get paid, and instead I have to move back to Nashville and move in with my mother or reenlist—which I really do not want to do." He was breathing hard. "That's why I'm here."

Tension stretched between them, taut like a violin string.

His words knocked the irritation out of her. "I had no idea. You never wanted to move back home."

Camden nodded, his jaw set. "No. And you always wanted to come back. Your parents' dream was yours too."

It was true. She never wanted anything else.

He inhaled and went looking through another rack of dresses that Viana had given up on an hour ago. "You don't ever quit, do you?"

He pulled out two dresses. "It's my military training. I joined as soon as I graduated. I skipped our class ceremony."

"I know." They'd broken up eight weeks before, but she'd still looked for him that day. "Why did you join the military?"

Camden sighed. "The pressure of family legacy is strong. But I guess, more than anything, I wanted to be a person of purpose." He visibly swallowed, his voice scratchy. "To be seen."

"And I didn't see you?" Viana whispered, her gaze riveted to Camden.

"No." He levelled a haunting stare at her. There was no anger in his eyes, no blame in his voice, just stark reality. "But my Dad didn't see me either—not as a real person with hopes and dreams—just something that he could bend to his will."

"I never realised how much pressure you were under." Viana exhaled softly. "You never talked about it."

Camden shrugged, his hand resting on a dress in the rack. "I liked what we had. I liked that you liked me without all the military stuff." A gentle smile touched his lips. "You just liked *me.*"

Viana's heartbeat furiously in her chest. *She just liked him.* And she had. They hadn't started talking about a future yet, but she sure had been thinking about it. "I'm sorry I didn't see you."

Camden pushed the dresses along the rack, the sound of rustling material and metal against the rod competing with, yes, the really bad Christmas music that filled the shop. Then he paused and looked over at her. "Thank you for that. I'm sorry I walked away."

Viana looked down at the floor, the carpet cream and thick, her heart squeezing as emotions rolled through her body. It was the first, real honest conversation they'd had since his arrival in Summer Shore. Raw and real—and it felt good.

"What about this?" Camden held up one of the dresses.

Viana perked up, curious, and grateful for the topic change. "How did I miss that one?" She stood, stretching her sore legs and examined the dress. "It might work. It's different, but not too different. Plainer, but it could work."

"And this one?" Camden held up the other dress.

This one was in the same style of the other one but was heavily embroidered and with more sparkling beads sewed along the hem. "This could work too," she murmured.

Camden's shoulders relaxed. "We need to hit the road. It'll be late by the time we get back. I had to get Lauren to pick up Ainslie and Lucas."

He was sacrificing his job to help her with hers. It seemed like superman was back.

"Yes, let's take these. I'll arrange with Nora, I think she'll let me bring back the dress that Ainslie doesn't want, and Ainslie will sort out payment." She leaned closer, lowering her voice. "Plus, Nora will get the surprise of her life when her dress shop is promoted after the wedding is announced."

Camden frowned. "I had no idea stuff like that was possible. Getting wedding dresses like this at the last minute."

"It happens more than you think. Usually, the wedding planner is utilizing all their contacts and calling in favors." Viana held one of the dresses, Camden had the other.

Viana thanked Nora and together they tucked the dresses, safe in their garment bags, into the back of the SUV.

"You're good at your job, you know that, right?" Camden asked as he negotiated them into the traffic and headed south to Summer Shore.

Viana didn't know how to feel about his compliment. "So far in my life, success means I lose people important to me."

The car hummed, the heating on low. It was colder in Montgomery than Summer Shore. Camden turned onto Route 331.

"Like your parents?" he said quietly.

And you. "Yes."

Did she mean him too? That question went unanswered. Cam gripped the steering wheel a little tighter. It felt safer to change the topic.

"You said that this wedding was needed...what did you mean by that?"

Viana spoke softly. "LOVElegant might have to close if this wedding isn't a success." She glanced at him and continued. "We're only averaging two weddings a month and that's simply not enough in this business. We should have at least one wedding each weekend, two would be perfect. And a few midweek ones would be the icing on the cake." Viana's shoulders sagged. "When the water main burst, and you showed up..."

"And now the dress?"

She nodded. "And you need this to be a hit as well."

Guilt slipped over Cam as easily as the waves hit the sand. "I'm sorry. Don't let my problems add to yours."

Viana laughed a short, humorless laugh. "But, don't you see, we need each other, or everything we've worked for falls apart." She looked over at him. "What if Ainslie doesn't like these dresses? Do you think, after this new debacle on top of everything else, that they'll still go through with the wedding?"

Cam tapped the steering wheel. "I think Lucas and Ainslie love each other and, as much as they hate what's happening, their decision to marry won't change." He kept his eyes on the road. "Maybe it's just my male opinion, but if you love someone, things like soggy grass and different dresses don't matter in the long run."

"They *are* crazy about each other." Viana let out a small sigh. "Ainslie's worried about her mom too. She's put so much pressure on the importance and perfection of this day on Ainslie. And I've had to put Florence on 'do not disturb' mode on my phone a few hours each day just to get anything done."

"That's tough." He looked out at the passing landscape, the rolling hills and farmland. It reminded him a little of Nashville. He loved that town, but he didn't love the complications that came with it. His gaze drifted to Viana. "Lucas looks at Ainslie like there's no one else in the room. He smiles that smile that only a guy in love does. And Ainslie will be gorgeous no matter what she wears."

Her gaze connected with his and the world narrowed, and it was nothing but them. No sounds. Just him and Viana. His heart thumped hard.

He shook his head and focused back on the road. Traffic slowed them down. "It's peak hour. We'll be free of this soon."

"You didn't answer my question before."

"What? About the military?" Cam slowed to let another driver in.

"Yes. I never knew you wanted to join."

Her question unsettled him. Brought up things he wanted to forget—about himself mostly.

"Was life in the military so bad, Cam?"

It was the first time she had called him that since he rolled back into her life. Hope filled his chest. Getting back with Viana was not even on his radar, but that didn't mean he couldn't find her as beautiful and as interesting as before—more so, really.

"Dad's pride is in the generations of Mayfield men being career servicemen—whether we like it or not. Jay loved it. I thought I would grow to love it." Cam tapped the steering wheel. "But Jay is out now too. Dad isn't coping well with his sons disappointing him and the family legacy."

Itchy, uncomfortable memories settled on him. Cam readjusted himself in the seat. "He only cares if I can do one of two things: follow the family tradition or manage on my own, but only as long as it's something he approves of." He laughed bitterly. "When I was ten years old, they forgot me at the fair. I was alone there for hours, until I found someone we knew, and they drove me home. I didn't have a phone back then. Dad was happy I was able to find a way without him—that's what a good military kid would do. I was ten, Viana, ten."

Her hand was on his arm. "You never told me that."

Why had he told her that now? He swallowed. "I—I don't think I've ever told anyone, honestly."

She squeezed his arm, the pressure sending sparks of attraction up and into his spine. "I'm sorry you went through that." Her gentle voice reached into the dark places he'd closed off years ago.

"Thanks." He swallowed back a rising lump of emotion. "But that's why I'm working so hard to make a go of my security business—I want to stand on my own two feet and hopefully make him proud at the same time."

The rest of the trip passed in a settled quiet. Not exactly relaxed, but at least the animosity that existed between them lessened. Viana was more comfortable around him now. And she liked the man he'd grown into. He was more assured and in charge than he'd ever been. And he was here with her, driving all over the place to help make sure this wedding went ahead.

But he had a stake in it too, she reminded herself. The effort he put in today wasn't just about her.

They made a quick drive-thru pit stop and ate in the car as Cam steered them into Summer Shore. The house came into view, and when Cam pulled into the driveway, Viana got out to open the gate. He rolled through, and she closed it behind them.

Maybe an automatic gate *would* be handy.

She met him as he climbed out of the car. Darkness had fallen, save for the soft glow of light coming from the windows on the lower floor, spilling out on the yard. Next to the car, under a magnolia tree, they were hidden in semi-darkness.

"Thanks for today." She put one hand in her back pocket. Standing there with him so close, regrets rolled through her. She wanted nothing but to make their past right, but what would that mean for their future?

"I was happy to help." His voice was low, quiet.

She shivered.

"Well, it was for both of us." She rubbed her forehead with a free hand.

Then Cam's hand was there. Over hers. Viana stilled. Her gaze was riveted to his. Slowly, with purpose, he gently massaged her temple with his thumb. Moving his thumb in firm but gentle circles along her forehead, relieving the building pressure and replacing it with a different kind of headache. Unwilling to stop herself, Viana leaned into his touch, letting his hand take the weight of her head.

"What happened to us?" she whispered, looking up at him.

Cam sighed and ran his finger down her cheek. "Oh Viva, I didn't know what I wanted—not really. And you always knew where you were headed," he said softly. "And I'm only now just figuring out what my path is."

Viana felt her walls collapse a little at his use of Viva, his own special nickname for her.

"I was so focused on my future, I didn't pay enough attention to us." She tripped over her words as she battled with the hurt that Cam inflicted on her...and the hurt she'd inflicted on him. "And then you left, and I was so angry. You left because I was too busy with my own stuff." *Too busy thriving.*

And ever since, she hadn't let anyone in, keeping herself from getting hurt, refusing to let another person walk away from her because of her dreams.

"But my breaking up with you and then leaving as soon as possible was cruel of me. We both had a lot of growing up to do." Cam's thumb continued to caress her cheek. The gentleness of it, undoing her bit by bit. His eyes were pools of calm water she wanted to sink into. Physically he had filled out since leaving college and joining the marines. He seemed taller too, his arms strong without being bulky.

Cam seemed to sense the change too. His gaze sharpened on her, traveling down her face, until it landed on her lips.

Viana inhaled, their past and the present colliding. She couldn't give her heart away again—the chance of losing him was too much of a risk.

The porch globe flickered on, splashing light across them. Viana jumped back, her hand on her chest, heart pounding.

"Goodnight." She grabbed the dresses from the car, and bolted into the house.

Cam had wanted to kiss her. She raced up the stairs, every footstep echoing in her head, along with the truth.

She wanted to kiss him too.

Chapter Six
Two days before the Wedding

"**A**ny more dramas erupt overnight?" Viana joined Lauren and Olivia in the kitchen. The third floor had been converted into a living space, complete with a kitchen, small dining area that opened onto a living room with a big, comfy L-shaped lounge and two snuggly reclining chairs, one bathroom with a dual sink—three women needed it—and generously sized bedrooms for each of them.

The breeze fluttered through the sheer curtains, and muted sunlight tried to break through the overcast sky.

"Not that I know of," Lauren piped up, coffee in hand. "I'm meeting with a new client for a wedding cake later today." She often baked cakes for weddings held at other venues too.

"Good." Viana stood by the counter, crunching a mouthful of Lucky Charms cereal. "Ainslie tried on the dresses last night. We're going to do another session when her mother gets here."

"Florence is coming *today*?" Olivia's eyes opened wide.

"Yes." Viana gave her a reassuring smile. Keeping everyone confident—including herself—was easier said than done, but she had to try. "We can handle Florence."

Lauren snorted. "You have Florence on 'do not disturb' mode most of the time."

Viana raised her eyebrows and grinned. "And you both should do the same if you want any peace." She felt her grin slip. "And with everything going wrong, we are not going to have much peace until the wedding is over."

Olivia gave a tremulous nod. Then she nodded toward Viana's cereal bowl. "Aren't you ever going to eat something else? You've been eating that stuff since high school." She wrinkled her nose. "You know it's full of sugar."

Lauren laughed.

"Longer actually." Viana took another defiant mouthful. "It's my thing, okay? I eat Lucky Charms for breakfast."

Viana's heart settled, up here on the third floor, there was no pressure, no deadlines, just their space to be themselves. Up here felt high enough to even chase away the memory of her almost-kiss with Cam last night.

Olivia put down her fork. "I think I've found a videographer."

Viana, glad of the topic change, sat on the dining chair, relief coursing through her. With two days until the wedding, it was cutting things down to the wire.

"I met him a few days ago." Olivia didn't sound confident, but something else stole across her pretty face.

"Who is he?"

"Sil--uh, Mac." Olivia looked down at her plate. "He's a scuba and snorkel instructor with a kiosk down by the pier. I've never seen such skill with a camera. Way better than the last guy." Her cheeks reddened.

"Oh, you have a crush!" Lauren's smile widened. "How'd you meet him? And why are you not telling us anything?"

"There's nothing to tell." Olivia's gaze strayed to the window. "I didn't want to say anything until I'm sure he'll work out." She paused. "We met on the beach when his black lab thought Sable was her new toy."

"Ooh, enemies to lovers, all those sparks." Lauren raised her eyebrows in Olivia's direction.

"Don't you talk." Viana pointed her spoon at Lauren. "Who's that guy I saw you with yesterday? When I was leaving town, you were out front of Castaways."

Lauren's face slipped into nonchalance. "No one you know."

Viana rolled her eyes but offered a teasing smile. "Keep your secrets then."

"Speaking of sparks—" Lauren nodded at Viana. "How are you and Cam getting along?"

Viana stood and washed her bowl in the sink, ignoring the loud stares of her friends. "Camden and I are fine. We're professionals."

Olivia stood and put her plate on the counter. "There's sparks, we can all see it." She gave her a quick hug. "I'll be back later."

"Have fun!" Lauren trilled after her.

Olivia flushed pink as she shut the door behind her.

Lauren turned to Viana. "Sure, you two are professionals. Whatever you say." She put her mug in the dishwasher. "It's okay to let your guard down." Her quiet words filled the room.

"You want me to let Camden back into my life?" Viana's gaze settled on her friend.

Lauren returned it with a pointed stare of her own. "No, not unless you want to. But you keep people—not us, but everyone else—at arm's length. Maybe Cam being here is a reminder to you that it's okay to let someone in...and I don't just mean him."

"So, what are you saying? Be open to romance?" Viana's hand went to her chest as she recalled Cam's gaze skimming to her lips. She could feel her cheeks heating.

"I can see something's been going on with you." Lauren shrugged. "I'm saying, be surprised by love."

Viana's phone pinged, grateful for the disruption. Lauren always had a way of pointing out things Viana would rather not think about. She loved and hated that about Lauren. She picked it up from the table and scanned the text message. "Florence will be here any minute. Ainslie and Lucas are good together, don't you think?"

"Fine, change the topic." Lauren said wryly. "Yes, they're lovely. Lucas is a bit..." she hedged.

"Into the fame?" Viana supplied with a grin.

"Yeah, but he still seems genuine." Lauren touched the hem of her t-shirt. "Fame is something I never want to experience again, and mine wasn't even on the level Lucas and Ainslie's is—but it was more than enough." Lauren stared into the distance. Viana's heart squeezed for her friend, who never talked in great detail about her former life. All Viana knew was that being a model had its perks, but for Lauren, the downsides had been numerous and leaving it behind had been her only option. "They've both been easy to work with and what a blessing that is."

Viana nodded. "So long as we avoid any more disasters between now until Saturday. But when they post all their wedding photos and videos, we're going to be beyond busy." Hopefully. That thought was so terrifying and exciting, it was enough to collapse her under the weight of all the pressure and expectation.

"You, okay?" Lauren eyed her.

Viana squared her shoulders. "It's a lot, just thinking about it, but yes. I am excited."

"Me too." Lauren grinned.

But not about Camden. Lauren's words followed her to the office downstairs. If news of the wedding didn't go viral after the fact, would their business still survive?

"Ainslie, honey, I'm here." The commanding voice of Florence Tucker blared through the house.

Viana closed her notes for the upcoming New Year's Eve wedding—their second wedding for December, shut her eyes and sent up a prayer for sanity and patience.

She walked out of her office on the first floor and smiled as Florence crossed the threshold. Short and stylish, with chin-length, silver-streaked hair and a purposeful stride that declared her presence in any room. "Hello, Mrs. Tucker. So lovely to see you again."

Florence did not smile back. Her brown eyes, sharp as her chin, bore holes into Viana. "So first it's the dress, and now the garden looks like a swamp. What's next?"

Viana fought to keep her smile. Dealing with difficult people came with the job, but that didn't mean she liked being blamed for things out of her control. Florence had put the screws on Viana from the moment Ainslie and Lucas booked The Summer House months ago, after a day trip they'd had to the area.

"Hopefully nothing. Rest assured, we've had worse issues than a little water in the yard and an AWOL dress."

Florence arched one eyebrow. "I'm glad to see you think my daughter's wedding issues are so trivial."

Cringing inwardly, Viana kept her expression neutral. "I didn't mean it like that." She took Florence by the arm and led her into the cozy sitting room. She needed Florence on side. "What I meant is that no matter how well planned a wedding is, there are always things that come up unexpectedly."

Florence eyed her, her frown deep, but she didn't reply.

Viana took that as a win.

"Mom?" Ainslie walked in, her face less strained than it was yesterday. Her brown hair was pulled into a messy bun and her outfit of jeans and black t-shirt managed to look put together, despite the tired circles under her eyes.

"Any news on my designer?"

"No." Florence glared at the room. "That man you hired to make your dress is clearly a fraud. I would sue him for breach of contract and emotional distress."

Ainslie sat down next to her mother. "Thanks for trying. But I just want to get married. I don't want to think about suing people right now—or ever." Ainslie muttered the last two words.

Viana watched them, her chest tight as she saw how tired Ainslie was, how angry Florence was. And there was nothing she could do to fix things beyond finding a dress Ainslie liked—which she'd done. But that only solved a physical issue, not the emotional battering Ainslie was taking with all the dramas they'd had so far.

Florence patted Ainslie's leg. "I'm not done yet. I'll find you a dress. If we don't, you'll have to cancel the wedding."

Viana held her breath, clamping her mouth shut. Panic needled up her neck and she felt the beginnings of a migraine coming on. And she would not rely on Cam—when had she started shortening his name again? —to fix it, with his facial massages, his wide, strong shoulders, and a chest she just wanted to lean on. Since when did she need Cam for anything? The image of Cam jumping over the fence with his stupid shovel danced across her mind.

Viana shook her head. *Get it together*. Florence could not pressure Ainslie into cancelling the wedding.

"Mom, it's fine. Viana found me two dresses yesterday." She held up her fingers. "Two. Come on, I want you to see them both." Ainslie ushered Viana to join them.

Together they trooped up the stairs into Ainslie's room.

It took both Viana and Florence to help Ainslie into the second dress.

"This one is my favourite. It's perfect." Ainslie spun around in front of the mirror in her room. "I can't believe you found one that fits and is so similar to my original. The only thing I need to do is wear higher heels to adjust for the length."

The dress was a capped sleeve, sweetheart neckline, natural waistline, chiffon dress that dropped and fell perfectly to the floor with a chapel train. It was perfect for a wedding at The Summer House. Viana could see the photos that Olivia would take on the stairs, on the porch. Hope surged in her chest.

"It's stunning." Viana sat on the bed, laughing in relief.

Florence eyed Ainslie as she spun in a circle. "It is better than the first one you tried on." She pursed her lips, her eyes narrowing. "But it's not as extravagant as your original one."

Ainslie stopped spinning and sent her mother a scowl via her reflection in the mirror. "Yes, well, my original one is who knows where. And as I recall, you insisted on a more upmarket dress than the one I had in mind."

"You're getting *married*. And you have fans expecting to see you in something spectacular. Not sweet and boring."

Ainslie drew in a shaky breath. "But I'm not getting married for the fans, Mom. I'm marrying Lucas because I love him." Then her eyes went wide. "You haven't said anything to anyone, have you?"

Florence stood and paced the room. "Of course I haven't. I haven't even told my best friend—" she pointed at Ainslie "—your surrogate aunt, I might add, that she's not allowed to come. How do you think she'll feel?"

Ainslie huffed. "You know we're holding a reception in New York after we get back from our honeymoon. Lucas and I have already inked new deals with four companies to capitalize on our marriage." She looked at the dress again, her face softening. "But this is *our* moment. It won't belong to the public."

"Fine." Florence went to the door. "Can I get food around here?"

Viana stood. "Of course, we have a limited breakfast menu for guests. Let me show you to the dining room where Anita can take your order."

"I can find it myself." Florence left the room, shutting the door with a sharp click.

"The rest of the party is coming tomorrow. Mom will have to be more chill with everyone else around." Ainslie seemed to be talking more to herself than Viana.

"Why don't I take both dresses upstairs and keep them safe there?" Viana helped Ainslie out of her gown, and together they maneuvered the dress into the garment bag and zipped it up. "You look so pretty in it."

Ainslie's shoulder sagged. "Thank you—for everything you've done." She headed to the bathroom to get changed.

"I only wish so much hadn't gone wrong." Viana's chest tightened. Nothing more could happen...right? She sent a silent plea heavenwards.

Ainslie called out from the bathroom. "I imagine doing this job, you get all sorts of crazy things happening." She stuck her head out of the door, grinning.

Viana chuckled as Ainslie emerged in her jeans and t-shirt. "A dog once ran off with the bride's bouquet. Snatched it right out of her hand and took off to the beach."

Ainslie put her hand to her mouth. "No."

Viana laughed. "There are great photos of the whole bridal party chasing the dog along the sand. Or there was that time when we had a storm, and the power went out. We had a beautiful candlelit ceremony inside, right in the foyer, in front of the grand staircase." Viana gave her a reassuring smile. "Your ceremony will be in the same place, under the arch, right in front the staircase, leading to the double doors, flowing out onto the porch."

Ainslie sat on the bed and sighed. "It sounds amazing. Better than my original idea."

Joy bubbled through Viana. They might just get out of this without any more scrapes. She took the dresses and walked to the door. "I'll see you later. Go and enjoy some time with your mom before all the guests arrive." Viana waved as she closed the door.

Anita met her on the landing, Cam in tow.

Her heart hammered at the sight of their serious expressions. "What's wrong?"

"I need you downstairs for a moment." Anita pushed her glasses higher up on her face. "Florence asked to know where the ceremony will be held, and I showed her. She doesn't like it and is demanding to talk to you. And I've got a prospective bride on the phone."

Viana looked at Cam. "And why are you here?"

He pointed to another door further down the second floor. "I'm on my way to my room."

"Oh." Viana then thrust the dresses at him. "Can you put them upstairs, third floor, while I go down and deal with Florence?" She pressed her hands hard into his chest, her eyes beseeching him. Here she was, needing him again, and there he was, coming to her rescue—or she hoped he would.

The thought struck like a slap. When had she ever let herself get to this point—hoping in Camden Mayfield? She swallowed. She didn't need to need him...not for anything beyond taking the dresses for the time being.

But the way he held her gaze, his voice low and husky as he dipped his head and offered a "yes ma'am" in response to her plea made her wonder if a part of her did, in fact, need Cam.

Being needed by Viana was a heady experience and one he would do well not to get too used to. It was only to save this wedding, and he would do what was needed to get them through the next two days.

He took the dresses and took the stairs two steps at a time.

Cam made it to the top and stared at a set of double doors. He looked up and down at either side but those were the only doors. Shrugging, he entered and found himself in the private quarters of the girls. A large living room with a combined kitchen and windows that overlooked the beach— the third floor had its advantages. On one side of the room, there were three doors he assumed led into their bedrooms.

Not knowing what else to do, he gently laid the dresses across the back of the comfy L-shaped couch. He was about to step out when something caught his eye. On a bookshelf, between two of the doors, on a high shelf, was a copper jewelry tree. Hanging from it were familiar shell necklaces, ones he'd seen Viana make, along with new ones. Sundial shells, small conche ones, and screw shells, all hanging from the intricately made tree.

It was her hobby, but one she didn't share with others. She could easily sell these and make money. They were stunning. He crossed the room and, without thinking, reached out and ran a finger along the shells. They tinkled when they touched each other. The grooves of each shell was light to touch, and he thought back to all the times she'd made a new one but never showed him. He only ever found out because she hung them on a thick string across her bedroom window. She didn't think he noticed things—not something like that anyway. But Cam noticed everything about Viana—she'd had his attention since the day she walked into his life.

Reluctantly he stepped away and turned to leave, then stopped in his tracks.

Viana stood at the door. "Ainslie came and rescued me. She convinced Florence to sit down and have breakfast. I said it was a good idea—you know, for security purposes."

Silence stretched across the room, the years shrinking between them.

"I didn't know you still made the necklaces." Cam watched as Viana walked slowly into the room.

She shrugged, running her hands along the dresses that hung over the couch. "It's just a hobby."

"They're amazing," he said quietly. "They always have been."

"Thanks." She wouldn't look at him.

Cam wanted to leave, but his legs wouldn't move. Being here with Viana felt right—for the first time since he'd walked back into her life. "How's Ainslie?"

Viana rubbed her temple with her knuckles. Cam's fingers twitched, he wanted to be the one to take the weight off her shoulders. "Despite everything that's happened, she's still excited." She looked up at him. "Still in love."

Something about that look in her eye...He swallowed. Was she still in love with him? No, there was no way. "One less thing to worry about."

Viana walked over until she was standing at the bookshelf with him. "And your plate too."

"But mine's not as important as yours." He watched as Viana touched her necklaces, running her fingers over them in the same way he had.

"Why do you say that?" She glanced at him "I thought we established that this wedding was vital to the success of both our careers."

"It is." The sunlight, the gentle sway of the curtains in the breeze, the sound of waves crashing on the sand. Viana's quiet statement matched the mood of the room and Cam didn't want to break it. "But it's your dream, the vision of your family. I'm standing inside the hopes and dreams of your parents, and you made it come true. That's what makes it more important."

Viana's face crumpled and her shoulders sagged, like whatever invisible weight she was carrying was too much for her. Cam touched her arm. "Hey, what's wrong?"

She wiped tears that traveled down her cheeks, and took a deep breath, clearly trying to steady herself. "It's not just the business." Another tear fell and Cam reached over and wiped it away with his thumb, not even thinking about what his actions might do to her or him. He hated to see her like this.

Viana stared at him, seeming to drink him in. He stared back, but then she blinked and went back to looking at her necklaces. "What's going on ?"

She looked around the room, appearing to drink in the cream walls, floor-to-ceiling windows, the French doors that led to the porch. "It's this house too."

"Viva, what do you mean?"

Chapter Seven

The use of Cam's nickname for her was her undoing. The compassion in his voice only added to the powerful pull that was taut between them.

"I'll lose the house, too, if business doesn't pick up." Viana swallowed the lump in her throat, but all it did was create a rock in her gut.

"What do you mean? It's yours, isn't it?" Cam's hand was still on her arm, and Viana hated how good it felt and how much she needed his presence.

Viana fought the tears that threatened to keep falling. "Yes, the house is mine, it was my inheritance after Dad died. My aunt looked after it in a trust until I turned twenty-one. I took it over then, but my aunt ran her bed-and-breakfast out of it before I came home five years ago. That was when Lauren and I started LOVElegant." The words tumbled out, like a release valve had been opened. "We took out a loan to renovate the top floor so we could live here—it's cheaper to stay on site with only people here a couple of days a week. But there's always the property taxes and the upkeep of the house." She inhaled a shaky breath. "And I get to be close to Mom and Dad." The thought was always there. The feeling of loss, still painful after all these years.

Cam's thumb was rubbing small circles on her wrist, sending goose-bumps pebbling up her arm. Did he notice? Did she want him to?

"You don't talk much about them." Cam stated it and there was no denying the truth in his words.

Viana touched the necklace around her neck and squeezed it for comfort. "That's because it was my fault."

His hand stilled on her arm. "How could that be? Weren't you twelve?"

Viana squeezed the necklace until the shell dug into her palm. Then she unclasped her hand and showed Cam the shell. "I made this when I was twelve. I used to make them all the time when I was younger. My Gramma, Mom's mom, taught me how to take the shell, clean it, shine it, attach it to the wire and then fasten it to the fabric cord." She breathed out before continuing, not wanting to be stopped now that she was talking. "After Mom died it was a way of feeling close to her. And it kept my mind off the fact that she was gone, you know?" A sob escaped.

Cam nodded, his hand was still circling her wrist.

"By the time I was nine, I was going to markets with Gramma to sell them. And I was doing well." Viana heaved a wobbly breath.

"What happened?" Cam's thumb resumed its circles on her arm. And when she glanced at him, his steady gaze infused her with strength again.

"Dad was going to take me to this market in Panama City Beach, right during spring break. I was so excited. Gramma was supposed to come, but she couldn't." Viana rubbed her forehead.

Cam reached out and began massaging her forehead, his voice deep and calm. "What happened next?"

"Dad didn't want to go. He was tired from finishing work on this house and I didn't care." Viana laughed, the sound hollow and dull in her ears. "I threw a tantrum, a twelve-year-old version of one, and begged him to take me. I bugged him and bugged him until he gave in."

"And it was a good day. I sold almost all my necklaces and then on the way home—" A sob caught in her chest, and it climbed higher, trying to escape.

"Was it the car crash?" Cam's hand had moved to the back of her neck, taking the weight of her head, as she leaned into him.

Viana nodded, unable to speak.

"And you were in the car?" He inhaled softly, his thumb caressing her neck.

She nodded again. "It was all my fault." She croaked out, then looked into his steady, compassionate gaze. "If I hadn't forced him to go, he wouldn't be dead."

"No, Viva." Cam hugged her to him and Viana allowed herself to share the burden she'd carried for so long. "No, it was not your fault."

Viana pulled back, clutching his arms, needing him to understand. "But I made him take me. And with Mom gone, now I have no one."

Cam ran his hands down her arms, the sensation immediately causing a contradiction. She needed that touch...yet it somehow made her want to run away. "Your dad was the adult. He wanted to take you because he loved you." Cam settled his hands on her shoulders. They weren't heavy, just solid, like his presence had always been. "Who was at fault with the accident?"

"The other driver." Viana stared hard at Cam, unable to make sense of her jumbled emotions and the way Cam affected her from head to toe and right to the center of her heart. "He was drinking and veered into our lane."

Cam closed his eyes and when he opened them, they were bright with unshed tears. "Viva, I'm so sorry you went through that. You never told me the details."

Viana touched the necklace, drawing strength from it. "I hate talking about it," she said hoarsely. "I hate that my drive to succeed killed my dad."

Cam sighed. "And I bet you think I left because of your success." It was a statement.

"Yes," Viana whispered.

The truth was out there, exposed. Viana couldn't hide from it. He knew her deepest fears now.

"With success comes loss…" Cam trailed out the words, his hands still firm and steady on her shoulders.

Viana exhaled until she felt there was no air left inside her. "I want my parents' dream—my dream—to work." She leaned her head on his chest, inhaling his familiar scent, leaning into his strength. "I need Ainslie and Lucas's wedding to be a hit. I don't want to lose everything my parents built." She looked into his eyes and curled her fist around his shirt. "But it's like a ticking time bomb in the back of my brain. I'm waiting for the other shoe to drop."

Cam leaned in, his forehead touching Viana's, his breath warm and gentle. "I'm not going anywhere. "You and I are in this wedding until the end…and maybe, we might have another chance at us…"

He breathed out the last word and, before Viana could process her actions, their lips met.

Kissing Viana was not part of his plans, not that he had plans beyond making this job a success and not going back to Nashville. But here he was, and he wasn't going to walk away from a potential second chance with the woman he'd never stopped loving.

Cam gently tugged Viana closer, and deepened the kiss, running his hand through her silky hair, remembering all the times they got lost in each other's kisses. All the times he knew he loved her but only said it once. All the times that they lost sight of each other.

When her hands reached around his neck, he tugged her closer and their kisses increased in passion. Cam wanted more than just a fleeting moment. He wanted something solid, tangible, and he wanted it with Viana.

He gently pulled back, giving them much needed inches of distance. "Viva," he breathed out her name. "We need to think before we get carried away."

A pretty blush stained her cheeks, and her lips were plump and rosy from his. His pulse pounded in his ears. He tugged her back, but into a hug, rather than passion. He settled her against his chest, and he loved the way she fit so perfectly under his arm.

"I'm sorry for hurting you all those years ago." He let his chin rest on the top of her head.

Viana tilted her head, so she peered up at him. "I'm sorry too." Her voice was soft, raspy around the edges too. "I was too busy for you, and I should have made you a priority."

Cam hugged her tightly. "It's okay. We were both broken then and maybe..." he hesitated. Did he want to officially get back together with Viana or was this just some bizarre stress reaction from a wedding that had so much riding on it? Was it stirring up old feelings? He didn't have any answers.

And he didn't want to go through the pain of losing her *again*. Was he ready for that risk?

"What are we doing?" Viana's question was loud in the too-quiet room.

Cam sighed. "I don't know."

Viana untangled herself from his arms and sat back, questions in her eyes. He immediately missed her closeness. "I think we need to try and move on from this." She stood, sorrow radiating from her posture.

Cam stood, scrubbing a hand down his face. Confusion reigned inside him, but he didn't want to argue with her. So she was having second thoughts already. History repeating itself? "Maybe you're right."

Viana stood, casting him a long, pained look before she hurried out of the room.

Cam looked heavenwards. "What is going on?"

There was no answer, not that he needed one, but voicing his question out loud felt better. And it served as a reminder that he wasn't alone in his walk through life.

Cam's phone pinged. He checked it and saw a text from Dad.

Call me when you can.

He headed to his room and shut the door. Might as well get it over now rather than delay. Cam pressed the video call button. Within a few seconds, Dad's face appeared on the screen, his hair regulation-short as always. Now gray peppered his temples. He looked more weathered, but it was the same man—rugged eyebrows, deep lines around his mouth and eyes, and his ever-familiar crooked nose. Cam recalled all the times he would run his finger along Dad's nose as a kid and try to straighten it.

"How are you?" Dad's deep timber was familiar as country music was to Nashville. Why did families have to be so complex? He loved his dad, but he wanted—no *needed*—to know his merit was based on who he was, not on whether he did or did not reup with the military.

"Good." Liar. But he was not going to discuss Viana with Dad. "The wedding is coming together, but there are some issues with the wedding dress, and other disasters. Bride and mother of the bride are stressed."

Dad's smile tightened. "That sounds like a normal wedding. Your mother lost her veil the morning of our wedding, and her mother was almost in tears. Turns out your cousin, Gabby, had taken it and was playing dress up."

Dad rarely talked about Mom. Their divorce hadn't been messy, mostly silent—like their marriage had been. "I can see her doing that. Wasn't she five at the time?"

"She was." Dad settled back in his chair and Cam could see he was in his office at his new base in Texas. A frown settled on his face.

Cam's stomach clenched. "Just say what you want to say."

Dad grunted. "Why are you not reenlisting in the service? You were on a great trajectory, and you strayed off the path."

Your path, not mine. Cam waited several heart beats before replying. "No, I'm not."

Dad's eyebrows drew together. "Both my boys walking away from job security and family pride. Where did I go wrong?"

Cam ran his hand down his face. "You didn't go wrong. We just don't want the same things you do."

"Starting your own security business is hard, almost impossible. You need to come back and find your place in the service." Dad's voice lowered, like his eyebrows.

"Since when have you ever cared what I did, so long as I took care of myself? You seem to like me most when I'm not needing you." All the old wounds were spilling out. "And now, you want me to drop everything and jump when you say how high?"

Dad's frown deepened and he shifted so Cam could see out the window. Texas looked like Summer Shore—wispy winter clouds and sunlight.

"It's because you're so independent, but you can follow orders. That's what makes a leader in the marines." Dad's voice dropped even lower. "I fostered that independence in you, so you could make a success of your life—and what you're doing isn't the right path."

"Thanks for the vote of confidence." Cam clenched his jaw, the pressure to comply was overwhelming. But he didn't want that for his life. In fact, all he knew was he needed his business to succeed, and he had nothing more beyond that. No room for anything but making sure he didn't go back to Dad. There was nothing worse than being lauded for being independent and then having that very freedom yanked away.

"Don't you care about the family legacy?"

Cam continued to pace, struggling with the emotions at war within him. "I do but legacy isn't everything." *And not at the expense of a relationship with your son.* But those words never left his lips.

"Well then," Dad spoke gruffly. "I guess I'll talk to you later." And the screen went blank.

Cam needed to do something to work off the adrenaline coursing through him.

He headed downstairs, did a perimeter walk, and as he did, he called several businesses who would change the gate to automatic and gathered some rough numbers for Viana. Then he checked every door on the porch on the ground and first floor. They were secure. Then he went and checked on the security lights around the property. The ground squelched underfoot, but at least it wasn't a total washout anymore. But the sodden, damp scent lingered in the air.

Viana walked out onto the porch holding bundles of flowers and plants. When she saw him, her cheeks flushed.

Cam went back to checking the lights, replaying their kiss as he pretended to focus, except he was tracking her every move around the porch.

Needing some space, he grabbed his laptop from his car and walked inside. He set it up on the reception table which was next to the front of the dining room.

Viana was hanging the bundles of greenery from hooks on the porch. She hung them at intervals.

As she approached, the familiar scent of lemongrass and lavender wafted over him.

Her favorite scents. She used to have a diffuser in her dorm in college. How many times had that scent reminded him of her?

"What are you doing?" Cam didn't look up, just kept his eyes on his screen.

Viana picked up a tablet and began checking off items. "Trying to get rid of the damp smell that's kind of everywhere." She peered around his arm. "What are you doing?"

He kept his eyes on his screen, the scent of her invading his space. "Double checking that the cameras are all working and pointing to where I need them."

"I see," she said softly. "I saw you walking around the property be-fore..."

"Perimeter check. Making sure there are no areas where people can enter easily." He moved an inch away from her. Viana smelled too good, and it was distracting him. "Your sandstone foundation with the wrought-iron fencing is very effective at keeping people out." He pointed to the gate. "The gate is still the biggest security risk. Anyone can push it open. I've checked all the external doors on the ground and first floor. They're all secure. I would recommend changing the locks on the back door that leads into the kitchen and the one that leads to your living quarters. They can be easily picked."

"Wow." Viana's exhale was loud in his ears. "You're thorough. Must be all that military training."

"It is." He knew he sounded curt, but he really needed her to back away from him, or he might just grab her and kiss her again. And he didn't need that, and she probably didn't want that to happen again. If she did, she wouldn't have left him upstairs so quickly.

Finally, she moved away from him. He exhaled, letting his shoulders drop.

Viana walked back and forth in the front of the stairs, noting things on her tablet. "Can you help me move this table out of the way?" She tapped the reception table. "We need to put it aside as we'll have people standing here on Saturday. It can't be here when the bride and groom are saying their vows in front of the staircase."

"Just tell me where it needs to go." Together they shifted the table to a corner, where guests could still check in, but it was out of direct sight of the staircase.

"Thanks." They weren't making any eye contact.

"This is actually a better spot for me to set up my station here during the wedding. Do you have a comms earpiece?" This time he finally looked at her.

She had an inscrutable expression on her face. "I do. Do you need to hook into mine?"

"It would be helpful for us to communicate throughout the day." She was still looking at him funny. "What?"

"I was just thinking...no, don't worry about it." She ducked her head and began rearranging items on the desk.

"Tell me."

After long seconds, she looked up. "Would you ever want to live in Summer Shore?"

Why had she asked such a question? It was clear their moment upstairs has been just that—a weak moment—for him. All it left in her was confusion and a longing she didn't know what to do with.

"Forget I said anything." Viana raced out of the room, to the back porch. Why had she asked such a stupid question? But seeing him there, checking doors, walking the perimeter, letting her know that locks were easy to pick. Even helping her move the table hit her right in the heart. It made her ache for something she didn't even realize she was missing until that moment. Someone to build a home with—a life with. And maybe it was their kiss that was stirring up all these confusing feelings.

A kiss she'd launched into with total abandon, and then ran out of the room the second she got her head on straight.

Viana let her thoughts rattle around while she tried to move the white arbor. It was too heavy and big for her alone. She knew that, but Anita was still talking to another client and Olivia and Lauren were not there. Huffing, she picked up one end and dragged it only a few inches before she couldn't do it anymore.

Cam walked through the door and saw her struggling.

Without a word, he picked up one end and nodded at her. Viana picked up her end and Cam walked backwards through the house. Together they placed it at the foot of the stairs.

"Thanks." Viana's gaze skimmed his before she found the world outside more interesting—more comfortable than being in Cam's space.

"In answer to your question before…" Cam's low, steady voice pulled her gaze from outside towards him—like a compass that always sought north. "I don't know if I'd ever move here, but small towns don't phase me." He paused, staring at her. "I guess I'd need the right reason to stay."

Viana's breath caught in her chest. "What are you saying?" Did he mean here in Summer Shore with her or some other random small town? No, there's no way he would want to tie himself to this place—to her—would he?

Ainslie's terrified shriek rent the air. "Mom! You did what?"

Chapter Eight

What now? Cam sprinted into the dining room. Fear jagged through his chest. What had gone wrong? He skidded to a stop, Viana stopping beside him. Her face blanched white. "What's going on?"

Florence, sitting at the table, halfway through her breakfast, put her napkin down. "What's the big deal? I only left a private message on that terrible designer's social media page."

Cam closed his eyes.

Viana squeaked.

Ainslie held up her phone, showing her mother the screen. "No, Mom, you left your berating message about my wedding on their public newsfeed."

Florence grabbed the phone and peered closely at it. "No, I went to the message section."

"That's not what happened." Ainslie was breathing hard, her lips white, her voice high and anguished.

Lucas walked in, running a hand through his hair, as if he'd just rolled out of bed. Which he probably had. "Babe, what's going on?"

Ainslie burst into tears and ran to Lucas, who enveloped her in a bear hug. "Mom posted about the wedding! There's comments already." Ainslie wailed into Lucas's chest.

"Mrs. Tucker, may I have your phone please?" Cam held out his hand.

Florence handed over her phone. Cam navigated to the page and clicked the three little dots and deleted it. Not before seeing more than one hundred comments and twenty-five shares. Great. His job had just gotten ten times harder.

"Florence, what were you thinking?" Lucas snapped, still hugging Ainslie.

Florence stood, her frown deep. "It was a mistake. I really thought I was writing them a private message." Her distress was genuine. "I'm sorry, sweetie. So sorry."

Ainslie finally pulled away from Lucas and faced her mother. "We have to cancel the wedding."

"Everything is going to be fine." Viana went over to Ainslie and put her hand on her shoulder. "It's okay. I've got this." But judging by her tight lips and pale face, she did *not* have anything.

Cam kept his expression neutral, but inside, he panicked. This wedding needed to go ahead. The other part of him tamped down the panic and went into work mode. He needed to get everyone to calm down first, then properly assess the situation. He needed to double check that no one knew where their location was. He was going to need some extra assistance. And this wedding had to happen. He could not have his first job be a failure.

Ainslie whipped out her phone and cried out again. "I've got sixty messages, asking about my wedding. And more keep coming in." Her phone was vibrating every few seconds. "They're all asking when the wedding is."

"Okay, let's all calm down." Cam stepped between everyone, palms up. "We need to take the panic down a notch. Everyone take a breath." He looked at Viana, silently communicating with her to help him get everyone to not jump off the proverbial cliff—including her.

Her cheeks pinked up and her shoulders straightened. Cam nodded and then addressed the little group. "They don't know where the wedding is," Cam said loudly over Ainslie's crying and Florence's apologies.

"That's right," Viana piped up. "That bit hasn't been revealed."

Cam looked sharply at Lucas and Ainslie. "Did you share anything in the last few days about where you might be?" He glanced at Florence. "What about you?"

Florence lifted her chin. "No, I did not."

Cam shifted his gaze back to Lucas and Ainslie. Both of them were scanning their phones.

Lucas held up his cell. "We posted about the cruise, but we didn't show anything telling."

"Can I see?" Lucas handed him the phone. Cam scanned the image, his body tense. All it showed was Ainslie and Lucas's legs dangling off the side of a boat, nothing but ocean in front of them. He flicked across to another image. This time Ainslie and Lucas were clinking two glasses of champagne, but part of the boat was visible. Cam scrutinized the image and then he saw it. In the corner, easy to miss, if one wasn't looking carefully, was part of the name of the boat they were on.

"This is a problem." He showed them the image.

"No way," Lucas said. "No one can figure out where we are based on that."

Denial was never an option. "You'd be surprised. As of right now, you three..." he pointed to Ainslie, Lucas and Florence "...are not to leave the house. You stay out of sight, is that clear? Call your public relations person and ask them how to handle this. Right now, no one knows where you are, but I expect that to change in the next twenty-four hours."

"Then like I said, we should just cancel the wedding," Ainslie said. "I'm not getting married with people stalking this place." She sent her mother a glare.

Florence wiped her eyes.

"Maybe we should postpone," Lucas added.

"No." Viana stepped forward. She looked at Cam. "Do we have only twenty-four hours until people figure out where they are?"

Cam exhaled. "Thirty-six hours tops." He would need to call Jay. And his ex-military buddy, Rowan, who was always up for an adventure. "Some of those fans would make great detectives. Pity they don't use their skills for something better than stalking their favorite influencer."

"So we need to postpone?" Ainslie was asking him.

"No." Viana cut across them.

Silence filled the room.

Cam shook his head. He hated what he was about to say—for everyone in the room, but unless another option presented itself, they didn't have any other option.

"None of us want to postpone, but in the interests of safety, we have to put that on the table as a real possibility."

Did he really just say that? Viana stared at him. Cam was all business. His expression was closed off, like he was compartmentalizing—which he probably was. It was like his presence increased tenfold within the room. Every eye was fixed on him—waiting for him to solve all the problems.

But that was her job.

Viana stepped into the center of the little circle. "Ainslie and Lucas, before you make a final decision, let's talk some more about this." She sent Cam a withering look. "I think we can make this work."

"How?" Ainslie said in a thick voice.

Viana started pacing, her mind running. Fear battled with her natural need to coordinate and problem-solve. Another location move? No, that would be too hard to pull off on such short notice. "When are the rest of the guests arriving?"

"Most are coming tomorrow morning." Ainslie replied, looking up at Lucas. "The last five are coming Saturday morning. Why?" There was a touch of hope in her voice.

An impossible idea started forming. Viana wasn't sure it could be done, but maybe, just maybe, it could work. She took a quick breath. "What if we held the ceremony tomorrow afternoon?"

Silence filled the room.

"Maybe."

"No."

"Yes."

Lucas, Cam and Ainslie all spoke at the same time.

Viana looked between the three of them. "That's not going to work," she laughed, trying to lighten the mood.

Ainslie smiled. "Come on, Lucas, let's hear Viana out."

Viana glanced at everyone in the room. Even Florence looked a little less defeated.

Cam was the only one not smiling.

"What's your plan?" His tone was as terse as his frown.

"If, and that's a big if, Ainslie and Lucas can get the remaining five people to get here tomorrow morning, and Lauren can swing it to get the cake ready by tomorrow, it could work."

Ainslie's face was now aglow with hope. Lucas massaged his chin, clearly thinking. Florence smiled a tentative one. As far as Viana was concerned that was a yes from her.

"Let's give it a try," Lucas said slowly.

Ainslie squealed and threw her arms around Lucas. "Get calling our Saturday arrival friends. I'll call our assistants. And Mom, can you call the makeup and hair stylists and see if they can get here tomorrow?"

Cam stepped into the conversation. "Right, if this goes ahead, we have a lot of work to do. But I'm insisting on the guests arriving at a different venue and I'll drive them over here. We don't want people finding out where you are."

"I can live with that. How are you going to manage it all?" Lucas asked.

Viana thought Lucas's question was a fair one.

"I'm going to call in some assistance of my own. And these two have worked in security before. Tobias, my previous boss, knows them and he can give you a reference. I'll get him to call you." Cam was texting on his phone as he spoke.

"Cool. Thanks man."

Lucas, Ainslie and Florence left the room, all of them glued to their phones.

That left the two of them alone.

Cam was still typing on his phone. "Can you call Lauren? And what about the minister? He needs to come earlier too. And vendors you've got coming in, I need to drive them to and from the house. We need to pack away the furniture on the porch that's not being used. You need to start setting up decorations now. I'll need to blackout some of the windows—"

"Wow! No, you're not. Hold up, Superman." Viana held up her hand. He was taking over. "I'll get to all that, I just can't think quite as quickly as you can. Give me a second to catch up."

Cam put his phone away, his lips pressed tight. "I have no idea how some of these fans will react if they find out the location."

"Most are harmless." Viana shot back.

"Yes, but..." he opened his phone and scrolled before showing her the screen. "See these? These are the screen shots I took of some of the comments on their social pages."

Viana scanned the comments:

I wish I was marrying Lucas. I love him so much. Why do you get him?

I don't know what Lucas sees in a bimbo like you.

You're just a fraud—I don't want to sacrifice my soul and moral compass to be like you.

Why can't you get a real job and act like normal people? If I was you, I'd drink myself into oblivion. No one would miss you.

"Oh," Viana whispered.

Cam put his phone away. "That's only a handful of hundreds. And most of them are just faceless trolls, but even if one of them acts on their words—"

"It'll be bad," Viana finished for him . Did her ambition cause this? Was this all her fault? Worry assailed her, but she took a fortifying breath.

There was no room for doubt anymore. "We're going to pull this thing off." She stared hard at Cam. In two days, he would be gone. And she would have lost nothing, secured her parents' legacy and thrived in the process.

"Alright, then." Cam checked his phone, the release of his gaze like a whoosh in her chest. "But you can't let anyone in or out of here without my say so."

"Fine."

"Good. We're on the same team, then." He put his phone away.

Hardly. It didn't feel like they were on the same planet, let alone the same room.

Chapter Nine
Wedding day

Cam met Jay and Rowan at the gate. He opened it for them, and they cruised through. Cam closed the gate and gave the street a scan. All was quiet. For now. The six a.m. sun hadn't emerged yet. The world was cool and quiet, waiting for the world to wake up.

Jay got out and Cam pulled his brother into a hug. "Thanks for coming at the last minute."

"Always." Jay slapped him on the back. Jay was just an older version of Cam, but there was no life in his eyes. His grief over Amy wore heavy on him.

"Rowan." Cam shook hands with his former marine buddy, whose motorcycle jacket, wide shoulders, and dark man-bun created the perfect intimidation factor to keep people away from the house. "You bring a suit?"

Rowan smirked. "I managed to find one."

Jay slapped Rowan on the back. "Let's go."

As they walked, Cam filled them in. "We'll need to do regular patrols around the property, we'll be escorting the guests to the site and doing deterrence if any fans or photographers show up. We'll get comms up, using one tap for good and two taps for need assistance."

They nodded.

A rush of gratitude peeled over him. "Let's get into the day."

Jay nodded and, like Cam, he scanned the surroundings. Rowan sauntered up the steps and walked through the door, Cam on his heels.

The bright lights, mixed with voices shouting back and forth, was like walking into what he imagined a movie set would be like.

Viana hurried past him, her hands full of tulle and the faux flowers. "The fresh flowers are being delivered now. I'm going to greet them." She stopped and looked at Jay.

"Jay. Nice to see you again."

Jay pulled Viana into a hug. "You too, Via."

"Wait," Cam interjected. "You can't just meet vehicles at the gate. You need to clear that with me."

Viana glared at him. "No, you need to let them in."

Cam gritted his teeth. "People will see the florist sign on the van. This is supposed to be low key."

Viana raised her eyebrows. "How else are they supposed to be delivered?" Before Cam could open his mouth, Viana kept going. "And before you say something ridiculous like you'll transfer the flowers to your car, and you'll drive here—that's just plain inefficient. And it's going to look funny if your car is always coming and going. This is a wedding venue. Flowers are expected to be delivered."

She walked off but turned at the door. "Oh, and there'll be a catering van coming today to use the kitchen. Would you like to cook the food in your car and then bring it in?" Then she walked outside.

Rowan coughed, but Cam heard his chuckle.

Jay looked at him. "Working with Viana seems to be going well."

Cam ignored them both. He led them into Viana's office, which was the new setup for his laptop and other equipment. He handed the guys earpieces, and they did a quick comms check. Then he handed them the run sheet for the day. "Keep a look out for anyone loitering around the place. I don't want to call the local sheriff, as that'll just draw more attention. But I will if I have to."

They both nodded, and he continued. "Let me help Viana with the delivery and then I'll introduce you to Ainslie and Lucas."

Cam left them and crossed the still-muddy yard to where Viana stood by the gate.

"You're cold." Cam noticed Viana hugging her arms.

"I'm too busy to be cold." She wasn't looking at him.

"Fine." He could play that game too. Except he couldn't. His gaze was drawn to her like waves to the shore.

Her hair was up in a neat bun, but wisps of hair had escaped and were curling around her cheek. And all he wanted to do was reach out and tuck those strands behind her ear, it didn't help that the early morning rays sent a pale pink hue across the sky, bathing her in soft light.

A white van approached, slamming into his traitorous thoughts. Summer Shore Florist was emblazoned across the side.

"Thanks for the assist, but I'm good here." She lifted her chin and, though he only had a profile in view, all it did was draw attention to her slender neck.

Cam forced his brain back to work mode—which wasn't hard. His body thrummed with tension. Similar to the waiting before their team went on a mission—they were poised and ready for anything. "I know," Cam exhaled. "But you've got it whether you like it or not." He opened the gate and walked up to the driver's side. "Morning, ma'am. Just doing a security check. Can I see your license please?"

"Camden Mayfield!" Viana rounded the van and tugged his arm. "I've known Betty and Grace my whole life. Go through." She waved them through. "You're acting crazy."

He rested his hands on his hips. "This is literally what I'm hired to do. I won't have you taking over and jeopardizing this opportunity for me because you don't like how I do it."

Viana stepped back, her face pale. "I'm jeopardizing *your* opportunity? What about mine? Last I checked we both needed this to work. The only thing I know right now is that you don't like how I do things. You want to run them your way."

Cam closed his eyes, the past flashing before his eyes. It was Viana all over again, needing to do things her way so she didn't get hurt. Cam opened his eyes and took her in—the hurt in her expression, the frown he wanted to smooth away. "If you don't trust me, just say so. You have to let me do my job right here and now. I'm not the same man who walked away from you. And I'm sorry I hurt you. So sorry."

An unfamiliar car pulled up across the road and a woman got out.

"Do you know her?" Cam glanced at Viana but then transferred his gaze to the woman.

"No." She looked at them. "I've never seen her before in my life."

The woman stood by the car, just staring at the house. Then she pulled her phone out and held it up.

Cam stiffened. This was not good. He glanced at Viana. "Go inside."

He heard Viana hurry away as he approached the closed gate, grateful for the high wrought-iron spires. It was not easy for the average person to breach them.

"Can I help you?" Cam called out.

The woman looked at Cam and even from this distance he could see she looked unsettled. Then she approached, a smile on her face. "I'm here for the wedding. I'm a friend of Lucas's."

Cam's gut tightened.

His earpiece crackled to life and Jay's voice sounded clear in his ear. "Everything okay?"

Cam tapped his earpiece once.

"Roger. Signal if you need help."

Cam went with the best option available to him. Deny and misdirect. "Ma'am, I have no idea who you're talking about—there's no groom on the schedule by that name."

The woman's face hardened for a split second before it relaxed into a fake smile. "Oh, well, I must have got my information wrong. Thanks for letting me know." And she turned and got in the car and drove away. He noted the number plate as the car disappeared.

"That was way too easy," Cam breathed out. With his internal antenna still on high alert, he scanned the street then touched his earpiece. "Can you look up this plate number?" He rattled it off.

"Done." It was Rowan this time.

Rowan and Jay met him at the porch steps. "Problem?" Jay said.

Cam filled them in, unease twisting like a snake through his gut.

Both of them scanned the boundaries of the property, their postures rigid.

Jay spoke. "I'll start making regular sweeps outside."

"I'll stay with the bride and groom," Rowan added.

"I'll keep checking guests in and out," Cam said. "Keep in constant comms."

They nodded and departed.

Cam went to find Viana. She was at the foot of the stairs, standing on a chair with the florist, weaving real and fake flowers around the white arbor.

When she saw him, her eyes grew serious. She hopped off the chair, barefoot. Her black skirt and white button-up top gave her that professional look, but he liked the bare feet. It made her more approachable.

"Who was that?" Worry lines creased her forehead.

"I don't know, but she was keen to see Lucas. Claimed she was a guest."

Viana shook her head vehemently. "No way. I have a picture of every person coming to this wedding—and she isn't one of them."

"I have the same info as you do," Cam said. "I want you to be very careful. You're in charge as much as I am. Do *not* let anyone in, that hasn't been vetted already—including people you've known all your life."

Viana sighed.

"For today, Viana. Please. I'm pretty sure this woman will come back. I didn't like the vibes she was giving off." Cam drilled his gaze into Viana's, desperate for her to understand the depth of worry that coursed through him.

"Of course." Viana glanced out the window.

"We've got six hours until the ceremony starts. The flowers are all set up. The chairs for the ceremony are set up. Catering will be here in the next thirty minutes." Viana bustled into the kitchen with Anita on her heels. "Can you make sure that everyone staying tonight has everything they need? And after I check in with Lauren, we'll move onto the table decorations. After that, we will have to set up the signage. Thankfully, we don't have to worry about a seating plan with such small numbers."

"Of course." Anita scuttled off.

Lauren was deep in cake decorating mode, her frown full of concentration as she sculpted daisies in fondants of different colors. A full tray of them lay on the table beside the two-tiered cake. Her phone buzzed every few minutes, but she pressed decline each time it rang.

"How are things going?" Viana leaned against the bench, grateful for the tiny reprieve in her day. She'd been on high alert ever since the woman appeared at the gate.

"Fine." Lauren didn't look at her as she sculpted another daisy.

Her phone kept buzzing.

"Who is Owen?" Viana keened over to look closer at Lauren's phone.

Putting the delicate flower down, Lauren snatched the phone away. "He's no one worth knowing about."

"So, there was something with that guy I saw you with?"

"Not anymore." Lauren finally looked up at Viana. There were no tears in her eyes, but a smoldering anger mixed with sadness. "It will be close, but I'll get the cake finished in time. The flowers will cascade down the cake." Topic change noted.

"It looks stunning." Viana squeezed Lauren's forearm. "I'm here if you want to talk."

Lauren grinned. "Only if you want to talk about Cam."

Viana groaned and tried not to think about him—but he was everywhere. "He's always near me, hovering like a pesky fly—"

"A handsome, well-built one," Lauren interjected, her cheeky attitude returning.

"Ugh. Let it go. We're not compatible."

Lauren started arranging the flowers in the style she needed them. "I did most of these yesterday, so they're good to be used now. And you're compatible, just both way too stubborn."

"He doesn't trust me," Viana said softly.

"You don't trust him either." Lauren continued to place the flowers on the tray, mirroring how she would place them on the cake.

"I don't. But it doesn't matter...he's leaving tomorrow." Her heart lurched at the thought. As frustrated and wary of him as she was, she could not hide the fact that she enjoyed his presence in her life again. And his kisses. Ugh. No, she was *not* going to think about something that wasn't possible. Besides, he wasn't sticking around, and if he did and she managed to get LOVElegant the success she knew it could be, he would still eventually leave, because a business like she dreamed about would drive him away in the end.

It was better to keep her heart locked away.

"Where's Livvie?" Lauren tilted her head, clearly assessing her design.

"Taking photos inside of Ainslie." Viana reached across to snag a broken flower and nibbled on the delicate sugar edible. She closed her eyes, letting it soften on her tongue and enjoying the tiny sugar rush.

She grabbed another broken flower. "Mac, the very handsome videographer keeps looking at Olivia the way you're looking at your phone. Something's up there too."

Lauren didn't reply.

"Fine. Have it your way." Viana gave her a quick shoulder hug before walking onto the back porch. No one would have thought that this area had housed all the wet items from storage. The porch sat empty of anything reminiscent in storage and it was swept clean and had been scrubbed.

"Hey." Cam appeared at her side.

Viana clutched her chest. "Way to scare a girl."

"Sorry. Here." He thrust a drink bottle in her hand and a protein bar. "You need to eat."

Then he was gone, talking into his earpiece, doing another perimeter sweep. Viana looked down at the bottle and the protein bar. He was looking after her—in the middle of all the craziness—he saw her.

But he would leave after this. It was what she wanted and expected.

Nevertheless, it didn't stop the hollow gnawing through her. Cam had indicated for the right reasons, he *could* stay in a place like Summer Shore. But Viana knew her history and it would only repeat itself.

Chapter Ten

Thirty minutes until the wedding started.

Viana and Anita had finished the table arrangements and decorations. The arbor was set up in front of the windows in the double front doors—shielded by pale pink and white sheer fabric that the setting sun would softly illuminate but would keep the potential prying eyes of fans out. Windows in the dining room were covered with the same.

"Help me with the floor runner." Viana motioned to Anita. Together they unfurled the satin runner and smoothed it out. "Now, let's do a lighting test."

Anita hit the lights and darkness fell across the room. Viana grabbed the remote from her pocket and hit one of the buttons. White fairy lights had been woven through the arbor to create a romantic atmosphere. She pressed another button, and the main light went on, but she controlled the brightness with a slow turn of the remote dial. The room slowly dimmed until the mood was just right—soft lights and the setting sun would be the crowning glory.

"How are the bride and groom faring?" she asked into her earpiece as she switched off the fairy lights and brought the room back into full light.

"All set," Anita said.

"We're good to go in thirty." Cam's familiar, deep voice sounded down the line.

Thirty minutes seemed so far away and too close, all at once.

Viana took a breath and went out on the back porch. It was so important to find a moment to breathe in the chaos of the wedding day. The sky was blue and the air cool but soft. She could stay here in this little cocoon of peace, but she needed to check in with Ainslie and Lucas. Anita was going to seat the guests any second and Viana needed to change into a wedding outfit. Her black skirt and white top was fine for now, but she had a pretty dress she wanted to wear.

A movement in the storage shed caught her eye. The door was ajar, and she saw the flicker of someone inside. Pulse kicking up, Viana crossed the yard and was almost at the door when a woman appeared, holding a pile of tablecloths.

Fear iced through Viana's veins when she realized who it was.

Where is Cam?

The woman continued forward as though she was a guest here rather than a complete stranger with no business being on the property.

"You need to leave," Viana said, doing everything she could to keep her voice steady as alarm bells screeched in her mind.

"I'm just grabbing the extra tablecloths in case we need them." She tried to push past Viana, still behaving as though she had every right to be here.

It was the woman from earlier. The one who said she was a guest but so wasn't.

"You're not one of the hired staff." Viana's heart was pounding, fear gripping her chest and squeezing hard.

"Yes, I am." The woman beamed, but she glanced at the house, her eyes raking the windows.

"No, you're not," Viana insisted. "You need to leave." She held her ground, even though she was terrified.

"Ma'am, you're trespassing." Cam's deep, strong voice called from behind.

You're here. "It's the woman from earlier." Viana's shoulders sagged, and relief poured through her at the sight of him. It was going to be okay.

Before Viana could react, tablecloths hit her as the woman threw them and rushed forward. Viana fell to the ground, landing hard on her wrist. She gasped as pain shot up her arm.

And then she saw the blade glinting in the woman's hand.

"She's got a knife!" Viana screamed, moving backwards along the ground. Pain radiated up her arm with each movement.

"Drop the weapon." Cam's steel hard voice sliced through the air. His face hardened. He moved towards the woman with speed and confidence. With a swift and clearly practiced kick, he knocked the knife from the woman's hand, tackling her to the ground.

Superman was back, but faster and stronger than before.

"Viva, are you okay?" He hauled the woman up, but his gaze landed on Viana.

"I'm f-fine." With her good hand, she pushed herself up, but her legs were shaking too much.

"Stay down, Viana," Cam commanded. He had the woman's hands behind her back. Viana clutched her arm and half-crawled, half-crouched out of the way, fear pressing her forward.

The woman struggled against Cam, trying to pull away from him. "Lucas, I'm here! Did you get the flowers I sent?" She looked around wildly. "I sent you flowers every week! I love you!"

Lucas ran out, his suit on and his eyes wide, face pale.

"Lucas, there you are!" The woman shrieked and a radiant, deranged smile spread across her face.

Cam tightened his hold on her, emitting a small grunt as she kicked her legs out, but he held firm. "Stay behind me." He glanced back at Viana.

He didn't need to tell her, Viana wasn't going anywhere near the unstable woman.

Jay ran to him and together, they got her under control.

Rowan sprinted across the driveway and helped Jay.

Cam released his hold on the woman.

Then he was beside her. "Viva, are you hurt?" Cam's hands, strong yet gentle, ran down her shoulders, as he gently helped her stand.

Viana stood on her shaky legs, Cam's arm around her waist.

He pulled her close, his lips brushing her forehead. "Lean on me." Breathing heavily and holding his arm, Viana leaned her head on his chest, letting him hold her up.

"Lucas, marry me!" the woman called as Rowan and Jay bundled her into the backseat of Cam's SUV.

"We'll drive her to the sheriff's office and be right back." Rowan's voice was clear in her ear.

Lucas charged at Cam. "How did she get in? You're supposed to stop stuff like this from happening!"

Cam was breathing hard, but he didn't let go of Viana. "I'm going to look into how she found her way onto the property. This should never have happened."

Lucan ran a shaky hand over his face. He glanced up at the window, where Ainslie's pale face appeared. He took deep breaths, resting his hands on his hips, scanning the yard. "No one else?"

"No, sir," Cam said.

"Good. Keep it that way." Lucas jogged back inside.

Cam stood for a moment, his head bowed, breathing hard.

Viana touched his cheek. "You were amazing."

His gaze pierced hers and then Viana saw it—the raw fear in his eyes. "You should never have been in danger like that." His ragged whisper tore through her.

Viana saw Lauren and Olivia at the back door, pale-faced and arms linked.

He wrapped his strong arm around her shoulders and touched her wrist. "Are you hurt anywhere else?"

She sucked in a breath through her teeth. "No."

Her bare feet were covered in dirt, her top streaked with mud.

"I assume Lucas ran to see Ainslie." She allowed Cam to help her across the grass. "You did an amazing job."

Cam's lips pressed into a thin line. "Regardless, I still need their recommendation if I'm going to have more work in this field." He heaved a heavy sigh. "How did she get in?"

He led her into the kitchen and onto the nearest stool. "Can I get you some ice?"

The catering crew had, like everyone else, stopped what they were doing to watch the intruder be carted off. One of them pulled an ice pack from the freezer and gave it to Cam. He pressed it against her wrist and held it there.

Viana sucked in a breath. The physical pain was not as overwhelming as the sheer proximity of Cam. His presence dwarfed her, but the gentleness of his actions stole her breath—and heart—away.

"It'll be alright." She eased her arm away, needing space or she might do something reckless and kiss him. Tell him to stay. Tell him he wasn't taking over her job but was working to look after them. Tell him she loved him.

Because why would he stay? They'd proven in the past that what he wanted and what she wanted were two different things. Surely the passage of eight years wouldn't change that.

But...what if? For a few seconds, they gazed at each other.

Then he switched off his earpiece and moved away. "It has to be okay." Then he walked out of the kitchen, speaking into his phone.

Viana was suddenly crowded by Lauren and Olivia. "Honey, are you okay?" Olivia hugged her, her face pale. "That must have been scary."

Viana inhaled a shaky breath. "It was, but I'm fine. The wrist is just sprained." She hoped that's all it was, but anyway, there was no time to think about that right now. "I'm going to get dressed and check in with Ainslie."

Ten minutes later, Viana stood in front of her mirror, staring at herself. Her wrist throbbed, but she'd taken some pain killers. The silver handkerchief skirt dress with its V-neck and sleeveless cut was pretty and flattering. She completed the look by adding butterfly clips to keep her long hair out of her face. She'd washed off the mud and now a pair of matching, peep-toe kitten heels adorned her feet. She'd also kept her makeup to a minimum, seeing as her sore wrist wouldn't let her do much more.

Taking another deep breath, she kept her wrist close to her chest, and she knocked faintly on Ainslie's door.

Florence opened it and ushered Viana in. "You poor thing. What a horrible fright that was."

"I'm fine," Viana lied, but right now, nothing was about her. "Oh, Ainslie, you look stunning." Tears sprung in Viana's eyes.

Ainslie was already in her dress, her two bridesmaids fussing over her. The pale pink gowns of the bridesmaids went perfectly with Ainslie's bouquet of pink daisies.

"Thank you!" Ainslie grinned, but concern filled her eyes. "Are you hurt? It looked so awful! I'm just glad it's over now. That woman, whoever she is—" she glared at the room— "would have found a way to get inside. I'm just glad Cam got her and you're okay."

Viana sunk onto the bed, still weary from lingering adrenaline. "I'm not worried. My focus is on getting you and Lucas married."

Florence stepped in and fussed with the hem of Ainslie's dress. "Olivia just left to grab some quick pictures of the boys before they head downstairs."

Ainslie squealed, giddy with excitement. "We're doing this! I'm getting married!"

Viana laughed. "Be at the top of the stairs in five minutes. I'll call you down once Olivia has your photos."

Viana stepped out of the room.

Cam was waiting at the bottom of the steps, his hands clasped in front of him. Viana's heart picked up into a gallop. As she held her arm close to her chest and descended the stairs, she couldn't help but stare at him, and his gaze tracked her every movement.

"You look..." He glanced away for a moment as she reached the bottom of the stairs. Then returned his gaze to hers. "Stunning." His raspy voice sent chills up her spine.

"Five minutes to go time," she whispered, unable to think of anything else to say because she didn't trust her heart anymore. Sometime between when he'd shown up and now, he'd taken her heart again and she could lie to herself as much as she wanted, but the truth was, she didn't want it back.

He could keep it. Even if he walked out the door and never came back.

"Five minutes," Cam whispered back, his eyes tracing every line of her face.

Sliding past him, Viana moved to the door of the dining room and signaled to the small group gathered that it was time to sit.

Olivia met her at the door. "Lucas and his groomsmen are coming down now. Mac will record Lucas's reaction when Ainslie appears in the entryway."

Mac was standing at the front of the aisle just behind the minister. He was holding a video recorder with a mounted microphone and a smaller digital camera strapped to his chest. When he saw them watching him, he cast Olivia a searching look.

Olivia looked away.

"Everything okay?" Viana asked softly.

Olivia fidgeted with her camera. "It will be." There was a stubborn tinge to her words.

Viana left it at that. There was no time to talk to her about her love life, or Lauren's, or even her own. A grin touched her lips. In the middle of their most important wedding to date, all three of them managed to get tangled up in romances none of them saw coming.

Lucas and his groomsman walked past, Viana giving them a thumbs up.

Lucas sent her a nervous grin.

Viana exhaled. Everything was going to be okay. The stress from earlier had melted away, and now Lucas looked like every other groom she'd seen—nervous and excited, unable to wait to see his bride.

Florence appeared at the door. She inhaled and a melancholy expression passed across her face.

Viana understood in an instant. It was hard watching your only daughter move onto a new phase of life—one where she wouldn't need her mother as much. Even for a relationship that was already fractious, Viana still felt for Florence. How many mothers had confided in her about the joy and sadness such a moment brought them? Too many to name.

Viana nodded at Anita, who started the music.

Ainslie appeared at the top of the stairs, bouquet in hand, her two bridesmaids adjusting the train of her dress. As she descended the stairs, Olivia clicked away.

The bridesmaids made their entrance.

Then Ainslie was beside Viana.

"It's your turn." Viana grinned. Cam came up beside her. Rowan was standing by the front door with his arms crossed in front of him. Jay stood near a window, his gaze scanning the room and the view outside. "I've got an off-duty police officer to keep watch," Cam said in a hushed tone.

Viana nodded, lost in the way Lucas sucked in a breath when Ainslie appeared in his field of vision. His eyes immediately watered, his smile huge.

Viana and Cam walked in last and stood subtly at the back of the room.

As Ainslie and Lucas joined hands and the minister began the service, Viana could feel Cam's gaze shifting to her and away again.

Her heart thumped and she snuck a look at him, and found his eyes trained on her.

Viana looked away, her breaths coming fast now. She wanted to move away from Cam to escape the feelings that he stirred up, but she couldn't disturb the ceremony. So she stayed put, acutely aware of him next to her, his arm not quite brushing hers.

"You may now kiss the bride," the minister announced.

As Lucas leaned in to kiss his brand-new wife, cheers erupted from the small crowd.

Viana stole another glance at Cam, who was murmuring, his hand on his ear, talking to Rowan and Jay. His handsome face was set in firm lines as he directed the other two to change positions. There was no denying his competence and skills.

Or the fact that he'd stolen her heart.

Again.

Chapter Eleven

Viana sat on a chair in the empty dining room. She fingered a flower she'd plucked from the table centrepiece, running her fingers along the petals, enjoying the quiet for a few minutes before they needed to pack up.

The guests had retired for the night when Ainslie and Lucas, still in their wedding attire, strolled in. Before she could even stand, Ainslie was beside her, hugging her. "You were amazing this week! Everything that could have gone wrong did and you didn't bat an eyelid."

"All in a week's work for a wedding planner," Viana quipped.

"I don't want your job." Lucas grinned. "I thought my job was stressful, but yours...wow. You pulled off a miracle."

"Thanks." Viana dipped her head.

"We're just going to have a quick word with Camden and then we're off." Lucas tugged Ainslie's hand, she flashed a giddy grin as she leapt up and followed her husband out the door.

The joy of seeing a couple happily married, the pride in a job well done bubbled up inside Viana. Mom and Dad would be so proud of her—she knew that deep in her soul. And she'd thrived—and lost no one—just as she planned. Well, not yet, anyway. Her heart thumped—Cam wasn't sticking around. Not that they'd talked about the future, or even what tomorrow might hold, but since he didn't know he'd stolen her heart, he couldn't hurt her. So his leaving was the right thing. Would she ever find her happily ever after?

Her best friends had their own issues to sort out. Outside on the porch, Mac and Olivia were engaged in a serious conversation. And when she last checked the kitchen after all the guests had retired upstairs, Lauren was ignoring the man, who Viana guessed was Owen, as she cleaned up the kitchen.

LOVElegant would live to see another day.

She hoped her heart would too.

Cam was packing up the equipment in his office when Lucas and Ainslie came in, holding hands. The reception was over, the bride and groom about to leave for their honeymoon in their car and meet the private jet Lucas had hired to fly them somewhere no one would find them for two weeks.

"I know you got stuck with this job at the last minute," Lucas said, all the cool, famous-guy persona gone. Now he was just a man in love, no need for pretense. "And I know I said some harsh stuff earlier."

"It was warranted. The woman climbed into the back of the catering van before it arrived here. She jumped out as soon as it passed through the gates, before I had a chance to check it." Cam didn't look away from Lucas. "That was a failing on me and my team."

Lucas dipped his head in ascent. "But, we all know, you can't plan for a determined person who's willing to take risks to get what they want."

"True, but it still shouldn't have happened." Cam looked between Lucas and Ainslie. "I understand if you're not willing to give me a recommendation." It hurt him to say it, but it needed to be said. He would accept their answer in stride—no matter what, he would find another way to be seen.

Ainslie let go of Lucas and pulled Cam into a hug. "You did amazing on such short notice, and you went above and beyond when so much went wrong this week. I wouldn't have a wedding dress if it wasn't for you and Viana. Or a wedding, if you hadn't taken that woman down." Her smile slipped, but she looked back at Lucas and grinned, love blooming in her rosy cheeks, bright eyes and unstoppable grin. "We'll be making sure everyone knows how good you are at your job."

Cam's chest filled with pride and the stress of the last week melted away.

"I appreciate that." He shook Lucas's hand. "Are you sure you don't want me to drive you to the airport?"

"No." Lucas took Ainslie's hand. "I've got this one. But I'll make sure we're not followed. The staff at the airport are very discreet." They left the room, hand in hand, eyes only for each other.

His thoughts turned to Viana. And just as the waves must land on the shore, he didn't fight the compulsion to search her out. He found her sitting in the dining room, on an empty chair under the twinkle of lights, shoes off, her wrist cradled against her arm.

He approached softly, lowered himself into a chair beside her. "Well—you did it."

Viana looked up as Cam took the seat beside her, lowering himself wearily into the chair. His shirt was unbuttoned at the top, his earpiece gone and the sleeves of his shirt rolled up to his elbows.

"No." Viana shook her head. "*We* did it."

For long seconds they stared at each other, Viana's heart thumping hard in her chest. "I know I said some things."

"So did I." Cam rested his elbows on his thighs.

"But," she inhaled, lips trembling, "I couldn't have survived this week without you."

Cam ran a hand down his face. "You asked me if I could ever stay in Summer Shore..."

Viana's breath stilled in her chest. "You said it would have to be for the right reasons." Her voice came out in barely a whisper. What was he saying? Did he want to get back together?

His gazed searched hers. "I did say that." He looked down at his hands, like he was trying to find the right words. He found her eyes again. "I was thinking, with all the publicity you're going to get, you might need some permanent security here and maybe an extra pair of hands around the place..." He trailed off, his voice raspy and low.

Tears sprung in Viana's eyes. She wiped them away, taking deep breaths. "I think it's worth the risk to be surprised by love."

And, taking the final leap of faith, she leaned over and kissed Cam, pouring all her hopes, dreams and fears into it.

Maybe one day someone would get to plan her wedding, after all.

SWEET ON Love

Tabitha Bouldin

Chapter One
Six days before the Wedding

She could do this. Lauren used her forearm to sweep hair from her face as she carried the small round plates with all her cake flavors to the main table in the center of Summer Shore Sweets. The blonde strands fell right back down, the length still too short for a proper ponytail.

"Lauren?" Audrey stuck her head out from the kitchen. "Can you grab that tray of cookies next? Nicole said she wanted to try those while she's here. I need to run next door."

"Sure." She arranged the plates in a circle, turning each one so they lined up between the two chairs where Nicole and her fiancé would sit. A quick sweep of the bakery helped ease the tightness building in her chest.

Audrey ran the bakery, and Lauren had her own kitchen at Summer House where she worked with her best friends. But Nicole had asked for her to coordinate with Audrey for her wedding, and it had been easier for them to work out of Audrey's kitchen.

Cool white marble stretched the length of the wall across from the frosted glass door. Circular tables were placed at strategic points around the dining area, each with wrought iron chairs covered with thick cushions inviting people to sit and stay for hours.

Audrey offered the perfect place to enjoy coffee and sweets while people watching or working in the quiet environment.

Deep breath. She pulled air in through her nose and held it. *Thank you, Lord, for the ability to work this job that I love.*

The exhale left her lightheaded but clear. She hurried into the kitchen and grabbed the tray of cookies from the stainless-steel table.

"Hey." A loud male voice snapped across the distance. "You can't take those."

"Excuse me?" She held the tray at waist level, her head snapping around to meet a pair of hazel eyes.

The man in front of her radiated a kind of cautious energy that darkened his eyes. Brown curls rested across his forehead and brushed his eyebrows. "You can't take those." He pointed at the cookies. "You shouldn't be in here. The shop's closed today."

"*I* shouldn't be here? What about you? Who are you?" She slammed the tray down so hard the cookies jumped and rattled. If he'd made her break any of the cookies, she'd never forgive him. "I'm calling the police."

"You're calling the police? I'm calling the police." He pulled out a slim cell and swiped the screen.

"This is getting out of hand." She held out a palm but already had her phone in the other hand. "I'm Lauren Stewart. I'm working with Audrey on a cake testing here in the shop today."

His fingers stilled on the screen. "Aunt Audrey doesn't do cakes."

"Aunt Audrey?" She looked him over again.

With the jeans and black t-shirt, he looked like half the people in Summer Shore. Including her. She almost grinned at their matched clothing but tamped down the smile to concentrate.

A conversation she'd had with Audrey a month ago came back to her. "Owen?"

He blinked slowly, dark brows slashing over stormy eyes. "How do you know my name?"

"I told you, I work with Audrey. She doesn't do cakes, but I do. We're teaming up for a wedding." The large black clock hanging over the stove hit noon and several low gongs rang to announce the hour. "I have to go. Our client will be here any minute."

Ignoring Owen, she picked up the tray again and walked backward through the swinging doors.

Owen followed her, his steps slow and precise. "You look familiar."

A twinge pinched her middle, and she averted her face, giving him nothing but her profile with a fringe of her hair blocking his view. "Yeah? Maybe we ran into each other at some point. You must have been here before."

"It's been a while. Eight years or so." He kept following her, his steps an echo to hers.

Eight years. That meant he'd recognized her from her life before coming back here.

Sweat beaded on her hairline and her palms turned clammy. She set the tray down—gently this time—and tensed. The feeling of being stalked poured adrenaline into her veins, and her past pushed her hands into fists. She wheeled to face him. "Stop."

He froze in his tracks, his mouth going slack as he raised both hands. "Whoa. Sorry." Without missing a beat, he took a large step backward.

Her lungs relaxed enough for a shallow breath. In most situations, she'd apologize for her potential overreaction.

Not this time.

Two quick knocks on the glass door brought the tension snapping into her spine.

Owen glanced that way and lowered his arms. "I think your client is here."

She didn't want to turn. Turning meant putting her back to Owen. After all this time, she'd hoped to be over this, but not all monsters hid under the bed. Some lived deep in your chest and clawed their way out at the most random times. Like now. "Thanks. Can you let her in?"

He assessed her with a sweeping look that saw too much. "Sure."

The back door opened and closed, Audrey's voice coming with it. "Lauren, I'm back. Listen, my nephew Owen is supposed to be here today."

"I'm here, Aunt Audrey." Owen crossed to the door, flipped the lock, and pushed it open. "Hi, you must be here for the cake tasting."

Nicole and her fiancé slipped past Owen, both wearing wide smiles. "I can't believe we're here. It feels like we've been waiting forever." Nicole bounded across the room and wrapped Lauren in an embrace.

Lauren took all the fear that Owen had stirred up and shoved it deep, deep down where it belonged. "Only a month to go." She returned Nicole's hug. "If you want to have a seat, we'll get started." She indicated the two chairs at the table she'd decorated with a white lace tablecloth and a bouquet of edible flower cupcakes for them to take home with them.

Owen took his time leaving. His gaze weighed heavy on her until he disappeared, his voice meeting Audrey's in a loud, joyous homecoming.

Lauren blocked out the sound to concentrate on her job. She sat across from Nicole and laced her fingers together in her lap. "I've set out each of the samples you asked for. They're all labeled, and I suggest you try them starting with the slice on the far left."

Nicole and Jack picked up their forks and cut into the cake.

"You mentioned a potential change to your RSVP list. Do you have that nailed down yet?" She focused on the details of the upcoming weddings and the differences between the cakes she'd be making.

"Yes. We're going up by twenty guests. Will that be a problem for the cake? We can pay more if we need to go up a size on the tiers." Nicole's excitement bubbled up and over, causing her to bounce in her seat.

"Not a problem." Lauren ran the calculations in her head, taking the current cake size into consideration. "As soon as you pick your flavors, we'll finalize the decorations." Talking cake was easy. She could prattle on all day about crumb and fondant.

It was what had given her hope after leaving her modeling job. A phantom shudder rippled down her spine. No time to think about any of that. It didn't matter anymore.

Nicole ate her cake, her eyes closing. She raised her fork in the air and sighed. "Wow. Okay. I'm not sure how I'm supposed to even try another flavor after that. I love it."

"You love anything chocolate." Jack grinned like a giddy schoolboy. "And so do I."

"One reason why I wanted you to start with this one." Lauren walked them through the flavors, encouraging them to sip water between bites to help keep the flavors from muddling together.

Nicole and Jack discussed cake with her, asking about combining flavors and which tiers would work best for their guests.

She loved that about them. They were concerned for their guests and what they might like almost more than they cared about their own preferences.

"The good news is that the entire top layer is just for you two. And there's the groom's cake to consider. You can have your favorites, and keep some of what I'd call the basic flavors for your guests."

"And the cookies." Nicole pointed her fork at the cookies Audrey had decorated. "Those are gorgeous."

"Yes, Audrey is amazing with royal icing." Every moment with the couple helped put her in a better mood. She despised the moments when the darkness won and had found no better way of battling her way free than with cake, conversation, prayer, and a bit of sarcasm when the right time called for it.

After Aunt Audrey's exuberant welcome, she had guided him to the counter—the same one where he used to help her roll out and decorate cookies—and all but forced him to try a new cookie recipe while sipping on a cup of black coffee.

He tried to ignore Lauren and the couple in the dining area, but Lauren's voice carried with a kind of excitement that he envied.

A soft nudge on his arm drew his head up. Aunt Audrey smiled down at him, her dimpled cheeks a little softer now, the lines around her eyes deeper. Her smile remained the same, that and her air of flamboyance that showed up in her pixie cut blonde hair and bohemian skirt with matching shirt. It all fit together with her bakery in swirls of pink and turquoise.

The kitchen held light and laughter, years and years of memories that rushed up to greet him.

"What do you think?"

He managed to keep his face averted, but his eyes darted to the left, toward the door that cut Lauren from his line of sight. "About?"

She rolled her eyes and smacked him on the back of his arm with the dish towel she always carried. "About the new recipe." Still grinning, she leaned down and gripped his shoulder. "I can already see what you think about Lauren."

Hearing her name out loud sparked all his senses to life. The bite of cookie he'd taken settled on his tongue, the brown sugar and cinnamon deepening the pecan flavor.

"The cookies are great. Best cookies I've had in years." Since the last time he'd been in the bakery, if they wanted to split hairs. "How's business?"

"Eh." Aunt Audrey ignored all talk of business whenever possible. Why should now be any different? "Looking forward to this wedding business. Lauren is talking about the two of us working together more often. She's the cake baker, and they usually have a caterer handle the rest of the reception. But who knows." She spread her hands and waved them while walking backward toward the ovens. "Maybe Nicole's wedding will spark something. Wouldn't mind getting to bake more fancy cookies."

"You and Lauren are going into business together?" He stiffened at the implications of such a move. Aunt Audrey was a magnificent baker, but she'd been taken in by some heinous crooks throughout the years.

His aunt had a soft heart. Too soft in his opinion. It wouldn't be the first time she'd been suckered by a pretty face and a sob story.

The oven timer beeped, and Aunt Audrey bent to retrieve the cookies. "Not exactly. She's already in business. She's part owner of a wedding business."

A wedding business? That was a new one. "Didn't think Summer Shore was big enough for something like that."

"Yeah, well." She set the pan on the counter and tested the cookies with the tip of her bare finger. "You never know what will happen over time. They work out of that big house near the beach. Summer House."

He knew the place. Everyone knew that house. "I feel like I've seen her before." The thought nagged at him from the minute he'd seen her sweep into the kitchen and pick up the tray of wedding ring shaped cookies decorated with exquisite diamond patterns done in royal icing. She was familiar in that gauzy, ephemeral way that fluttered at the edges of his mind but never took hold.

"She grew up here. Maybe you ran into her before she left. Before you both left." Sadness infiltrated her voice and drew her eyes into deep wells of soft blue. "And now you're both back."

Not for long. Not if he could help it. Aunt Audrey wouldn't be happy when she heard the truth, but it was for the best. Small town life had never really suited him. He'd never felt at home here. His fault. He'd never really tried even though she did her best to give him peace and a sense of hope after losing his parents and being shuttled off to nowhere USA his senior year.

He'd fought the system, trying to claim his independence so he could stay in his hometown.

Aunt Audrey fought back...and she won.

"Owen?" She gripped his shoulder. "Is everything okay?"

"Sure." He rolled his shoulders back and pasted on a smile. "Anything you need me to do while I'm here?"

The smell of fresh cookies and coffee mingled in that perfect aroma that made him want to pull up a chair and stay right here in the kitchen for the rest of the day. Anything longer than that and the old need to wander kicked in.

"You can stop acting like you're fine and tell me why you called in the middle of the night to let me know you'd be coming to see me." Fisted hands landed on slim hips, and she looked at him the same way Mom used to when he'd broken the rules. "And why you showed up a day early."

"That's a long conversation."

Drawing out a long harrumph, she dragged a stool away from the counter, the screech grating on his eardrums, and sat. "I have all day."

"Don't you need to open the store?" He shot a look at the door, but there was no hint of Lauren. Had she slipped out the front door, leaving it unlocked for anyone to come strolling in?

The swinging doors opened, and Lauren eased into the kitchen, the empty tray in her hands. She stopped at the sight of him, her mouth falling slack for a single heartbeat before it firmed and her expression hardened.

Aunt Audrey watched the exchange, her head swinging from Lauren to him as her eyebrows shot upward. "How did it go?"

Lauren set the tray in its original spot and started toward the doors. "Great. Nicole and Jack loved the cookies. She needs to increase the amount by a minimum of thirty to account for some additional guests." She slipped into the dining area, leaving the doors swinging behind her.

Owen stood and stretched. "I should go. Thanks for the cookies." He picked up his dirty dishes and carried them to the sink, taking the time to wash them while trying to ignore Lauren's return to the kitchen, this time with a stack of empty plates and forks in hand.

Tension thickened the air, seizing his lungs and causing a pinch in the vicinity of his heart. She stopped at the end of the counter and set the dishes down. Her black Converse cut a cute silhouette against her slim fit jeans and black t-shirt. But the look in her eyes when they met and clashed with his held more warning than a train barreling down the track at full speed.

That glare told him not to look, and to stay far, far away. He relived her reaction when they first met and the twinge of sympathy turned into something cold and demanding.

Who had hurt her to the point that she'd turned intolerable to greeting a stranger?

Was it *any* stranger or only those of the male variety?

The *drip, drip* of water from the kitchen sink created a background to the clock ticking over the stove. His aunt's kitchen was a stainless-steel and chrome paradise, though nothing she did would be complete without the splashes of paisley, pink, and turquoise spread throughout the room.

Aunt Audrey asked Lauren a question, but the buzzing in his head kept him from hearing the answer.

Her problems were not his to handle. He'd learned a long time ago to keep his nose out of other people's business. Except his aunt's. It was up to him to protect her from those who saw her sweetness and decided to take advantage.

"We're really excited about this upcoming wedding." Lauren's entire stance changed when she brought up the wedding. The tenseness evaporated, and a smile that reminded him of the beauty of a sunrise spread across her face in that same slow cascade.

He dragged Lauren's dishes into the sink and scrubbed them clean. The kind act gave him a chance to continue listening, just in case he needed to step in and keep Lauren from convincing his aunt to invest in some escapade or lend her money for some asinine reason.

It had happened before.

"You'll be baking the cake here for Nicole and Jack, right?" Aunt Audrey held out a cookie to Lauren, who took it, broke it in half, and nibbled on the edge. "We discussed it last week, but I want to make sure I have everything ready."

"If you're sure it's not an imposition. We can bake here, then I'll drive everything to the venue and do the last-minute details on the cake there. It's three tiers, so I'll need to assemble and decorate on site." A dreamy look softened her face.

Owen dropped the plate he'd been washing, and it landed in the soapy water with a loud splash. "You bake here? Are you sure that's a good idea? What about the insurance?"

Aunt Audrey made a face at him, the puckered one that she used to give him when he complained about her feeding the stray cats in the alley behind her shop. "It's not a problem, Owen. Lauren is licensed, and anyone who works for me is covered on the insurance."

"But she doesn't work here."

"Sometimes I do." Lauren faced him, arms crossed and a fire deep in her eyes. "If it makes you feel better, you're not insured to wash dishes, so if you break something, it comes out of your pocket."

He couldn't be sure, but it almost sounded like she was trying to use sarcasm and wit to make him more comfortable. It didn't work, but he appreciated the effort. There was only one way to fix this. He'd have to talk to Frank, his aunt's lawyer, and make sure Lauren hadn't made herself too comfortable with his aunt's business.

"I need to go. Viana and Olivia are expecting me. I'll be back in a few days to start baking." Lauren hugged his aunt and waved at him.

Aunt Audrey waited until Lauren exited through the back door before she stood and crossed to him. "What's going on?"

"Nothing." He wouldn't tell her he suspected Lauren had ulterior motives for wanting to come here and bake. His aunt believed the best of everyone. Even after being betrayed, she continued to open her heart and her home to anyone. Even if they didn't deserve it.

Like him.

Chapter Two
Six days before the Wedding

Lauren rarely stress baked. Tonight was an exception as she whipped eggs until they turned frothy and threatened to curdle. Groaning in the emptiness of the third-floor kitchen she shared with her best friends, she set the bowl on the counter and gripped the edge. "It's nothing."

"What's nothing?" Olivia walked in through the open balcony door, her pet rabbit Sable tucked under her arm. She stroked the rabbit's back and scooted onto one of the stools that lined the other side of the counter across from Lauren.

With the homey kitchen surrounding her, Lauren almost gave into the urge to tell Olivia the truth she'd spent years hiding. She was not okay. She was not as strong and capable as they thought. Sure, she baked fantastic cakes and decorated them with the skill of someone who'd been in the profession for years.

But she was broken.

One moment alone in the kitchen with Owen when he surprised her proved that she hadn't healed. Not completely. It helped that he stopped and apologized when he realized he'd made her uncomfortable. He was probably a good guy. He obviously loved his aunt, if his attempt at interrogating her this morning was any indication.

Olivia swept her shoulder-length brown hair behind her ears before setting her elbow on the counter and cupping her chin in her palm. "Is everything okay?"

"Yep." The lie came easily…too easily. She dumped sugar and butter into her stand mixer and turned it on low. The steady, metallic sound eased her frayed nerves better than any conversation. Except prayer. "How was the beach?"

Olivia suddenly found the counter an excellent place to stare. Which meant she was trying to hide something. "Great. Sable enjoyed the sand."

The butter and sugar whipped into a creamy mixture, and Lauren added the egg in a slow drizzle. Calm. Precise. Everything about baking made sense. There was an order to things. She knew if she added the right ingredients at the right time, she'd end up with a perfect end product.

Unlike modeling with all its chaos and instability. Her hand spasmed around the measuring cup handle, causing the egg to slosh into the bowl. She winced but kept going, turning the mixer back on to finish adding the ingredients.

Olivia patted Sable, occasionally talking to the rabbit in a low whisper. When Lauren turned the mixer off again, she motioned at the counter. "What are you making?"

"Red velvet and pistachio cookies." While she loved the predictability of baking, sometimes she deviated from a recipe or tinkered with a classic to give it a new twist. But only when baking for herself.

Olivia's nose wrinkled until it resembled Sable's. "Is that supposed to sound appetizing?"

"What? It'll be great." She laughed when Olivia continued staring at her like she'd lost her mind. "Okay. Maybe they won't be great. It's an experiment."

Owen had thrown her into a downward spiral, and the only way she knew to recover was to bake and pray. It was her process, and it always worked for her. The strange combination of flavors were an homage to Owen with his contradicting personality. One minute he'd apologized to her, and a half hour later he was worrying over the possibility she'd cause an insurance problem.

It didn't make sense. What was he doing back here anyway? She set the measuring cup down harder than intended, and the loud *clang* of glass on marble startled Sable, causing the rabbit to squeak and jump across Olivia's lap.

"Sorry."

"It's okay." Olivia carried Sable to his indoor enclosure and settled him with a treat. "You sure you don't want to talk about it? I know I'm not Viana, but you can tell me."

She made it sound like they never shared secrets. Lauren tried to keep her shoulders from drawing up close to her ears and maintained her calm façade. "It's nothing. Just nerves, I guess. I'm not used to having two weddings in the same week. I'm supposed to start baking for Nicole and Jack in a couple days. And I start Ainslie's decorations tomorrow."

"Is there anything I can do to help you?" She returned to the counter but remained standing.

Lauren offered her a warm, genuine smile of thanks. "If I think of anything, I'll let you know. The main thing is sticking to my schedule." She tapped her phone where it sat on the counter. "I have it all laid out. Daily task lists and everything."

"If you start to fall behind, let me know."

"I will. Thanks." Their friendship had always been like this, and it was the reminder Lauren needed that she wasn't alone. They always helped each other if they were needed. No questions asked. It had been that way since high school, through college, and into the opening of LOVElegant, the wedding service business that she and Via built from the ground up five years ago.

Olivia returned to the balcony and settled in one of the Adirondack chairs they'd collected through the years. The third floor was a collection of all their tastes with several converging elements they all needed.

Lauren loved every inch of it, but the kitchen would always be her favorite. She scooped the cookies onto baking sheets and popped them into the oven, then worked through cleaning up her mess.

The sight of the sink of soapy water brought Owen to mind. She tried to stuff the thoughts back down, but they lingered, twisting and tangling her insides until the coil of tension grew too tight to bear.

Her phone pinged a text message notification that she swiped to open after drying her hands on one of her favorite towels. She'd found the lavender towels embroidered with butterflies at one of Summer Shore's festivals and ordered enough to stuff the kitchen drawer to overflowing.

Viana pretended to complain, but she loved them too. Otherwise she wouldn't have called the woman and ordered ten more when theirs began to grow ratty at the edges.

Lauren grinned and tossed the towel aside before turning her attention to the message.

> Hey, L. Can't believe you're ignoring my calls. I took the liberty of updating your portfolio in case you change your mind and decide to come back where you belong. M.

Marvin. The man who'd been her manager and friend during her modeling days. Her teeth locked as a full-body shudder pebbled her skin with gooseflesh. A picture appeared beneath the message, one she recognized from what Marvin called her glory days. She stood in front of a brick building, her long blonde hair dyed almost silver and hanging in a long cascade almost to her waist.

The slinky, black dress showed every dip and curve in her body, though she'd starved most of the curves away until she was all sharp shoulders and hips. Even her face had a hollowness to it, a sharp edge Marvin had played up with black eyeliner and heavy makeup.

Seeing that picture on billboards and city benches had been a wake-up call she'd desperately needed. The saying that a picture was worth a thousand words rang true, only for her, it had been worth her life.

Not long after Marvin released that summer's portfolio, she'd started getting late night hang up calls full of heavy breathing and deep male laughter. She'd never been afraid to leave her apartment for a walk in the park, until the night when she'd felt someone following her, heard their steps match hers as they stayed in the shadows.

Then the flowers and gifts arrived. Each one addressed to her pseudonym, Laura Grady. The first time it happened, she'd blown it off as nothing more than a fan showing their appreciation. As time went on and the gifts became more frequent, the steps in the shadows more sinister, she'd started hiding in her apartment.

Marvin called her paranoid.

She could have lived with that. Could have suffered through the fear and discomfort of popularity.

The final straw came with Marvin's insistence that she lose *more* weight. He claimed ten more pounds would guarantee her a spot in Riot or Fair Daily, the two leading magazines in beauty and health.

She'd been walking home from a rare trip to the supermarket for chicken and asparagus for her dinner when he called, and by God's leading intervention, she'd stopped at the crosswalk between Smith and Locos streets. Right in front of a billboard plastered with the image of her in the black dress.

For the first time in her life, she hadn't recognized herself. She'd quit her modeling career that day, packed her apartment, and moved home. A week later, her long blonde locks were chopped into a shoulder-length, blunt cut with black roots that she maintained religiously.

And in the six years since, she'd managed to mentally box up that year of fear, wrap it in chains, and sink it to the bottom of her subconscious.

Until Owen.

Owen shifted his weight in the uncomfortable plastic chair and met Frank's curious gaze head on. "You're sure?"

"Positive." Frank tapped his index finger on a green folder he'd pulled from the filing cabinet within minutes of Owen's arrival. "Your aunt has iron-clad contracts. I should know. I wrote them." He gave a self-satisfied smile that normally annoyed Owen but Frank was too genuine to be annoying. And Frank cared about Aunt Audrey.

He almost asked again, just to make sure there was nothing Lauren—or anyone else—could do to hurt Aunt Audrey's business, but that risked driving a wedge of discontent between him and Frank. The man didn't like being questioned, especially about his contracts, and Owen had walked the knife edge of offending him since he walked into the office.

"Okay then." Owen forced his knees to unlock and stood, holding out a hand toward Frank. "Thanks for seeing me like this, and for taking care of my aunt."

Frank shook his hand, his grip strong as ever. "No problem, Owen. You've always been a bit overprotective of your aunt. Can't really say I blame you, what with your history."

"And that year she nearly lost the business because of that investment." A breeze stirred through the office when the front door opened. The salty tang ruffled Owen's hair and put an urge to walk in his bones.

"She's learned her lesson about that." Frank adjusted the files on his desk. "It's good that you worry about her, Owen. But don't forget to leave room for a few of God's surprises along the way. You never know what you'll miss if you keep everything locked in so tight you see danger everywhere."

His aunt gave him the same spiel.

The only thing he knew was that he owed Lauren an apology. "Enjoy the rest of your day."

"You too." Frank waved him off with shooing motions. "Get out on the beach or something."

Owen glanced at his jeans and sneakers. Yeah, a walk on the beach might help.

He exited the small office, stopped to check the street for oncoming traffic, and jogged across. A quick duck between a row of shops and he reached the boardwalk that led to a dock and a series of steps that deposited him at the water's edge.

Hands in his pockets, he toed off his sneakers and tucked them beneath a blue bench where they'd stay out of the tide. Gulls swooped and dove overhead, their calls mixing with the crash of waves. He'd missed this.

Years of working in a small booth as he called sports games for radio hosts meant the most time he spent outdoors was when he worked baseball games. A phantom ache in his shoulder caused a wince. One wrong pitch and he'd ended his baseball career before it began.

"Heads up!" A feminine voice shouted the warning from behind him.

Owen turned just in time to snap the Frisbee from the air before it sailed into his nose.

A dog bounded toward him, yipping and bouncing with a frantic fervor. The golden retriever slid to a stop in front of him, panting, tongue lolling out one side of its mouth.

The woman who'd called out jogged up behind the dog. "Hey. Sorry about that. The kids were playing, and their throws went a little wild." She held out a hand for the Frisbee, and he passed it over. "Thanks."

Movement behind her pulled him away like a puppet being directed by marionette strings.

Lauren. She walked with the kind of grace and poise that made dancers weep with envy.

After how he'd treated her in the shop, he cut a path straight toward her, waving when she glanced his way.

She stopped dead in her tracks. Large sunglasses covered her eyes, and she wore a baseball cap tugged low over her forehead. She'd changed from her jeans to a pair of yellow shorts. "What are you doing here?"

The coldness in her voice pulled him up short.

"Are you following me?"

Realization dawned. "No. I came from town." He thumbed over his shoulder. "I saw you walking, and I'd already decided to apologize. Seemed like a good opportunity."

He took a good, long look at her, that same feeling of familiarity tickling the edges of his memory. Where had he seen her before? Not here. He knew that for sure. Somewhere in the city.

She swept a hand through the ends of her hair, almost like she thought it was longer and was trying to pull it over her shoulder.

"That's it." He snapped his fingers and shook his head. "I remember you now."

"Oh?" Her sunglasses reflected his face at him, reminding him to temper his expression. "And where do you remember me from?"

"You're Laura Grady. You did a modeling job for Sunset Weekly. Your picture was on the billboard at the stadium where I worked." He almost smiled, but the way she stiffened stopped him cold.

"You're mistaken."

"It's none of my business." He ran a hand through his hair and down the back of his neck. "I'm sorry for how I acted earlier."

"It's fine." She walked past him to the water, not stopping until she stood ankle-deep in the crashing surf. Her arms remained locked over her stomach.

"No." He almost reached out for her but stopped with his hand outstretched.

She arched a brow that angled over the rounded edge of her sunglasses. "No, what?"

"It's not okay." The need to explain worked through him with enough force that the words exploded from him. "Aunt Audrey has been through a lot. I worry about her, and I took that out on you. That's not the kind of man I am. I'm not usually rude and judgmental."

"Only when it comes to your aunt." Her lips twitched in an almost smile.

"She's all I have."

Lauren's chin dipped, and her grip on her elbows tightened. "I know how that feels." She took a deep breath that lifted her shoulders. "Does this mean you're not going to be mad when I show up to bake with your aunt?"

"Not a bit." He used his index finger to draw an X over his heart. "I promise. I might even be convinced to help."

"That's not necessary."

"Not even after I tell you I have a degree in culinary science?" He grinned when she snapped around to face him. "Never used it, but I always loved baking."

"You're not what I expected." A low laugh rolled in time with the crashing waves. "Guess we surprised each other."

"How so?"

She bent to scoop a handful of damp sand and let it drip between her fingers. "I thought you were stalking me. You thought I was going to hurt your aunt. Not sure how you thought I'd manage that, but stranger things have happened. It's sweet that you're so protective of her."

Her words took a minute to sink in. "You thought I was a stalker? Why?"

Her sunglasses hid her eyes, but not the tightness around her mouth. "Long story. And one that doesn't matter anymore. I'm out of that life. I'm *not* Laura Grady. Laura was a persona, a job. Nothing more."

"And someone stalked you." It wasn't a question. Now he understood her reaction to him, the way she shied away and kept herself closed off, in control. "I wish I hadn't scared you. It wasn't my intention."

"You don't have to walk on eggshells. I'm over it." As though trying to prove herself, she dropped the last of the sand and held out a tiny spiral shell. "Truce?"

"Didn't know we were at war, but sure." He took the shell.

Grinning, she flicked her sandy fingers in his direction, splattering his shirt with wet flecks of sand. "I'm sure Audrey's glad to have you back." She turned and walked away, making her way between the dues that led to a large, three-story white house with large columns.

Chapter Three
Five days before the Wedding

Two weddings on the same day. What had she been thinking to agree to that?

Lauren carried her coffee to the front porch and leaned her hip on the white porch railing. Birds twittered from the large magnolia tree in the yard, and Lauren caught a glimpse of feathers and a sharp beak before the bird ducked into the thick branches.

Two weddings wasn't impossible. All she had to do was make sure all the decorations were prepped and the cakes baked. As soon as she finished Ainslie's cake for the two p.m. wedding on Saturday, she'd head straight to the shop and pick up Nicole's cake.

"You look lost in thought." Olivia carried Sable to the porch swing and sat, using her toe to push the swing back and forth.

Lauren sipped the rich brew and crossed her ankles so her weight rested on her right heel. "Mentally preparing for the drama. What about you?"

"You think it'll be bad?" Olivia stared at Sable. The quietest of their group, Olivia avoided drama. She'd been the peacemaker as long as Lauren could remember.

While Ainslie and Lucas wanted a small wedding despite their massive social media following, pulling it off was going to be one of the hardest things they'd ever done. But they needed this job.

She took her time formulating an answer that might soothe Olivia's fears while being honest. "I think her mother is a bit aggressive, but we know what we're doing and this is going to be an amazing wedding."

Viana joined them, her phone clutched tight in her hand and a worried frown drawing a line between her brows. "They'll be here any minute." Viana checked her phone.

"Relax, Via." Lauren forced her body to obey her own order. Nothing good ever came from being uptight all the time.

Viana gave her a look. "Easy for you to say."

Olivia continued to swing back and forth, the rabbit in her lap content to nuzzle her forearm. "I love that Ainslie and Lucas are having a December wedding. It's sweet that they'll be married and on their honeymoon when Christmas rolls around. And the best part is, no one will expect a wedding at this time of the year."

Lauren checked the sky. It wasn't supposed to rain, but the movement gave her a chance to look toward the beach. Why did she want to go for a walk when they had clients arriving? "Who knew a guy responsible for making men around the country style themselves after Cary Grant in skinny jeans with a too-cool attitude would fall in love with the princess of the best ways to live each day? And then, together, they've become a fashion powerhouse."

Viana ran her hand up the post where she'd stopped. Lauren leaned closer for a better look at the engravings Viana traced with her fingertips. Viana let out a long sigh. "This wedding is so important. Obviously, we need more than two weddings a month, and we already had to lay off the cleaning staff. We can't let Anita go, too, since we need her on the front desk and as my admin assistant. And we really need to keep our kitchen and grounds staff."

Viana swiped a finger across her phone screen, then opened her laptop.

Olivia gave Lauren a helpless look.

Time to remind Via how awesome she was. "Between Ainslie and Lucas, they're going to more than put us back in the black, they're going to put The Summer House on the map." Lauren squeezed Via's hand.

"Lauren's right." Viana glanced at her phone. "And Ainslie's mother is a pain, but that just comes with wedding territory."

"Oh yeah," Lauren pulled up one of her favorite memories and smiled. "Remember when that bride changed the cake design five times before the wedding?"

Viana giggled along with her. "You almost tore your hair out dealing with her."

Lauren took another sip of her coffee. The slight bitterness as it cooled made her wince. "I still get stressed when I think about that particular wedding but thank the Lord you handled the lion's share of that wedding party." She tipped her cup in Viana's direction, saluting their leader.

"We're all ready?" Viana looked at Lauren.

Lauren finished the last of her coffee and raised her mug before setting it on the rail. "All the preliminary design has been done. And I had the final meeting with Ainslie and Lucas, and they're happy."

"What about you, Livvie?" Viana asked.

Olivia hesitated long enough for Viana to arch her brows before Olivia's quiet answer came. "My videographer quit."

Uh-oh. Thick silence settled over the trio. Waves crashed in the distance with the steady drum of a heartbeat.

"Did he give a reason?" Viana crossed to stand beside Olivia.

Olivia patted Sable and shrugged. "He hates the mother of the bride. He won't work with her."

Viana pressed her fingertips to her temple. "This isn't the worst problem we can have. Not by a long shot. It's one videographer. It's not like the bridal party got stranded on the boat the morning of the wedding."

"Or like when the groom arrived late after getting a speeding ticket on his way to the wedding." Lauren added.

"Or when that hurricane broke the bridge, separating the wedding parties." Viana tossed back.

"Panhandle living." Lauren laughed. Man, it felt good to laugh with her friends. After her ordeal with Owen, she needed this levity, even if it came with disappointment.

"I'll find someone." Olivia made it sound easy. Her gaze cut to the ocean, and an unfamiliar look brightened her eyes.

What was that all about?

Viana patted Olivia's ankle, then Sable's back. "I know you will, but you don't have to do this alone. We're in this together."

"Pot calling the kettle black there, Via?" Lauren laughed under her breath, loving nothing more than to razz her best friend to help calm them all down before they panicked. "I love you, but, woman, you are the most independent of the three of us." Lauren stretched her arms high in the air. "We're here to help you just as much as you're here to help us."

Five years of working with Via, on top of the years of friendship before that gave her keen insight into the wedding planner. Olivia might have only joined them a year ago, but she fit right in with their dynamic, especially since they'd all known each other since high school.

No one looked convinced yet, so Lauren continued. "We've never done a wedding with so much riding on it."

Via nodded. "Ainslie and Lucas want a private wedding that they can share with all their fans after the fact."

Olivia glanced at Via. "I want to give them the best, but now…"

"You're worried you're not up to this job?" Viana asked. "And you won't find a suitable replacement in time?"

Olivia hesitated briefly before she nodded.

"We're *not* up to this—"

"What?" Olivia interrupted, eyes wide.

"No one is ready for an event like this, but we can do this. It's twenty people max. We handle that all the time. We also handle difficult brides, difficult family members, hurricanes." Viana looked at Lauren and Olivia. "It's just last-minute jitters. It happens with every wedding. And it should. Because we care about giving the bride and groom an amazing day with a lifetime of memories that make them smile every time they think of it."

"You know, if you didn't sound like such a sergeant major, it might have been a more inspiring speech." Lauren tapped her empty cup on the railing.

Viana threw her head back in a loud laugh. "I needed that."

Olivia joined in, though she wasn't quite as boisterous as Viana.

"But there is one thing different with this wedding." Lauren grabbed her mug. Did she have time for one more cup of coffee before Ainslie and Lucas arrived?

"What's different?" Viana asked.

Lauren raised her eyebrows. "We have an actual bodyguard with this one."

Viana checked her phone again. "We've never worked with security before. I hope he's not some blockheaded guy with no sense of what's needed." She played with her shell necklace, her one sign of uncertainty, before concentrating on Olivia. "Let me know if you need any help getting a videographer."

"I'll find someone. Your support—both of you—means everything to me."

Lauren hugged Olivia. "We've had each other's back since high school, that doesn't change now."

Viana joined them. "I know you're worried, but like we said before, this kind of thing happens at weddings all the time. If you haven't found someone soon, let me know and I'll put out some feelers as well."

"Thanks." Olivia smoothed Sable's fur. "When I was coming home, I saw the city maintenance crew setting up."

Lauren made her way around to the other side of the steps to get a better view of the driveway. "They're probably doing the routine maintenance. It was on the town's social media page last week. I hope they'll be finished before the wedding. You know how long these jobs take. Sometimes, it's like they're not even working."

Their combined laughter put a smile on their faces.

Olivia followed her stare toward the gate. "It's funny how we all came home. Life's best laid plans."

Viana laughed, but the sound held no joy. Lauren shot a look at her before movement at the gate pulled her away. "Ainslie and Lucas are here."

Two vehicles rolled down the gravel drive and pulled to a stop.

Lauren held her breath to settle her nerves. Show time.

The back door of the gray Range Rover popped open.

"We're here!" Ainslie's chipper squeal could puncture eardrums, but it was the kind of sound that made everyone around her instantly at ease.

No wonder her social media following rose every time she spoke. Giant sunglasses hid Ainslie's face the same way Lauren's did. Incognito mode activated.

Owen had still recognized her.

Her stomach flip-flopped, a sense of warmth spreading through her.

Lucas joined Ainslie, the two of them heading toward the house with bright smiles that promised a wonderful wedding.

Viana hurried down the steps, her arms wide for a hug. "Welcome! I'm so excited you guys are here. I want you to use the next four days to just relax. No one knows you're here and we want to keep it that way."

"I knew why I wanted you three to do this wedding." Ainslie hugged Viana, then turned to embrace Lauren and Olivia. The hug was quick, Ainslie's excitement swirling as she turned to look around. "I love this place so much. I can't believe your parents built this. It's like the perfect hideaway."

Yes, absolutely perfect for getting away from the world with its criticism and backbiting. She'd rather be here than anywhere else.

Lauren let Viana do her thing while she concentrated on her checklist. She'd have to start working on the flowers soon if she wanted to guarantee plenty of time for any mishaps.

There were *always* mishaps with weddings.

He'd always wanted to be a cowboy. Owen hooked his thumbs in his beltloops and rocked on his heels. "What do you think?"

Barbara, the owner of the one and only horse riding stable along the beach smirked at him. "Missing the hat."

"Eh." He batted the words away with the ease of snatching a pop fly from the air. "No one wears cowboy hats in Florida."

She pointed at her head, where a black Stetson perched on her steel gray curls. "Says who?" The smirk widened. "It's part of the business, son. You want to help me out with the rides, you wear the hat."

"I'm not wearing the hat." He loved arguing with Barbara. They both knew he'd give up and follow her orders, but they had too much fun to stop the tradition from his youth.

Soft footsteps crept up behind him, and before he had a chance to turn, someone jammed a hat over his eyes.

"Wear the hat." Lauren danced around him, blue eyes alight with laughter and mischief.

His heart thudded loud enough to drown out everything else. He palmed the top of the hat, pushing it into place and trying to settle his erratic pulse. "What are you doing here?"

"Bringing Barbara her weekly cake order." Lauren pointed toward the office at the end of the barn. "I heard you two arguing. Thought I'd help out. You're not going to win against her."

"Never planned on it." He couldn't think straight with her smiling at him like that. The whole world seemed brighter when happiness shone from her.

A horse stuck his head out from the stall beside Owen and shoved his head into Owen's arm. He repeated the motion when Owen turned and scratched the gelding's neck. "Do you ride?"

"I've ridden before but not often." She dug a hand into her pocket and pulled out a handful of carrot pieces. "But I always bring snacks, which means I'm their favorite visitor."

"Oh yeah?" He picked up a bucket of feed that he'd helped Barbara scoop out when he first arrived and shook it. "Should we put that to the test?"

"That's cheating." Lauren's breezy laugh was followed by the crunching of carrots from the gelding.

Barbara snorted a sound not unlike the horses and rolled her eyes. "You two going to help me out or stand around flirting all day?"

Flirting? He wasn't flirting.

Lauren continued patting the gelding. "I can't stay long."

"More cakes to bake?" Owen worked his way down the barn aisle, emptying feed into each of the buckets in the stalls.

"I have clients. You two keep it PG in here. There are kids around." She stomped and muttered, but every word sounded too chipper for anger. If anything, she seemed pleased by the turn of events.

"Barbara." Lauren admonished the woman's retreating figure by drawing out each syllable of her name.

"You heard me." Barbara gathered up the reins of the horses she'd saddled up earlier and walked them to the rail where a group of people began lining up next to the split rail fence.

Kids and parents laughed and chatted with the kind of frivolous energy that he'd seen many times from vacationing families. They were all excited, the kids thrilled with the idea of riding horses on the beach.

He understood. He'd been one of those kids the first time his parents brought him to visit Aunt Audrey when he turned eight. They'd brought him every year after that, and one of his favorite things to do was come to Barbara's and ride on the beach. It made him feel free, like nothing in the world was impossible. Nothing could hold him down or hold him back.

That feeling had continued for years. Until he'd blown out his shoulder and destroyed his dreams of playing in the major leagues.

"So. What kind of cake are you baking?" He concentrated on not letting his churning emotions loose on his face.

Lauren was in a good mood, and he wanted to keep it that way.

"You really want to know?"

"Why else would I ask?" He shot the answer at her with a softness that he hoped showed his genuineness.

She bundled her short hair in a ponytail and twisted a band around the strands. Several fell and framed her face, the edges brushing her chin as a breeze flitted through the alley. It brought the salty tang of the ocean and the waves.

Horses nickered and stamped where they waited for their riders as Barbara gave her safe riding speech. He'd heard it enough to have it memorized.

"I'm supposed to have two cakes ready for weddings on Saturday." Lauren's shoulder brushed his. When had she gotten so close? She reached past him and smoothed the mare's forelock before he dumped food into her bucket.

"Sounds intense. Need any help?" He offered without thought, certain she'd turn him down.

Lauren didn't strike him as the type to accept help.

"I have it under control." She dropped her hands away from the mare, brushing them together before easing them into her pockets and stepping to the side.

He had expected the reaction, but for some reason, it still bothered him. "If you change your mind, you know where to find me. I haven't baked in a while, but I still remember all the tricks. And I have a home-made fondant recipe that is to die for."

"I make my own fondant too." The sunshine returned to her smile. "Let me guess. You use marshmallows?"

"Yep. It's a little finicky and prone to breaking if you don't get it right. But the flavor is worth the pain." He could almost taste the marshmallow and powdered sugar.

"I agree." Lauren held out the last carrot stick to a gelding on the other side of the barn. "I have to go. Have fun out there." She winked at him, the playfulness so shocking he dropped the bucket he'd been holding. It clattered and banged sideways, then rolled to a stop at the toe of her boots. With her boots and jeans, she looked ready to swing into the saddle and take off on horseback alongside Barbara. "Hat suits you. Maybe you should consider joining Barbara full time."

He'd never been speechless before, but that did it. She was across the parking lot and striding toward the beach by the time he recovered. Too late to chase after her, not that he'd risk scaring her again by doing that.

Barbara and the group rode away, leaving him alone in the barn. She had others to help with the horses, but they were all prepping more horses for the upcoming rides scheduled, including the group he was supposed to lead.

He didn't have time to mull over what Lauren might have meant with her wisecrack about the hat.

Chapter Four
Four days before the Wedding

aylight had barely broken over the ocean when Lauren swung onto her bike and pedaled into town. Early morning hours were her favorite, and the short ride down the boardwalk invigorated her. She parked behind Audrey's shop and opened the narrow door that led into the kitchen. Music made a sweet melody that tickled her ears with the rise and fall of chimes mixed with a soft crooning.

"Audrey?" Lauren checked her hair and stopped at the sink to splash water on her face before washing her hands and grabbing an apron from the hooks.

Like most other things in Audrey's shop, the apron had a flamboyant air in the flared skirt and ruffled edge. Lauren chose one with a pink background and white hibiscus flowers in full bloom. The string wrapped around her waist and she tied it in the front, pulling at the material until it fell in comfortable waves over her jeans.

Audrey hadn't answered her, but that wasn't unusual. She often became so immersed in her work that she didn't hear anything.

Lauren pulled her phone from her pocket and swiped to the first recipe she needed to finish today. The bottom layer of Nicole's cake was the most important as far as structure. It would hold up the remaining tiers. Creating a masterpiece for Nicole started there, at the base. Without a firm base, the whole cake would fail.

Which made her lemon pound cake a perfect option for the most important layer. Thankfully, Nicole had loved the recipe. Not that she couldn't tweak the flavors to match whatever Nicole wanted.

She rounded the counter where Audrey kept all her mixing bowls and the stand mixer, already reaching for the largest bowl that she needed. Her hand hit something soft and warm, not firm and cold. She snapped it back with a hiss and jerked her head up.

Owen sidestepped away from her. "Sorry."

"No. My fault." She must have smacked him in the back with her hand, and he was the one apologizing. "Had enough cowboying for the week?"

He grinned at her over his shoulder, the white of his apron drawing out the dark brown in his eyes. "Not even close. But I told Aunt Audrey I'd help her today." He motioned at the bowls she'd been reaching for. "Which ones do you need?"

"These." She reached past him, pulling the entire stack of bowls toward her.

Audrey walked around the far side of the counter, her hair pulled back in a neat bun and a paisley apron tied around her waist. "There you are. I was about to send Owen to see if you needed help."

"Took the scenic route." She scooted the bowls into a better position and picked them up, tucking them under one arm. "You have to see what I made this week." Grinning at the memory of the look on Olivia's face, she showed Audrey the red velvet and pistachio cookies she'd made. "Christmas cookies."

Audrey's face turned an alarming shade of magenta. "What is that?"

Lauren explained her recipe, breaking into the occasional giggle as she told them about Olivia's reaction. "They didn't taste horrible."

"I'm sure they were fine." The tight sound that emerged from Owen bordered somewhere between laughter and pain.

Audrey covered her mouth with one hand, then the other. A laugh slipped through. She squeezed her eyes shut and shook her head.

"What?" Lauren looked from the phone to Audrey and back. "What's so funny?"

"Nothing." Audrey snorted even as she tried to smother her laughter.

Owen patted her shoulder, but instead of helping, it caused her to burst out with a loud guffaw. He locked eyes with Lauren and shrugged. "I have no idea what's happening."

"It's nothing." Audrey flapped her hands in the air like they were bird wings. Tears streamed down her cheeks, and she snorted while trying to drag in a breath. "Here." She walked backward toward the main counter. "Come see."

Lauren set the bowls aside and followed.

Step by step, Audrey led them to the shelf where she kept cookies that were too old to put in the case for sale.

"I've never seen her like this." Curiosity pinched Owen's face. "This is weird. Maybe she's been breathing too much powdered sugar."

Lauren elbowed him. "Stop that."

"Look." Audrey wiped her eyes and swept aside a silver dome covering a platter.

Green cookies with red flakes covered the platter's fluted edges.

Owen leaned over the counter and poked the cookies with one finger. His eyes narrowed. "What are they?"

"Christmas cookies." Audrey and Lauren said it together, flinging their arms around each other and laughing so hard they both nearly crashed to the floor.

Grinning but shaking his head with a kind of exasperation Lauren had become used to when it came to hers and Audrey's antics in the kitchen, he spoke. "You both made Christmas cookies, but in inverted color patterns." He picked up a cookie and bit into it. "What are they?"

"Pistachio cookie with frosted coconut that I dyed red." Audrey wiped the last of the tears from her eyes. "I believe we both suffered a bit in the execution of our ideas."

"And maybe in flavor choices," Lauren added. It wasn't the first time she'd combined the wrong flavors and come up with a dud. Many of her ideas worked, which was what kept her trying. If she wasn't so burned out on being in front of a camera, she'd even thought about starting her own baking series on YouTube.

No way in the world she'd put herself out there like that again. It wasn't worth the risk for her.

"It's no wonder you enjoy baking here." Owen took another bite. His mouth puckered. "There's a strange flavor in here. Maybe the food dye on the coconut?"

"Beets." Audrey used the hem of her apron to pat her face dry. "I used beets to turn the coconut red. That's what you're tasting." She covered the cookies, still chuckling under her breath. "The side section is all yours, Lauren. I'll be working in the front to make the sugar cookies. Mildred's watching the register."

The chime from the front door rang out, followed by a low hum of voices, then Mildred asking what cookies they'd like to purchase.

Lauren backed toward her stack of bowls. "Thanks, Audrey."

"Why are you baking the cakes here?" Owen tagged along at her elbow, his presence not as alarming as that first encounter.

She might even think she was getting used to him, except she didn't want to. "Your aunt likes the company. I like the company."

"And I have commercial grade freezers and refrigerators," Audrey called out from her hunched position over the lump of sugar cookie dough.

"So do I," Lauren shouted back. She headed to the pantry and pulled the ingredients she needed from the shelves. "I don't like transporting large quantities of cakes. Even taking the tiers in separate sections to the venue and putting them together is a risk. Plus." She paused to check her list against the items she held.

Owen took the container of flour and the sugar from her. "Plus?"

"Plus I like baking with Audrey. It's fun." She baked in the kitchen at Summer House all the time with Davia, but the vibe here with Audrey put her more at ease sometimes. "What about you? What brought you back?"

Was he here to stay?

The tub of butter slid from her grasp, almost dropping to the floor before Owen caught it, his reflexes faster than she thought possible.

"Nice moves." She blurted it out without thinking, the way she lobbed quips with Viana and Olivia. Her cheeks heated when Owen arched a brow.

He walked backward out of the pantry, keeping her in his line of sight. "Former professional pitcher. Still got the reflexes." He mimed snapping a baseball glove together while setting the flour, sugar, and butter on the counter beside her bowls.

"I remember. You played in college, right? Audrey mentioned you planned on going pro." She tightened her ponytail when it slipped, sending several strands of hair across her cheeks.

"Yes to both. Pro didn't last very long." He rolled his arm a couple times and winced. "I've been working as a radio announcer."

She should have remembered that. Audrey talked about Owen a few times a year, and sometimes she even turned on a game as he announced the plays.

"I've baked cakes to your work before. You make games fun." She opened the containers and began measuring out her ingredients using Audrey's kitchen scale.

Owen reached for a bowl. "Can I help?"

She smacked his hand without thinking. "Not yet. I have to set everything up first."

"You smacked me." He pulled his hand to his chest and rubbed it with his fingers.

Shock and embarrassment scrambled her brain, stopping her in the middle of pouring sugar into the bowl she'd set on the scale. "Habit. I have to keep Olivia and Viana out of my ingredients when I'm working. It's like a game that we play."

"I'm not mad." He grinned as though to prove he meant it, and it wrinkled the edges of his eyes, making him appear younger. "I'm surprised."

"Surprised?" That was new.

He propped against the wall in what Marvin used to call a signature bad boy pose. Arms crossed. One ankle propped over the other. All he needed was a leather jacket to pair with his jeans and he'd be ready to walk onto a movie set.

"Yep." He tucked his hands tight to his ribs. "You don't seem afraid of me anymore."

"Oh." That.

"I thought I was scarier than that. Figured I at least deserved a few more days of terror."

She snorted a laugh so deep it burned her nose. "Yeah, you're terrifying. You with your puppy dog eyes and apologies."

"Not to mention my devastatingly handsome cowboy good looks." He framed his face in his hands and blinked.

"You should take that comedy show on the road. From what I've heard, you have a perfect voice for radio. Comedy's a close second." She resumed her measurements, greased and floured her pans, and set the oven temperature.

Most people would treat her with an excess of caution after what she'd revealed. But she'd told Owen she was okay, and he took her at her word.

Owen picked three apples from the basket behind him and juggled them in the air. "What do you think? Clown show or straight up comedy?"

"Comedy. No need covering that pretty face in garish makeup."

He dropped an apple on the counter. It bounced and skidded toward her bowls, clipped the edge of the bowl of sugar, and spun toward the floor. Owen watched it happen, everything about his expression moving in slow motion.

Lauren held out a hand to stop him from trying to grab the apple. "It'll be less of a mess if you let it fall. Audrey will use it to make apple tarts or something before it bruises."

The apple rolled to the edge of the counter, spun twice and tumbled toward Owen. He grabbed it and bit deep. "Or I'll eat it."

"That works too." The process of adding ingredients and working through the recipe combined with the sweet aroma of Audrey's cookies and the soulful music from the radio. "Here." She held out a bowl of cake mixture toward Owen. "Use the scale and separate this into the pans. Each one needs to weigh the same so the layers match each other."

"Why is that important?" He took the bowl, the three pans she indicated, and the scales. "Can't you cut the cakes to match?"

"I can, and I will have to trim them some, but this makes the process quicker." She started on the second batch of batter. It would take both, and maybe a third to create the height she needed for the bottom tier.

Owen worked with the kind of casualness that showed he found everything in his life easy.

"How long are you staying in Summer Shore?" She had been meaning to ask, but it became more important when her heart decided it wanted to pitter-patter every time she looked at him.

The last thing she needed was develop a crush on Audrey's nephew.

"Not long. I had enough vacation time for three weeks."

Three weeks. Good thing she had no plans on any kind of relationship. She was too busy. *Hear that, heart. He's not staying. You're not getting attached.* The fluttery feeling intensified when Owen looked her way, that boyish gleam giving way to a serious expression as he bent to check the scales.

A man who accepted her directions and followed them with minimal questions. If she was ever going to marry someone, it would be a guy like Owen. He understood her and he wasn't afraid to tell a joke.

He had to find a way to get Lauren talking again. Her sharp remarks kept him on his toes, and he loved that she didn't hold back. The whole comedy show routine was a risk, and she'd jumped at the challenge. "What else are you making today?"

A fresh lemon scent billowed out from the oven when Lauren removed the pans and set them on the counter. "Not much else today. These need to cool, then I can start icing and stacking them. They'll need to cool overnight to help the weight settle."

"Wow. More complicated than I thought."

"Let me guess," she removed the oven mitts and set them on the counter. "You thought it was as simple as baking the cakes, slapping some icing on, and throwing the cake rounds on top of each other." Coming from anyone else, it might sound accusatory, but Lauren grinned the whole time she spoke.

"Well...yeah." He played into the moment, hopping onto the empty counter behind them and dropping his laced hands between his knees.

Aunt Audrey had finished her cookies already and left them alone in the kitchen. He'd thought she planned on being in the kitchen all day, but he wasn't going to complain about the extra time with Lauren. She'd flinched when he said he was leaving soon.

It was minimal, but he'd seen and taken note.

If he had to guess, he'd assume she was attracted to him. Same as he was to her. If things were different, he'd consider asking her out on a date.

"What else is there to it?" He loved the way her eyes sparked when she scoffed at him.

The moment stretched thin, the space shrinking to nothing more than the two of them amid the swirls of lemon-scented air. She tapped the edges of the pan with her bare fingers. "That's all there is to it. Cake. Icing. A little fondant. Speaking of, how steady are your hands?"

He held them both out. "Why?"

She showed him a picture on her phone. "This is the cake topper Nicole wants. And it should be edible."

He whistled and took her phone, examining the design. An outline of a couple dancing stood in the foreground, the space behind them a rippling curtain with a swag of pale pink flowers attached to white columns. A second, larger frame of rippling curtains, flowers, and columns rose behind the first, creating a large piece that would definitely be a show-stopper.

"I have the fondant and the gumpaste. But if you're offering to help, I'll take that too." She dumped the cakes onto cooling racks and ducked beneath the counter, coming back up with two white tubs labeled in a careful script that must be hers.

She could ask for the moon and he'd do his best to bring it down from the sky for her.

"Steady as a surgeon. Tell me what to do." He hopped down and clapped. "Are you making all the flowers by hand or using icing once the background is made?"

"Let's see how the rest of it goes." The crack of the tub lid coming loose punctuated the words.

Within minutes, she had the fondant and gumpaste rolled out in thin sheets. She handed him an Exacto knife and held up one of her own.

He clinked his blade against hers. "I don't suppose you printed off any templates for us to use?"

"What? You can't freehand something like this?" She *tsk*ed. "And here I thought you were a master cookie maker."

"Cookie eater. Mediocre baker. And I've never done anything like this before, so I have no idea if I'm capable."

"You're willing to learn. That means a lot." She backed up a step and set her knife on the counter. "As it happens, I did make templates."

"Great. Let's get to work." He waited for her to hand them over, but she stood and stared like she'd never seen him before.

A flush colored her cheeks, and she tugged on her ear. "There's a problem."

"What?"

"I forgot to bring them."

He lowered the knife to the counter, setting it alongside hers. "That is a problem. I suppose I could try to make it myself." He closed one eye and angled his head to the side. "Or. We could go get them."

"We?" One hand splayed over her chest. "Do you think I need help picking up a stack of papers and bringing them back here?"

"Nope. I think I'm nosy and I want to see what you three have done with Summer House since turning it into a wedding venue." He considered the cakes on the counter. "They still need to cool, right? There's time."

Her mouth worked but no words came out. He knew that look. He'd given it and received it, usually for the same reason. She didn't want him coming with her.

"Or I can stay here." He put physical distance between them. It didn't make the sudden ache in his heart lessen, but it gave him a chance to breathe air not coated in the smell of her shampoo.

When had he leaned in so close that the scent invaded his head?

"Owen..." Her phone rang and she dove for it like a runner stealing home. "Viana?" A piercing shout of guttural noise pierced the quiet. "Whoa, Via, slow down. I can't understand you. What happened?"

Her eyes narrowed and she rubbed a hand across her forehead.

Owen made himself scarce, but he couldn't help keeping an eye on her from across the kitchen.

What looked like panic flickered in her wide eyes. "What do you mean the yard is flooded? What about the house?"

Lauren paced, one hand on her hip. "Okay. Okay. I hear you." She turned and looked over the counter. "I can't leave yet, but I'll be there soon as I can."

"Go." He took a step closer. "Tell me what to do and I'll finish the cakes for you."

She shook her head. "Via, I'll be there soon. Camden will help you with the yard." Her laugh trickled out. "Sorry. Couldn't resist."

What was it about her laugh that made him willing to turn the world upside down just to hear it again? They were nothing to each other. He barely knew her.

What's this all about, Lord? You and I both know I'll take off in a couple weeks and might never come back. Summer Shore isn't home. Home doesn't exist for me.

He'd gotten used to that feeling over the years of wandering from city to city, using his career as an excuse to never settle.

"You should go." He drew his thoughts away from the buried dream of finally feeling like he belonged and concentrated on Lauren.

"You don't know how to care for my cakes." Her smile popped dimples into her cheeks. "But you can help."

"What happened?"

A sigh drove the grin away. "Burst water main on our street. The yard where we were going to hold the wedding is flooded. I need to go help my friends figure out what to do next."

Within minutes, they had the cakes covered in simple syrup and wrapped up for cooling.

"I can come with you. You said something about Camden helping. I can help too." He held out his hands, flipping them from front to back. "These hands are good for more than baking. I can pick stuff up. You know, carry it around. Like these bowls." He picked up the stack of dirty bowls and carried them to the sink. "You could save me from ruining my hands washing more dishes."

"I could. But I won't." She patted his shoulder in passing. "You can save your aunt's hands by washing the dishes for her."

"Good point." Why was it so hard to watch her walk away? He dug his hands into the soapy water, using it as a distraction to keep from trying to convince her to let him tag along.

He was a lot of things, but desperate wasn't one.

Chapter Five
Three days before the Wedding

One day at a time. Lauren stopped at the edge of the beach and dug her heels into the coarse sand. Wind and waves and quiet time with God. That was all she needed to settle her thoughts and figure out how to finish both cakes.

A bell jangled nearby, and she turned toward the sound. A man dressed in red board shorts and a Santa hat stood on the end of the boardwalk, his bell clanging as he drew attention to the bucket where people dropped donations for the local toy drive. The middle-aged man was a staple of the community, and the most ambitious bell-ringing Santa in Summer Shore.

"Hey, Tony. Running kind of late, aren't you?" She made her way over and dropped a few bills into the red bucket.

Tony tipped his Santa hat. "Last-minute addition to the toy drive. One of the churches a few towns over needed help finishing out their gifts. Thought I'd come down and see what I could shake loose."

"You're a good one, Tony." She gave his shoulder a pat and moved toward Castaways, her favorite thrift store, for a quick shopping spree before she ducked into Audrey's to check on her cakes for Nicole. What she needed was an extra set of hands.

Owen stood near the front windows, his arms loaded down with brown paper bags.

She almost ducked into the alley, hoping to avoid him, but that made no sense. Neither did the way her pulse raced, but she attributed that to the rush of adrenaline that kicked up every time she thought about working with him again.

"How'd things go with the flooding?" He shifted the bags to one hand. "Is there anything I can do to help?"

Here was her chance to ask, to finally break out of her 'do it all yourself' mentality and let someone into her life. It should be simple. She trusted Via and Olivia and never had trouble asking them for help.

"Actually…" Her throat pinched. "I'd love some help."

"Great." The way his voice pitched higher with excitement stopped the guilty feeling in its tracks.

After helping clean up last night—and annoying Viana about Camden—she'd spent hours in her kitchen rolling out daisies for Ainslie's cake. The varying colors would look amazing once she finished the design, but the tediousness of rolling and cutting each one caused her hands to cramp late into the night.

Worth it. She loved making wedding cakes enough to put up with the days when it seemed like everything was going wrong. No job was without trials and the occasional mishap.

"We're moving the wedding indoors, but that won't change anything about the cake." She started into Castaways. "Find anything interesting?"

"Tons." The boyishness she'd noted before returned to his face. "They had a bunch of vintage cookie cutters. I thought Aunt Audrey would love them. Huh." He hefted the bags higher. "They might come in handy for you too. You could cut fondant with them."

"I prefer to hand cut my designs, but that's a great idea." Especially for things like flowers where she needed several hundred of the same design. "I use templates all the time, but cookie cutters are a great idea." Stop talking. Why couldn't she stop blathering on like a fool?

"Are you headed over to the bakery?" Head back, he eyed the sky. "I was on my way there. I can walk with you."

"I thought about doing a little shopping, but I'd better get to work. Cakes won't bake themselves." And the decorations wouldn't pop into existence because she wanted them to. Nicole's design would take hours even if she cut it perfectly the first time. The fondant needed to dry and every single flower glued into place with the edible glue paste she preferred.

So many steps to each part of the cake. They scrolled though her mind the same way Marvin's directions used to every time she stood in front of a camera.

She made a decision, though it came in part because she knew the house would be empty today. "Do you want to help cut out flowers?"

"I'd like nothing better." He said it with enough conviction that a lightness entered her chest.

Shaking her head at his enthusiasm, she added, "At the house."

A car rolled to a stop two stores down the street. Ainslie and Lucas emerged, along with Florence, Ainslie's mother.

Lauren checked the sidewalk in either direction, watching the people walking along the sidewalk to see if anyone recognized the social media couple. No one paid any attention, and the sudden tension that had frozen her lungs released.

"Hey. You okay?" Owen touched her elbow, cupping it gently in his palm.

She let the warmth of his skin seep into her and spread. "Yeah. Fine." It took a little effort to pull her smile into place. "Ready to go? You can meet me at the house if you need to drop those off first."

The bags rustled in his grip. "I'll bring them with me. They might come in handy, and Aunt Audrey won't mind."

She'd left the house feeling slightly defeated at everything that had gone wrong the last few days. It was nothing definitive, only a sense that things were falling part. A gnawing discomfort that things always fell apart eventually.

I'm sorry, Lord. I don't mean to let the intrusive thoughts get in the way of our relationship. I don't want to feel this way, like the world is going against me. I'm not part of the world. I am part of Your kingdom. This world is temporary.

Did that mean that she would never fall in love and marry?

Images of Viana and Camden came to mind. She'd seen how they looked at each other, how Camden tried to take care of Viana. Her friend didn't make it easy for him, but he hadn't given up.

Olivia would tell her not to give up on love. Then again, Olivia was spending an awful amount of time with her own Prince Charming.

She thought she was being sneaky, but Lauren spotted them on the beach this morning when she walked onto the balcony to drink her morning coffee.

They kept pace with each other along the boardwalk, across the beach, and up to the gate that Camden had insisted they keep closed. She wasn't opposed to his demand, but it complicated things when she drove.

Owen stopped and stared at the house. "I'd forgotten how massive this place was. I only really saw it a couple times from a distance. You run the whole business from here?"

Answering his questions gave her the distraction she needed. "Yes. Viana takes care of the wedding planning side. She's the business side of the whole operation, plus she does the decorations. I bake and decorate the cakes, and Olivia does the photography and videography."

"Sounds complicated." He stopped in front of the magnolia tree and pinched a green leaf between his thumb and forefinger.

"We figured out how to make it work." She led the way around to the back of the house, stopping to check on the flooded yard. "This is where we planned on holding the wedding." The smell of dampness remained thick in the air.

Sodden decorations hung limp along the railing. They'd been optimistic that some would dry out in time for the wedding, but Camden had shown up with boxes and boxes of stuff for Viana to choose from in case nothing was salvageable.

"This way." She entered the main foyer, waved at Anita where she sat behind the reception desk, and pushed open the door to her kitchen.

The feeling of coming home always hit hardest right here, on the threshold of the space where she found comfort.

White counters met white cabinets with chrome handles that matched the stainless-steel appliances. She'd always preferred sleek, clean lines and a minimalist approach. The kitchen reflected that while giving her space for everything she needed for her best work.

Owen set the paper bags on the glass top kitchen table and dug both hands into the depths. "What kind of flowers?"

"Daisies. Different colors." She pulled the pan of flowers she'd cut last night from the refrigerator and showed him. "Like this."

"Ah. I don't think I have anything that can help with that. Except these." He raised both hands and wiggled his fingers.

"Those will work." She returned the pan to the refrigerator and brought out her colored fondant. "The templates are over there. Some can be cut in whole flowers, but not all. I need some of them to have individual petals."

"That way they look more authentic." He crossed to the counter and flipped through the templates. "What about the centers? Are they all yellow?"

"So far, yes. I haven't found another color that makes sense." She carried her box of cake tools to the counter on the far end of the kitchen, the one closest to the private staircase they all used to move between floors.

The fake cake she crafted years ago stood on a turntable in the center of the counter. Different sized tiers were stacked in a cabinet overhead, each round of Styrofoam covered in cling wrap to keep particles from contaminating her products.

She took the extra step to cover them in fondant just to be safe before she cut out a flower petal and held it up against the replica of Ainslie's cake. "I need different sizes to make a waterfall of flowers. They're going to start here." She pointed at the top of the cake. "They'll be pasted on top of each other and come around like this." She used the tip of one of her smoothing tools to make a line in the fondant.

Owen moved to stand beside her. He concentrated on the cake, and she alternated between the cake and the warmth that spread through her every time his weight shifted toward her and their arms touched.

This was so not appropriate. He was the wrong guy, it was the wrong time in her life. Nothing about the way he made her feel made sense. Why now? Why him?

Her mother always said that love rarely made sense. She claimed she'd known from the moment she spotted Lauren's father that she'd marry him someday.

Fifty years later, they were still as in love—maybe more so—than ever. They had the kind of forever, lasting love that had survived hardship and heartache because they trusted each other and they trusted God.

That was the kind of love she wanted.

Owen continued to stare at the cake. He pinched the turntable and spun the cake around in a dizzying circle. White fondant blurred with the white subway tile on the backsplash. A single flash of color snapped around, the single petal she'd anchored coming loose and spinning across the counter.

She picked it up and twirled it the way she would a real daisy, tempted to bring it to her nose and sniff deep enough to push all the uncertainty away. The phantom aroma of wildflowers filled the empty space in her heart long enough for her to stop imagining a life with Owen.

"Think you got it?" She picked her favorite tools and arranged them how she liked.

Owen retreated to the table and hauled a bundle of material out. He shook out the folds and slung the apron string over his head.

"That's...bright." She shielded her eyes with one hand. "Did you find the sun and decide to wear it?"

"You don't like it?" Owen smoothed both hands down his front, his palms glancing over the sunshine yellow material.

A laugh started at the depths of her stomach and rolled up. "I think it's wonderful. And it matches mine."

"Yours?" He gave her a once-over that coming from anyone else would have made her uncomfortable. But Owen was the kindhearted sort who made the look sweet.

Talking to Owen reminded her of her friends and how they all worked with each other to make weddings come together.

She walked backward to the tiny closet where she kept her aprons and pulled her favorite from the hook. An entire beach scene stretched across the front in brilliant yellows, pinks, and blues. A thick ruffle ran around the edge from hip to hip, and the tie wrapped around her waist and came together in a rising sun the same color as Owen's apron.

"We're a matched set." He grabbed her hands and twirled them in a circle.

It was easily the most ridiculous thing she'd ever done in her kitchen, and yet Owen made it all normal. He lived with the kind of innocence that belied the pain he'd shown her when he spoke of losing his career as a professional pitcher.

A rush of dizziness forced her to stop, her laughter so deep and rich that her sides ached.

Voices trickled in from the foyer, and Lauren held up a hand. "Shh."

Owen froze, his eyes going wide. "What?"

"That's Olivia." She almost gave into the urge to run to the door and spy on her friend when she heard the masculine voice join Olivia.

The words were faint, but she caught enough of them to understand they were talking about the wedding. Was this the same man she'd seen Olivia walking with on the beach this morning?

"Come on." She turned away from their voices, pulling Owen along behind her. "We need to work."

They bent over the counter, each with their own roll of colored fondant. Purple for Owen, and pink for her.

Olivia and her friend made their way around the front rooms, their voices rising and falling close enough that Lauren used the app on her phone to play music to give them some privacy.

If Olivia wanted them to know about her adventures at the beach, she'd tell them.

Just like Lauren would eventually tell them about Owen. Maybe. Probably. Once she figured out what was going on between them.

Her vision misted, blurring the petal's soft edges. Her low-key lifestyle on the beach wasn't what he wanted.

A shrill ring startled her in the middle of slicing out a petal, sending her knife skidding across the counter and carving a trench in the fondant.

"Careful." Owen stood with his knife poised, concern deepening the concentration carving a furrow between his brows.

She swiped her phone to answer. "Camden, you're on speaker."

"Hey, Lauren. Sorry to call you like this, but I need a favor."

Her eyebrows rose so fast her head ached. "What's up?"'

"Can you pick up Ainslie and Lucas from the spa in town? I'm not going to be back in time."

"You don't sound disappointed about that. You and Viana having a good time dress shopping?" She smirked at Owen when Camden spluttered. "Relax, Cam. I won't tell her. And I'll pick up Ainslie and Lucas."

"Thanks." If the man sounded any more relieved to have the couple taken care of, she might have to take offense that he'd pawned them off on her. "They'll be ready in half an hour."

She couldn't blame him for wanting to help Viana in the save the dress debacle. Viana wouldn't stop until she'd fixed the problem, and Cam was the kind of man who couldn't tolerate standing by and being useless.

"Problem?" Owen waited until she ended the call to speak up. He was the curious kind but not invasive.

She moved to the sink to wash the powdered sugar and fondant from her tools. "I need to pick up our clients. Can you help me put everything up?"

"I could get them for you. Or stay here and work on the flowers."

"No, that's okay. I'm sure Audrey wants to spend time with you before you leave." It might be easier to admit the truth to him, but it meant trusting him with the secret they'd all been keeping.

Ainslie and Lucas wanted a quiet wedding, without their millions of followers knowing. Telling one person—even one as quick to agree to help as Owen—risked the wrong person finding out and ruining their perfect day.

"I can drop you off at the shop. It's on my way." It took a bit of effort to pull her grin into place and hold it there.

Owen followed her lead and washed his tools, then began covering the petals for their trip to the refrigerator to rest alongside the rest of her work. "If you need help with anything else, you know where to find me."

Was it her, or did he sound disappointed?

"I still have a few days to pull everything together. If I can finish baking cakes tomorrow and cut out the rest of the decorations, Saturday will run like clockwork." She'd said it often enough.

"You know the saying about best laid plans." Owen dried his hands and cleaned up the last of the mess from the counter. "Seems like every time I decide something for myself, God laughs and I end up on the other end of the country."

"Do you enjoy it?" She'd wanted to ask before but hesitated to hear him put words to his departure.

The way he paused before he resumed scrubbing at a spot on the white marble caused her heart to stutter with a wicked flare of hope.

Ridiculous. She was being ridiculous. Wedding fever and nothing more. She refused to develop a crush on the cute baker, especially knowing he'd never choose to stay and she would never return to a life outside of this one.

She'd spent enough time traveling all over the world for her modeling career. Never again.

"I'm not sure enjoy is the right word. It's like I'm searching for something. Every time I take a new job, I think I've finally found it."

"It?"

He put a certain inflection on the word, a seriousness that drew the air in close.

Owen met her gaze, his full of longing. "Home."

Oh. She knew that feeling all the way to her soul.

"When my parents died and I came to live with Aunt Audrey, I lost everything. All these years later, I'm still looking for that sense of peace, of being in the place where I belong."

"You sure it's a physical place you can find that will bring you peace?" The question popped out against her will.

Owen's stare was cold enough to freeze the ocean. "What do you mean?"

"Nothing. Forget I said anything." She grabbed her keys from the basket by the door. "I have to go. You ready?"

Lips pressed tight, he followed her through the house and out to her car. She'd known the question would end everything the minute it left her. Better now than after she'd gotten more attached.

Chapter Six
Two days before the Wedding

Sleep was impossible after the way she and Owen left things. If she was a better person, she would have tried to clear things up with him before they reached the bakery. Instead, she lingered in silence.

Owen had left the car without a word. Many men would have slammed the door or shown their displeasure in some other way. Not Owen. He remained quiet and solemn.

She'd tossed and turned all night before finally giving up at dawn and heading to the kitchen she shared with Olivia and Via. A full pot of coffee took too long, so she settled for a single serve cup that she carried to the counter.

Olivia joined her before she'd taken the first sip.

"You look chipper this morning." Lauren smiled into her cup when Olivia blushed and ducked her head. "I'm glad."

"It's a beautiful day. How could anyone be sad on a day like this?" She waved toward the balcony doors, where waves thundered against the shore.

"True. And we have a wedding to finalize."

Olivia busied herself with dragging a pan out from beneath the counter and cracking eggs into a bowl. She whisked them with the same focused energy she put into her photography, adding them to the pan and stirring them around with a spatula.

The intensity in her expression silenced Lauren. She sat with her back to the kitchen, her gaze locked on the ocean. Her list of tasks increased with every day that passed. She finished the first cup of coffee and returned for a second as Viana joined them.

Viana stretched and yawned. "Any new dramas erupt overnight?" She didn't wait for an answer on her way to grab the box of Lucky Charms from the cabinet.

Olivia took her plate of eggs to the living room and sat in one of the two matching recliners.

Lauren shook her head. "Not that I know of. I'm meeting with a new client for a wedding cake later today." With Nicole and Ainslie's weddings this weekend, she needed more work for the upcoming months to keep her busy.

Viana scooped a bite into her mouth. "Good. Ainslie tried on the dresses last night. We're going to do another session when her mother gets here."

Olivia had just bitten into her eggs, but the mention of Ainslie's mother caused all color to flee from her face. "Florence is coming *today*?"

"Yes. We can handle Florence." Via's smile held confidence and not a shred of doubt.

That was why she was the main face of the business. She handled Florence with ease and made everyone else confident they could as well. She grinned and snorted, playing into the moment. "You have Florence on 'do not disturb' mode most of the time."

Viana raised her eyebrows and grinned. "And you both should do the same if you want any peace. And with everything going wrong, we are not going to have much peace until the wedding is over."

Olivia forked up another bite of eggs, chewing and swallowing before she grinned. "Aren't you ever going to eat something else? You've been eating that stuff since high school. You know it's full of sugar."

Lauren laughed so hard she nearly fell off the stool. She caught herself with a hand on the counter, saving her coffee from sliding onto the floor as Olivia revived the years' old argument.

"Longer actually." Viana scooped up a giant bite as though to annoy Olivia. "It's my thing okay. I eat Lucky Charms for breakfast."

The booming laughter of friendship warmed the room, causing Olivia to lower her fork.

A pensive look tightened her eyes. "I think I've found a videographer."

The way Via suddenly relaxed showed how stressed she'd been.

Olivia continued, rushing through her words like she was afraid they'd slip away. "I met him a four days ago."

"Who is he?"

"Sil––uh, Mac. He's a scuba and snorkel instructor with a kiosk down by the pier. I've never seen such skill with a camera. Way better than the last guy." Olivia ducked her head, but not before Lauren caught the sight of her flushed cheeks.

Delight danced through Lauren's veins and widened her smile until her cheeks ached. "Oh, you have a crush! How'd you meet him? And why are you not telling us anything?"

"There's nothing to tell." Olivia hesitated, eyes locked on the window. "I didn't want to say anything until I'm sure he'd work out. We met on the beach when his black lab thought Sable was her new toy."

"Ooh, enemies to lovers, all those sparks." Lauren clasped her hands beneath her chin and wiggled her eyebrows. She loved a good romance trope. What would hers and Owen's be? Opposites attract?

"Don't you talk," Viana pointed her spoon at Lauren. "Who's that guy I saw you with yesterday? When I was leaving town. You were out front of Castaways."

Busted. "No one you know." Not entirely true. Viana and Olivia had both met Owen years and years ago, but it was unlikely either of them remembered him.

Viana rolled her eyes like a true professional. "Keep your secrets then."

Time for a diversion, and she had the perfect one up her sleeve. "Speaking of sparks. How are you and Cam getting along?"

Viana stood, hurrying around the counter to the sink, where she scrubbed her bowl. "Camden and I are fine. We're professionals."

Olivia followed Viana and cleaned her plate and fork. "There's sparks, we can all see it." She and Viana hugged. "I'll be back later."

"Have fun!" Lauren laughed when Olivia shot her a dirty look from the door as she picked up her bag.

Lauren made a decision on the spot, as she often did with her friends. Viana hadn't asked for advice, but she offered it anyway. "Sure, you two are professionals. Whatever you say." Lauren put her mug in the dishwasher and gave her a side hug. "It's okay to let your guard down."

"You want me to let Camden back into my life?" Viana's hard gaze locked on Lauren.

Lauren could retreat, or she could double down. She knew Viana, and she had a good feeling about Cam. "No, not unless you want to. But you keep people—not us, but everyone else—at arm's length. Maybe Cam being here is a reminder to you that it's okay to let someone in...and I don't just mean him."

"So, what are you saying? Be open to romance?" Viana's hand went to her chest, and a blush flared in her cheeks.

Well. Well. What was that all about?

"I can see something's been going on with you." Lauren tried not to pry, even though curiosity dug in hard. Viana deserved a chance to tell them in her own time. "I'm saying, be surprised by love."

What if she took her own advice? Owen's face flashed in her mind, and that soft feeling in her middle stretched to her heart.

All the years of keeping love at a distance threatened to crash all around her. They were not compatible, but her heart refused to take the memo.

Viana's phone pinged. She picked it up, and her business voice took over. "Florence will be here any minute. Ainslie and Lucas are good together, don't you think?"

"Fine, change the topic. Yes, they're lovely. Lucas is a bit..." She trailed off.

"Into the fame?" Viana filled in the silence with Lauren's exact thought.

"Yeah, but he still seems genuine. Fame is something I never want to experience again, and mine wasn't even on the level Lucas and Ainslie's is—but it was more than enough." She swallowed hard and stared toward the water. "They've both been easy to work with and what a blessing that is."

Viana nodded. "So long as we can avoid any more disasters from now until Saturday. But when they post all their wedding photos and videos, we're going to be beyond busy."

"You okay?" If there was anything she could do to help, she would. It didn't matter that her own schedule was filled to bursting. They were a team. They helped each other.

Viana straightened and pocketed her phone. "It's a lot, just thinking about it, but yes. I am excited."

"Me too." Agreeing was too easy. She'd been excited—and nervous—about this wedding since Ainslie booked it. The threat of their discovery put an anticipated edge into every step. Lauren tried to hide the threads of fear that came every time she saw a stranger in town. Every new face was a new opportunity for Ainslie or Lucas to be recognized.

They'd had their fair share of stalkers over the years. Lauren had almost asked Viana not to take on the wedding. It brought up too many old memories, too many fears.

But she refused to let fear rule her.

Except when it meant handing over her heart to a man who might not cherish it.

"Good gosh almighty, son. You gonna ride that horse or stand there and pet him to death?" The grizzled voice held enough laughter to float a submarine.

Owen turned to face the hunched old man whose white hair fluffed around the top of his head like a cotton ball. "Haven't made up my mind yet."

"Psh." Bernard flapped one hand and used the other to push his hair out of his eyes. "Better make your mind up quick or he's going to make it up for you."

As though to prove Bernard's point, the gelding snorted and stomped a front hoof right alongside Owen's boot. He patted the arched neck. "Yeah, okay. We'll go out."

The sleek Gypsy Vanner was Barbara's personal horse. She'd thought it funny when she named him Gypsy and bought all purple tack for the sixteen plus hand horse that reminded Owen of a Clydesdale. His size made him intimidating to most of the riders despite his striking black and white spotted coloring and perfect training.

She'd started letting Owen ride him when he visited eight years ago, and he'd been thrilled to find the gelding healthy and Barbara more than willing to let him take her horse out for a ride.

Except he kept standing at the edge where the trail started, the reins loose in his grip as Lauren's words tumbled in a constant loop.

"Hey, Bernie, can I ask you something?"

Bernard shoved his hands in his back pockets and rocked from heel to toe as he grinned wide enough to make his eyes crease. "Well, sure. Can't guarantee you an answer, but I'll give it my best shot."

He wasn't going to get a better opportunity than that. "How do you know when you've found home?"

"Home?" Bernard said it with a wry twist to his mouth. "Like the place?"

Owen nodded, uncertain how else to explain it, but he gave it his best shot. "I haven't found anywhere that felt like home since I lost my parents."

"Hmm." Grunting and rubbing a hand over the top of his head, which made his hair stand on end, Bernard squinted at the sky. "That's a serious question, son. Not sure I can answer that one right off the top of the old noggin, but I'll give it my best shot."

"I'd appreciate that."

Bernard pointed at the trail. "But then you gotta take that poor horse out for a ride. He's been almighty patient with you."

"He sure has." He patted the arched neck. "I'll let him have a good run on the beach."

"All right then. You're not going to find the kind of home you're looking for."

Cold so deep it froze the blood in his veins took over his whole body. He barely managed to push words through his numb limbs. "What do you mean?"

"You're looking for the home you had with your parents. You can't find that, but you might be able to find a different kind of home. The years you spent here with your aunt might not have felt like home because you were grieving." Bernard took a long look at the ocean, avoiding eye contact with Owen. "When you suffer a tragedy like you did, it changes your whole perspective."

Yeah, he'd figured that out. What did that have to do with the hole in his chest? "I don't understand."

"You're looking for what you lost, and you ain't never going to get that back. Home is a whole lot of things, different things for different people. If you're looking for people who love you, then that's right here." Bernard stabbed his finger toward the ground.

He'd never thought about it like that. Home had always been a feeling, a sense of finding the piece he'd been missing. But he'd never get that piece back. His parents were gone. All he had left of their love was memories.

"How do I make this feel like home?" He ran the leather reins through his fingers and followed Bernard's gaze toward the ocean.

"Have you asked God if this is where you belong?"

"Working on that." He'd thought his relationship with God was strong enough that he'd know when God wanted him to stop moving and settle down. He'd expected to feel it, way down deep where his grief lingered. "I thought it would be easier."

"Nothing easy about grief, or about coming home when the wandering is the only thing keeping you from falling apart." Bernard turned a grieving look Owen's way. "Trust me, son. I ran from my grief too. Thought it helped. Thought all that moving around gave me purpose. Wasn't till I stood still and the grief caught up with me that I realized I'd never dealt with it. I'd run from it. Every time I started to feel anything, I'd take off."

He knew what Bernard would say next before the man even took a breath. "You think I'm still grieving and I've been running away this whole time?"

"Didn't say that. Said that's what I did. But I tell you what, if what I said poked some kind of hot spot that made you angry, then maybe I gouged the wound and you should take a look at why it bothered you." Bernard hooked his thumb toward the horse, then the ocean. "Go on. Get out of here."

Owen tried to respond, but everything that threatened to come out of his mouth would be said in anger. So, he grabbed a handful of Gypsy's mane and launched onto the broad back.

"Have a good ride." Bernard patted Gypsy's flank. "Think about what I said."

He managed another nod before tapping his heels against Gypsy's sides. The gelding lumbered off with his slow walk. Owen hadn't ridden bareback in years, but it all came back to him before Gypsy stepped fully onto the trail and raised his head to scent the air.

"You smell the ocean? We're going down there." He tightened his thighs and his core to keep his balance and aimed Gypsy at the winding trail that took them beneath the arching canopy of branches and along the shore. They'd break into the sand a few feet away, on a stretch of beach that was almost always empty.

He needed empty, needed a few minutes to process what Bernard had said. It was similar enough to what Lauren said that he had to consider he'd overlooked something major all these years.

What was home? Aunt Audrey believed Summer Shore was home because she'd always lived there, had inherited the store from her parents, and never experienced the wanderlust that struck Owen.

Was it a need to wander, or had Bernard hit a homerun with his assessment? *What am I doing, Lord?*

Gypsy snorted and tossed his head, sending his black and white mane flying. They left the trees behind and stepped out onto the pristine beach. Gypsy pranced, his large hooves churning up clumps of sand.

"You want to run?" Owen knew the answer without asking, leaning forward and gathering up handfuls of mane. "Let's go." He made a kissing sound and Gypsy launched forward with enough force to send sand splatting the tree trunks behind them.

Every stride rattled up his backbone. A laugh tore from his throat. The wind ripped it away in a breath and tossed it aside. He'd missed this. All of it. Time with Aunt Audrey, helping at the stables and in the bakery.

Time slowed here. Instead of feeling rushed, like every day needed to be packed with enough activity to drive fatigue into his bones so he'd manage to sleep at night, he found comfort in the quiet.

And that was his answer, wasn't it?

If he wanted home, he had to find the place that gave him peace.

That place had been under his nose all along. Why had he always ran away?

Gypsy's hooves thundered on the damp sand when he guided the big horse toward the surf. His galloping strides smoothed. Owen knotted the reins and dropped them to spread his arms out. He closed his eyes, head tipped to the sky.

Home.

The feeling he'd chased for so long had merely been waiting for him to realize the truth. He left because he didn't want this place to be home.

Finding home meant he was learning how to cope with his grief and move on. It was what his parents would have wanted, but he'd resisted.

Owen opened his eyes and let the wind rip the tears from his face and throw them into the surf. The wind stung his cheeks, and Gypsy's headlong gallop slowed when the beach curved toward another stretch of trees.

He leaned back enough to ask Gypsy to slow, and the gelding eased his speed down by degrees until they were walking in fetlock-deep water.

"Thought for a minute you were going to take off across the water."

He knew that voice. In a matter of days, he'd memorized every-thing he could about her. Turning, he tented a hand over his eyes and scanned the beach.

Lauren stood in the shade a few feet away, her hands tucked in the pockets of her loose jeans. She wore yet another black t-shirt, this one with capped sleeves that showed off toned arms and a golden tan. She pushed a pair of sunglasses over her eyes and walked toward him.

"Hey." Of all the things he could've said, that one word might be the worst. He dropped his hand and stopped Gypsy, then slung his leg over the horse's neck and slid to the ground. "What are you doing out here?"

"Oh, you know." She shrugged and dug her feet into the sand. "Giving myself a pedicure."

"Sounds nice. How's wedding stuff going?" No sooner did he ask than her forehead tightened into that series of lines he'd come to understand meant she was stressed. "That bad?"

"No. It's fine. I should be baking right now, but I just finished a tasting with another client, and Viana has booked a wedding for the new year." She rubbed the notches in her forehead, smoothing them out with a huff. "It's good. I love my job."

"You don't have to explain to me." He led Gypsy closer. "But if you're looking for a distraction, I happen to have one."

"What?"

"Ride with me." He grinned easily despite the way his heart took flight and soared away.

Lauren looked Gypsy over, her expression impossible to read be-hind the sunglasses. "You want me to ride bareback with you? Why? You planning on throwing me in the ocean because of what I said?"

"Nope." He knelt and cupped his hands together. "I'll even give you a boost. You can ride and I'll walk if that makes you more comfortable."

"Why are you doing this?" Suspicion laced her voice.

Waves crept up the shore, dampening his jeans. The answer tried to stick in his throat, but he pushed through. "Because you were right. And you look like you need a break. Horseback riding is great therapy for emotions."

"Yeah? Says who?"

"Me." Another wave crashed, this one high enough to slam into Gypsy's knees and soak Owen from the thighs down. He leaped up and back with a howl.

Lauren's mouth rounded in an O a split second before she roared with laughter. "I'm sorry." She held her ribs. "It's not funny, but I can't help it."

He couldn't help joining her, laughing at his own expense. "Are you going to ride?"

"I don't know. I've always said I'd never get in a car with a man I didn't know. Not sure how that translates to horseback rides."

"Well." He shook hair from his eyes, then flicked damp sand at her like she'd done him days ago. "You've already been in a car with me, so that's not a valid argument."

"True." She wiped her eyes. "Go on. I'll ride behind you. You can't help me up then get in front of me."

He grunted but swung back onto Gypsy.

She clapped with a surprised grin. "Nice moves, cowboy."

"Keep saying that and you're going to make me think you actually like me." He extended his hand. "Up you go."

Still grinning, she grabbed Gypsy's mane and jumped up behind him. "Where we going?"

"Anywhere you want." He turned Gypsy around so they faced the empty beach again. "How fast do you want to go?"

"Just like this." She gripped his shirt, gathering the material along his ribs and holding on.

"I'm sorry I stopped talking to you the other day. You were right." He hadn't been ready to hear it, but that was beside the point. It was time he learned the truth about himself.

He felt her shrug in the way her arms moved beneath his.

"I should have kept my mouth shut."

"No." He patted the back of her hand. "I never want you to be afraid to tell me the truth."

"It's not like there will be many opportunities for that since you're leaving soon."

Her voice was too controlled, too careful. Unable to see her face, he had to guess what the tone meant.

"What if I wasn't leaving?" He glanced over his shoulder when her breath puffed across his neck.

"What do you mean?" Her grip on his shirt tightened.

He eased Gypsy further up the beach until they were in the loose, dry sand. "I'm not leaving. I haven't figured out the logistics yet, but I'm tired of running away. I want to stay here. I want to make a home here."

She turned so silent and still that he worried she'd gone into some kind of shock. "Why would you do that?"

"Because..." Was he really going to throw it all out there? "Because I like you, and I'd like to get to know you better. And Aunt Audrey has been asking me to come home for years. It's time. No more running and trying to hide from myself. This is where I belong."

"You don't know anything about me. The only thing you could possibly like about me is how I look." Without warning, she pushed away from him and slid off Gypsy's back.

He turned the horse and joined her in the sand, landing less than a foot away. "Wrong. I know a lot about you."

"Like what?" A tremble shook her arms.

Shoot. He'd stuck his foot in it again. Only one way out now. "I know that you're funny. You love your friends. You're an amazing baker."

The shaking stopped, but she locked her hands together behind her back.

"Everything else I need to know about you, I'll learn over time. Like your favorite flower." He raised one finger. "And your favorite color." Another finger. "Favorite food."

The smile started slow but spread until her cheeks lifted the sunglasses. "You can add that I overreact to that list."

"Nope." He tapped the reins against his palm. "You don't overreact. You're cautious, with good reason."

"It's this wedding." She released a quiet sigh. "It's got me on edge." She didn't explain, and he didn't push for answers.

"It will be over soon."

Her phone rang. She groaned and palmed her pocket. "Sorry. That's Viana."

"Maybe she's calling with good news."

"Unlikely. This wedding has been one problem after another." She answered the phone while walking a few feet away from him.

Seconds later, she took off her sunglasses and pinched the bridge of her nose.

He stood with Gypsy and waited for her, but he knew the minute she faced him that their impromptu date was over.

"I have to go home. There's been another problem."

"Anything I can help with?" He wanted to be there for her, no matter what that meant. He'd never experienced this kind of attraction to a woman before. It was more than physical. He wanted her trust.

"I don't want to impose. You've helped so much already."

"Impose." He took her hand and squeezed her fingers. "What do you need?"

"Give me a ride home. I'll tell you on the way." She stared up at him, her bare toes touching his boots.

The urge to kiss her nearly overwhelmed him. He locked it away, completely unwilling to take advantage of her vulnerability for his own gain.

Chapter Seven
Wedding Day

Focus. She had to focus. Last night's debacle played out with every daisy she formed and set on the tray to her right.

Ainslie's mother posted online about the wrong wedding dress getting sent to Ainslie and the couple's followers had latched onto the information. They were going to figure it out.

Camden thought so, and as much as Lauren wanted to believe the best in people, her experience warned that something awful might happen. It was the reason they'd all voted to have the wedding a day early.

Now she had to finish Ainslie's cake today. Like right now. She'd told Owen everything. He'd listened without interrupting, then offered to help.

The fool man didn't know when to quit. He made her like him more with every passing day, and he wasn't even trying. That might be *why* it was so easy to fall for him.

She'd texted him this morning, telling him she had everything under control here but she wouldn't mind if he wanted to work on the cake for Nicole. His aunt had been expecting Lauren to stop by today too, but there was no way she'd make it.

This wedding had to be perfect. Florence had been adamant from the beginning, and it was her mistake that put it all at risk.

Her fingers twitched around the soft fondant, squishing the intricate petal into mush. Lauren tossed it aside and cut another.

Footsteps moved overhead, down the steps, and across the foyer. Lauren hadn't bothered to even look up to see who might be coming and going. It didn't matter.

Owen was staying. That was the other thought that refused to leave her alone.

Her phone pinged, and Owen's face popped up on the screen. She swiped to read the message.

Owen:

> You're amazing! You have this. It's going to be a great day.

Her cheeks heated, and she used the back of her hand to brush the smile away. No distractions.

Once this was over, she'd take the time and figure out what happened next. Owen was a good guy. He'd proven that time after time.

She'd almost kissed him last night. The horseback ride had been exactly what she needed, and she hadn't even known it.

Owen had a way about him, a kind of silence, that helped her.

Viana and Olivia said she was calm and always in control. What they didn't realize was she'd had to be. Being a model forced her to put all her emotions away. They were not safe, and they always showed up on the camera. She'd learned to hide them. No matter how she felt, she remained stoic and in control.

Owen gave her the chance to take off the mask and be herself. Now that she'd experienced that kind of freedom, she might never be able to go back.

Another flower joined its friends on the tray.

What if he changed his mind and left?

Her phone buzzed again. She ignored it, resting her elbows on the counter and sculpting yet another pink daisy.

Viana walked in, talking to Anita over her shoulder.

Lauren ignored the conversation. If it had anything to do with her, Viana would say so. Until then, she had plenty to keep her busy.

Her phone pinged again, this time with an image attached to the message. She opened the picture and smiled. Owen stood in the center of Audrey's kitchen, his yellow apron in place and a handful of fondant tools in hand. Another image popped up, this time of the fondant wedding cake topper that she'd been working on all week.

Owen had all the pieces cut out and laid on a sheet of wax paper to dry.

He'd really taken her need for assistance seriously and was putting in every effort to help pull things together.

"How are things going?"

Lauren had gotten so engrossed in the flowers and Owen's pictures that she hadn't heard Viana approach.

Her friend leaned against the bench.

"Fine." She concentrated on the next flower, ignoring her phone when it buzzed again.

Viana stretched over the counter to peek at the screen. "Who is Owen?"

She was so not ready to have this conversation with everything else going on. Not to mention Viana and Camden and Olivia and Mac with all their relationship stuff.

Better all around if she kept this to herself a little while longer. At least until she had a better idea *if* anything was happening.

She set the flower on the tray and pulled her phone close, keeping it out of Viana's line of sight. "He's no one worth knowing about." Not yet, anyway.

"So, there was something with that guy I saw you with?"

"Not anymore." She had work to do first. Owen had made it clear he was interested but he wouldn't push her. "It will be close, but I'll get the cake finished in time. The flowers will cascade down the cake."

Viana might not take the bait and switch in conversation, but with the amount of stress she'd been under to move the wedding up a day, it might work.

"It looks stunning." Viana squeezed Lauren's forearm. "I'm here if you want to talk."

Lauren found her opening and launched. "Only if you want to talk about Cam."

Viana groaned and rolled her eyes. "He's always near me, hovering like a pesky fly—"

"A handsome, well-built one." Lauren interrupted with a laugh.

"Ugh. Let it go. We're not compatible."

Lauren dropped her gaze to the tray, rearranging the flowers how they made the most sense for decorating. "I did most of these yesterday, so they're good to be used now. And you're compatible, just both way too stubborn."

"He doesn't trust me." Viana whispered the words, but hurt lingered in the way she palmed the edge of the counter and swallowed hard.

"You don't trust him either." Lauren continued shifting the flowers into small piles.

"I don't. But it doesn't matter. He's leaving tomorrow."

Maybe not. She'd thought Owen would leave too, but he'd decided that he wanted a home here. For how long? Could she risk putting her trust in him, knowing he might up and leave at a moment's notice? "Where's Livvie?"

"Taking photos inside of Ainslie." Viana snatched up one of the broken flowers and nibbled on the edge. "Mac, the very handsome videographer, keeps looking at Olivia the way you're looking at your phone. Something's up there too."

Lauren barely resisted glancing at her phone.

"Fine. Have it your way." Viana gave her a quick hug around the shoulders and walked away.

She fully planned on having everything her way. Pushing back the same errant strand of hair, she straightened, arching her back to ease the ache in her lower spine and took in the empty kitchen.

A tight feeling invaded her throat. What was she hoping to accomplish by pushing Owen away? After their adventure yesterday when he'd told her he planned on staying here, she'd shut down. Fear once again took control and tried to drive her back into the hard shell she'd created to protect herself.

Nothing protected her from her own heart.

Falling in love hadn't been in her plans. She'd told Viana to let herself be surprised by love, because Viana and Camden had history. They'd been in love and things didn't work out.

Lauren was pretty sure Viana had never stopped loving Camden.

And then there was Olivia. She and Mac went together like cinnamon and sugar.

Where did that leave her and Owen? It wasn't like they'd had any real conversations about their future. It was all hopes and dreams and feelings.

Emotions that knotted themselves up in her middle and confused her.

"Lauren?"

The sound of her name spun her around so fast she knocked her elbow against the tray of flowers, sending them spinning sideways. She caught them before they crashed to the floor. "Camden. You scared the daylights out of me."

"I didn't know people still said that." He chuckled, but the look turned bashful when he caught sight of her frown. "Sorry. Didn't mean to scare you. Got someone at the gate asking for you."

"For me?" Who in the world would be asking for her? Fear clawed its way up her throat and drew all the moisture from her mouth.

Had her stalker found her?

"Says his name is Owen. Tall guy, dark hair. Reminds me of Jensen Ackles."

Her entire body sagged. "I know him."

"I took a picture." Camden flashed his phone screen in her direction. "That your guy?"

She couldn't help laughing at the way he said it. "Yeah, that's my guy. You can send him in."

"He knows about the wedding?" Camden's eyebrows slashed together. "Any chance he's told anyone else?"

"He doesn't know everything. Just that we had a change in wedding plans and that I need help." He was supposed to stay at Audrey's and work on Nicole's cake, but she wasn't surprised to hear he'd come over to check on her.

"I'll walk him in." Camden pocketed his phone. "Anyone else you're expecting today?"

"No." She resisted the urge to fix her hair as Camden headed out to get Owen.

She concentrated on the flowers, finishing the last one and adding it to the collection as Owen walked in with his apron draped over his arm and a baseball cap pulled low over his forehead. "Sorry if I caused a problem."

"It's fine." She motioned for him to join her. "You're just in time to help before I have to go change."

"Change?" He eyed his jeans and black shirt. "Guess I should have thought of that. But since I'm not a guest, I'll hide out in the kitchen while you do your thing." He winked.

"I could find you a tux." She tapped his shoulder, guiding him around to the counter. "If we get this done in time. Sit. I'll grab the cake."

She'd finished the icing and fondant a few hours ago, and the flowers should stick just fine with a bit of water and her edible glue.

"I didn't come here to crash the wedding." Owen put his apron on and tied it tight. "You stopped answering my messages, and I finished everything I could on Nicole's cake, so I thought I'd offer to help."

"I'm glad you did. Things have been crazy here."

Olivia stuck her head in the door. "Thirty-minute warning."

"Thirty minutes?" Owen glanced from Olivia to Lauren, his eyes popping wide. "You're going to decorate that in thirty minutes?"

"No." She set the two-tier wedding cake on the turntable and handed him a bowl of water and another of the glue, along with a bottle of aerosol edible glue. "*We* are."

"Got a picture for me to look at?" Owen didn't hesitate to jump in. He rounded the counter so they stood on opposite sides. "Want me to start at the bottom? We can meet in the middle."

"Yes. Perfect." She showed him the picture she'd used for inspiration, then used one of her smoothing tools to mark the lines on the cake for him to follow.

Viana's voice carried from somewhere close by. Lauren couldn't hear the words, but the pitch of her voice sent her flying across the kitchen. "Something's wrong."

"Right behind you." Owen's steps matched hers as they ran across the kitchen and onto the porch toward the flooded side yard with its small storage shed where Viana kept most of her decorations.

A strange woman shoved Viana. Lauren leaped forward, but Camden beat her to the woman, tackling her to the ground and pinning her arms behind her back.

Owen's set a hand in the small of her back as Olivia joined them. "It's okay. Camden has it under control."

He did, but that didn't stop her heart from threatening to burst at the sight of Viana cradling her wrist to her chest. What was the world coming to that a couple as wonderful as Ainslie and Lucas were forced to deal with the insanity of crazed fans?

No one should have to deal with that.

"Are you okay?" Owen dipped his head to whisper into her ear.

Her head twitched in a shaky nod.

Lucas barged onto the scene, his anger rising as he berated the team for allowing the woman to sneak past them.

She couldn't listen to this. With Owen's hand still on her back, she took a step away. The whole situation brought up a rush of old memories. "I have to finish the cake."

Owen stayed with her, not once dropping the point of contact between them. He didn't say a word, but he seemed to understand that she needed a minute to compose herself.

When they reached the kitchen, he ran his hand up and down her spine when she bowed over the counter and dropped her face into her hands. The first breath pinched, but the second came easier.

"Guess I'm not over it like I thought." She'd known she hadn't fully processed those months of being stalked. She'd shoved them down and covered them up.

"You don't have to rush yourself." Owen's hand continued to stroke her spine. "You went through a terrible ordeal. There's nothing wrong with being sensitive to what just happened."

How did he understand her so well? They were basically strangers.

"I don't have time to process now either." She pushed upright and smoothed her hair. "Let's get this cake finished." Then she'd go upstairs and change into her dress, attend the wedding while she smiled and pretended everything was fine.

Then, after it was all over, she'd sit down with Owen and have the talk they both needed.

Chapter Eight

Weddings were beautiful events that Lauren hoped she was always able to see as a heartfelt union between two people who loved each other the way Ainslie and Lucas loved one another.

Of all the weddings she'd baked for and attended over the last few years, theirs was one of her favorites.

Their vows were wholesome and heartwarming, and the final kiss had been the kind that brought tears to her eyes.

After helping Olivia with her hair, she'd changed into her standard pale blue dress with the cap sleeves and swirling skirts. Owen had declined her offer of a tuxedo, which was a real shame because she would've loved to see him dressed up.

Someday. The lingering promise was far too tempting. There was a huge difference in spending a few hours a day for a week with a guy and promising in sickness and in health for as long as they lived.

And yet, her silly, fluttering heart still refused to accept the truth of it all.

Every time she looked over at him in the kitchen as they cleaned up after the wedding, he wore a goofy smile that caused her breathing to stutter.

"Want to go for a walk?" He held out his hand.

Lauren arched a brow and threw the sponge she'd used to wipe down the counters at him.

He caught it in midair, laughing and tossing it into the sink. "Is that a no?"

"No." She crossed her arms loosely over her stomach, her usual way of anchoring herself. It gave her a sense of security. "That's me asking you to finish up here. I'll be right back."

She yanked off the low heels and jogged up the stairs to the third floor. Viana and Olivia were off taking care of their own stuff, leaving the entire floor empty and quiet. Lauren breathed in the silence and calmed her racing pulse.

Within minutes, she'd changed into her jeans and t-shirt and shoved her feet into a pair of ballet flats.

Owen waited for her at the bottom of the stairs, hands in his pockets and a soft smile raising his lips.

"What?" She paused halfway down, her hand on the rail.

He climbed up to meet her. "Just thinking how beautiful you are. It doesn't matter if you're wearing a gown or your jeans. You have the kind of beauty that shines through from your heart."

A small part of her wanted to argue, to tell him not to call her beautiful, but it felt nice to be appreciated. Owen made it clear that he saw more than her outward appearance.

"You just made it impossible to compliment you without sounding like I'm making it up." She stood a step above him, which put them eye to eye. "Jerk move, cowboy."

"Nah." He reached for her hands and cradled them in his.

She rolled her eyes with a playful huff. "I thought we were going for a walk."

"We are. But I couldn't wait to tell you that I'm falling for you." He grinned that sweet, innocent smile that made his eyes sparkle. "I'm sweet on you, Lauren."

"No one says that anymore." She leaned forward. "But I know the feeling. You're growing on me, Owen." Grinning, she kissed the corner of his mouth. "Like a barnacle on the hull of a ship."

His snort of laughter rumbled out, and he wrapped both arms around her waist. "You meant like this?"

She squealed when he lifted her off the stairs and into his arms. "Put me down."

"Make me." He carried her all the way to the bottom of the stairs and out onto the porch.

Their laugher rode the breeze that fluttered the magnolia tree and brought a slight chill to her bare arms.

"Can you believe it's almost Christmas?" She rested her forearms on his shoulders when he lowered her enough that her toes touched the deck. He settled his hands at her waist and dropped his forehead to hers.

They'd stood next to each other several times, even standing face to face as they discussed cakes, but it had never been this intimate. She felt every point of contact, and a shiver of anticipation spiraled through her.

"What do you want for Christmas?" He brushed his nose alongside hers.

Her fingers tangled in his collar. "You."

"Are you sure?" He stayed close, their lips a breath apart. "Once I give you my heart, that's it for me. There's no taking it back. I've spent years looking for where I belong, and now I know why I couldn't find it. I was looking for you."

"I can't be your home, Owen." She tightened her hold on his shirt. "You have to find peace for yourself, not through me. If you can do that, then my heart is all yours."

What was that supposed to mean? Owen took a minute to process her words. "I have found peace." Hadn't he? Lauren made him happy. Being with her gave him a sense of homecoming that he'd searched for.

"Have you?" She hugged him tight. "What happens if we have a fight? We barely know each other. If we disagree on something, are you going to leave because you no longer feel like you're home?"

The challenge in her tone stopped him from answering without thinking. He wanted to promise that he'd never leave, even if they had a disagreement. But she had a point. They didn't know each other.

What fear did Lauren face that made her question him? She always mentioned him leaving like it was a deal breaker.

"I'd like to think that if we disagree, we'll figure out how to talk through it."

Her breath whispered over his cheek. "I hope that too, but people tend to hide things from each other. Sometimes it takes years before we're comfortable enough to tell someone—even someone we love—that we're unhappy about something."

Her fingers at the nape of his neck were a distraction, but he focused anyway. "Have you ever told your friends about what happened to you?"

She shook her head. "Like I said, sometimes we hide things from each other."

"But you told me." He had to believe that meant something. "You trusted me enough to talk about it."

"True." She agreed easily enough, but there was still a kind of hesitation in the way she looked at him.

"What?" He couldn't stand not knowing what bothered her. It made him want to beg her to talk to him, to tell him everything that he needed to know to help make her life easier.

All the time he'd spent praying for God to guide him had led him here, to this moment with Lauren. If he'd messed it all up and this wasn't what he'd been meant to do, he had no idea where to go from here.

Lauren didn't speak for a minute, but her eyes were full of thoughts and emotions that flickered past in rapid succession. "I kept telling myself I couldn't fall for you because you were leaving. I didn't want to fall in love with someone who didn't feel as rooted in Summer Shore as me. Kind of silly, isn't it? I just told you I can't be your home, but I wanted you to make this your home."

"Sometimes we don't know what we want, even when it's standing right in front of us." He drew his arms tighter around her. "That's not the problem here. I know exactly what I want."

"What's that?"

He kissed her, letting his lips answer the question his heart had begged to answer from the beginning. Home could be a place. It could be a person. Lauren might not want to hold the responsibility of being his home, but that was okay. What had started as attraction turned into a deeper connection, the kind of love that lasted lifetimes.